I0668382

If Wishes Were

Dragons

A DragonEye, PI story

Karina Fabian

Laser Cow Press

ROCKLEDGE, FL

Copyright © 2020 by Karina Fabian

All rights reserved. No part of this publication may be reproduced, distributed or transmitted in any form or by any means, without prior written permission.

Laser Cow Press
Rockledge, FL
https://fabianspace.com

Publisher's Note: This is a work of fiction. Names, characters, places, and incidents are a product of the author's imagination. Locales and public names are sometimes used for atmospheric purposes. Any resemblance to actual people, living or dead, or to businesses, companies, events, institutions, or locales is completely coincidental.

Cover art by Dawn Grimes
DragonEye Logo by Len Fabian

Book Layout © 2017 BookDesignTemplates.com

If Wishes Were Dragons/Karina Fabian -- 1st ed.
ISBN 978-1-7334471-7-1

Dedication

To my fellow adventurers: Purch D&D group, Catholic INTJ Gamers, and of course, my husband and kids. Huzzah for zany predicaments and unpredictable dice rolls!

To Cesar Chacon, for being a crazy-enthusiastic Vern fan and a wonderful encouragement.

Beware of *artistes* and genies granting wishes.

Contents

Chapter One: No Such Thing as an Idle Wish

One of the hardest things I've had to learn is confession. It is not natural for us dragons to admit we're wrong. Under normal circumstances, it's a rare occurrence. We act according to our nature, and if the other sapient species have a problem with it, then they just need to "embrace diversity," as you Mundanes say.

Having lived with humans (and under the Catholic Church) since my encounter with St. George, I've had to adapt to human ways. Which means I fail to live up to their expectations—a lot. Hence, confession. When you're a dragon being forced to go against nature to conform to the standards of another species, it's not always easy to know what's a sin and what isn't. So sometimes, I end up confessing something that isn't really a sin, but more of an...unfortunate turn of events.

Of course, when the priest is also a good friend, it doesn't mean I get off the hook.

"What do you mean, you lost your job?" Father Rich demanded. "It's only been a day!"

We were at a picnic table in the open area of Los Lagos's Renaissance Festival. The festival attracted bigger crowds every year thanks to the opening of the Gap between Faerie and the Mundane. All around us, people were bustling about in costumes that ranged from authentic to in-your-dreams. They munched on turkey legs, trying not to spill grease on their outfits, and sipped fairy mead which was authentic this year as it was actually made by a clan of the little people in Faerie. I'd made sure they removed the magical effects, however. Having your entire clientele fall asleep for 20 years would be hard on business.

What should not have been hard on business was having a live, genuine Faerie dragon on the payroll. Not a fire-breathing dragon, of course. I couldn't breathe fire anymore. I hadn't breathed fire since my battle with St. George. However, it made things easier for the festival organizers since they didn't have to worry about extra insurance or fire codes. I'm telling you, though, after the morning I'd had, I was wishing God would return my flames to me.

"It wasn't my fault," I said again. "I don't even know how I insulted her. If I insulted her. She seemed to take offense at anything."

I paused to glare warningly at a lookie-loo who had stopped to gape at my magnificence and was lingering to eavesdrop on my conversation. A family took the pause as an invitation and dashed up requesting a photo. I posed, a fake smile on my face. Only an hour ago, I'd have made five bucks every time Daddy the Smartphone Photographer said, "Hang on. Let me try one more with this filter."

I was raking in some sweet treasure, too, until this human wearing a sword and a leather bikini that was supposed to be her "barbarian armor" approached me and said she wanted to have my half-dragon babies.

"All I did was try to tell her it was impossible. She's the one who decided it was because she was fat."

"Who's fat?" Owen, one of the members of my gaming group, asked as he took a spot at the bench. Two spots, really. He was dressed as the half-orc fighter he usually played in-game, and no one wanted to be near his spiky shoulder pads.

He set down a tray loaded with food in the middle of the table, put a basket bearing a turkey leg in front of himself, and passed a basket bearing a His Majesty's Burger and King-sized Fries to Father. Speaking of fat, I wondered if I was going to have to confess that I wasn't nagging him about his diet. Of course, that "confession" would have to be to his sister, Sister Bernadette. She'd made me promise to keep track of his calories. If she found out I was letting him cheat on his diet, he and I would both be in for some serious penance.

I was glad to see Owen eating, though. He'd seemed run down lately, but he'd brushed off our friends' inquiries when they noticed him moving slow. They'd attributed it to him being sad that the group was breaking up as people moved away. I knew better. Something about him "smelled" off. He seemed in good health and spirits today, though.

Our other friends took their spots at the table. Linda had chosen to dress as her LARPing character, Lady Estel. Only her D&D character wore bikini armor—not the best choice for a cool autumn day even if she wasn't too self-conscious to wear it. Samwise was dressed as a fighter and had augmented his ensemble with a set of fairy wings he'd purchased earlier. He'd done more shopping, it seemed. He set a plastic bag on the ground by his feet. His dog, Thunderpaws, sniffed at it, and he snapped his fingers to order him to stop.

The little corgi, too, was in costume: leather armor that covered his furry chest and back. His ears peeked out from a leather helmet. Sam had used his bridle-style leash to mimic an actual bridle, and a Barbie-sized fairy rode Thunderpaws' back, holding reins. I'll bet he got as many photos taken of himself as I did of me. Now, he'd get more.

"Vern got fired," Father said, then rolled his eyes at my cry of protest. "It's not a sin, Vern, and they're going to find out, anyway."

"What?" Linda exclaimed. "How could you get fired from that job? All you had to do was stand around and be yourself."

I narrowed my eyes at my friends, daring them to take a swing at the slow ball she'd just pitched. Ray bit his lip, but mostly in show. He was dressed as a minstrel and enjoying the opportunity to play a part since he'd always been the dungeon master in our games. He had a lute on his back. He knew three chords, which didn't stop him from treating any shy damsel, child, or older lady to an impromptu song, which was the same song with slightly different words.

As Father gave them a summary, it occurred to me that I had given him material for his first ballad.

Owen passed me a burger. "That's tough. So, is it because you called some chick fat?"

"But I didn't! She said it. How would I know? I'm a dragon. I judge human weight by how long before I'm hungry again. Besides, in Faerie, plump women are more desirable."

"And you said that?" Owen asked.

"Something to that effect."

Father crossed his arms and leaned back. "So, you agreed she was fat."

I tossed my head in annoyance. Several people around us went for their phones. I was getting used to that. It was more fun when I got paid for it.

"You see?" I said to my friends. "That's exactly how she took it. It went downhill from there."

We shared a moment of silence for my lost job, and everyone turned to their food.

Linda followed her bite of inauthentic fries with a sip of anachronistic soda and said, "I don't know. I'm on Vern's side here. She propositioned him and made trouble when he turned her down. Sounds like sexual harassment to me. Maybe we should ask Scott."

Scott Youngman, Esquire, was the lawyer who had helped me when the Los Lagos chief of police put me under house arrest to make it look like he was protecting the community. Long story. Captain Beavers is gone now, but so is Youngman. He'd moved to DC after losing the lawsuit against the nuclear power company that was partly responsible for creating the Gap. The defense countered that, tragic as the accident was, the company could in no way have predicted the opening of a portal in a dimension no one even knew existed. The judge agreed. Youngman lost the case but caught the attention of a big law firm that then hired him. I guess that meant he won, after all.

"Can an androgynous species be sexually harassed?" Owen asked.

"What?" I demanded. "Are you saying I'm undesirable because I'm asexual?"

He pointed his turkey leg at me. "Touché! They didn't run you out or anything? Can you hang with us the rest of the day?"

"Yes," Linda pleaded. "This may be the last time we get to do anything together."

Our group was breaking up. Ray, who had been our dungeon master, had gotten an offer from an animations company in Orlando and was catching a flight to Florida tomorrow. Linda was leaving next week to work in some museum in Chicago. Sam had graduated and was looking for work. It figured that just as I was making friends in the Mundane, they'd leave. Anything concerning humans ended so quickly.

Like my job.

Once upon a time, I had enjoyed the companionship of other dragons, my immortal family who understood me. We hunted monsters and battled demons. We held the reverence of all the other species. Our word was second only to that of the angels. I wondered if I'd ever see that life again.

I answered, "Unless someone else wants to raise a stink about things I never said. Or they get tired of people doing things with me for free that they'd been charging for this morning." I turned to the four-year-old who was poking at my thigh with his wooden sword. I swung my head close to his snot-nosed, chocolate-smeared face so he got a good look at my teeth. When I had his attention, I growled.

As he ran screaming for his mommy, my friends at the table—and a few bystanders—laughed. Thunderpaws stopped nosing at Sam's bag long enough to add his barks. That earned us a few more sympathetic giggles from the people around us.

Father dropped his head into his hands and groaned. "Seriously, Vern? Do you think that's going to endear you?"

I bit into my burger without bothering to pick it up out of the basket and feigned innocence.

He sighed. "I wish I knew how Saint George handled you."

I snickered. "You wish you could whack me with your sword and have God approve, like He did George."

He folded his hands and turned to look at me frankly. "There are days, yes!" he admitted.

Linda sighed. "Wouldn't it be fun, though? I mean, to have a real adventure instead of playing at it? I wish there was a way to make it happen."

Owen said, "Yeah, well, if wishes were horses..."

"Or dragons?" Linda quipped. "What would you wish for, Vern?"

"I don't wish," I said, with a little more force than I intended. There were a lot of things I'd wish for—have wished for—in my years living under humans. None had ever been granted, and I doubted any ever would. I'd given up voicing them. It just added more sting to the disappointment.

Linda shrugged it off. "How about you, Sam? Don't you wish you could actually be a fairy knight with real magical powers?"

"Wouldn't that be cool? And Thunderpaws could be my valiant steed."

She grinned, then leaned back to look at the little corgi, who was pawing at a paper bag at Sam's feet. "Hey, what is up with Thunderpaws, anyway? Are you hiding treats in that bag?"

Sam clucked with annoyance. "No. Those are in my pouch, like always. Thud, sploot!"

Immediately, Thunderpaws' little legs splayed, and he sank flat onto the ground. I heard an older lady coo. Sam left his eager-to-please pup in that position for a 10 count, then released him and tossed him a treat. Thunderpaws snatched it from the air, chewed happily, then went right back to fussing at his bag.

"What's wrong with you?" He snatched up the bag and put it in his lap.

"There must be some smell he likes," Linda said, then her voice got singsong. "Was it that shopgirl's perfume?"

Sam's cheeks went pink.

We'd all taken an interest in Samwise's love life—or lack of it. He was a little portly by human standards, and he didn't have what Linda called "LoTR good looks," but he was considerate and loyal, just like his namesake. I'd have expected him to have a mate or at least a steady stream of potentials.

Then again, some half-dressed trollop wanted to have my dragon babies. I do not understand Mundanes' ideas of romance.

Linda continued. "What if we go back to the shop and find something for Thud? Then you'd have a chance to talk to her again. What was her name—Beth?"

"Betts, and what's the point? She'll be going back to Faerie next week. Besides, the only reason she was talking to me was to sell me the lamp. She probably just liked Thunderpaws, anyway."

"What lamp?" I asked, suddenly suspicious.

"Just this cool old oil lamp. Looks like something out of Arabian Knights. I thought we could use it in a campaign sometime...if we ever play again in person. Look."

He started to pull it out of the bag, but suddenly, Thunderpaws leaped up and grabbed the handle.

"Thunderpaws! No!"

I caught a glimpse of a brass veneer that hid what I knew was a truly beautiful interior. Even worse, I now scented the magic that was just barely seeping out of the spout. "Leave it alone! Don't touch it."

But Sam was too occupied with wresting it from his dog.

Linda kept talking, "It isn't always about Thuddy. Someone will see your worth. I just wish I could be there when it happens."

"Stop wishing!" I said. Owen gave me an odd look, and Father smacked my flank with the back of his hand. The others, meanwhile, retrieved the lamp.

Linda said, "Oh, gross. It has drool. Here." She grabbed a napkin.

I stood, almost toppling Father beside me. "No! Don't rub that lamp!"

Too late. Suddenly, I, Father, my friends, even the corgi, were engulfed in blue smoke.

Then, we were gone.

Chapter Two: St. George & the Dragon, Re-Enacted

When awareness returned, I was standing in a desert, near the coast of some sea. Rain drizzled on me and made the sand sticky and wet. All around me, I felt a shimmer of energies in a huge dome around me. A magical shield had me penned in.

A long, deep gash in my belly burned like fire despite the cool rain. Even though it bled freely, I could feel poison entering my bloodstream. Nausea and weakness swept over me; I blinked away the dizziness. Not poison—poisons. To one side lay a knight's lance, its tip sticky with ichor. The scent was familiar and evil. Some knight had run a demon through with that lance—an iron lance!—then stabbed me with it.

The demon was gone—killed before I was finished with him. I'd needed that demon for something. I couldn't remember what, but I knew it was important—and some uppity knight ran him through before I could get whatever it was I had needed.

There was the knight—staggering to his feet and reaching for his sword while his faithful steed wisely backed away.

Iron mixed with demon blood burned in the wound. My temper burned with it.

"You idiot!" I said it in my own language, so the knight heard unintelligible roaring. I accentuated it by breathing flame with all the fury I could muster. He'd understand that.

"Father God!" he cried out and fell to one knee, his arm up as if holding a shield. And as if he had a shield, my fire splashed on some invisible force and splayed harmlessly away. The drizzling rain became a torrent and doused the flames.

Cute trick, but I wasn't done with him. I swept his legs out from under him with my tail.

He fell hard but managed to swing at my tail with his sword. Though awkward, it had a lot more power than I'd have expected. The blade smacked against my scales, shattering one, and bruising the skin underneath.

With a roar of pain, I pulled back and made to breathe fire again, this time with more focus and heat.

"God of mercy! Aid me!" the knight cried out.

A sudden zephyr gathered the rain into a hard stream and threw it toward me.

I ducked.

The water raked across my scales, and I felt holy magics tickle my back spikes. That was close. If I'd gotten a mouthful of that, it could have extinguished my fire. Permanently.

Wait. How did I know that? Suddenly, this fight was starting to feel familiar.

Or maybe not. A second blast of wind caught me in the chest. The force of it flung me backward until I slammed into the barrier. My barrier. Some instinct made me spread my wings so that when I hit the shield, my back took the brunt of the blow and kept me from shattering my already broken wing bones.

How had I known to do that? And why had I made a barrier to pen myself in with a vengeful knight?

I dropped to my feet, shook the rain out of my eyes, and took a good look at my opponent.

Even with dragon sight, I could not make out his expression through the rain. There was no doubting his stature as he drew himself tall and called out, "By the name of Jesus Christ, our Lord, surrender yourself, foul beast."

Lightning flashed as a brief gust set his dark, wet hair to flying and pressed his chainmail and clothes tight against his arms and legs. Square jaw, broad shoulders, wide stance...

...belly fat?

Something was wrong. This fight felt too familiar, yet too different.

I didn't have time to think about it further. The knight—no, the paladin—rushed at me. Paladins are worse than knights. If there was anything more annoying than a knight or a saint on a mission, it was the combination of both in one self-important, monofocused, human form. In the heat of battle, they wouldn't listen to reason. Basically, you won, you lost, or you wore them down.

I threw myself at him. Yet, fast as I moved, he moved faster. Inhumanly fast. No human was that quick, not even with magic.

I fell flat on my face as he skipped away. Frustration and morbid curiosity overtook my pride. "How are you doing that?" I demanded.

He didn't reply, but God did.

I lashed out with my tail. The paladin rolled out of my way, grabbed a rock, and threw it at me.

It struck my flank, a mere tap, but it shook me, nonetheless. I should have dodged that easily, without even thinking about it.

He wasn't getting faster. I had gotten slower. Human speed.

He stood, hands on his knees as he fought for breath. "Submit," he panted.

"You're not getting off that easy."

I lunged for him again. I had planned to use my whole body and smash him against my shields as he had done with his rain attack. However, at the last minute, I pulled myself short and merely tackled him instead. I pinned him, arms and legs.

Lightning flashed. Finally, I was able to get a good look at his face. And it all came back to me.

"Father Richard?"

Suddenly, the horse charged, reared, and kicked me in the shoulder with her hooves. My weight shifted and I compensated fast to avoid squashing my friend.

Father Rich took that opportunity to bring up his sword arm and bash me in the jaw with the hilt.

I backed off, seeing stars, jaws and shoulders stinging from my new injuries.

Father staggered upright, then ran at me.

I slipped in a puddle and my feet flew out from beneath me. I flopped onto the cold beach and howled to God in my own language. "All right! Enough. If I promise not to eat this human, can you at least make it stop raining?"

As if to test me, my bezerker paladiny friend lunged forward to smack me with his sword. At least exhaustion was finally taking its toll on him. He didn't manage more than a hard spank. I contained my counterattack to a dirty look.

"Get up and fight!" he panted.

"No," I told him.

"Fight me!"

"Stand down. I give up, okay? You win this one." I looked again to the heavens. "I surrender! Thy will be done! Now, can you please halt the rain?"

The sky once again thundered. I thought I detected a hint of smugness. Then, the rain stopped, the clouds cleared, and the day burned hot.

The paladin—Father Rich—wiped his hair off his face, looked at the sky, then turned to me. His eyes widened with recognition. "Vern?"

"Finally!"

"What the..." He sputtered as he looked around, taking in the sand, the horse, the lance as if for the first time. He closed his eyes and took a shuddering breath, then tried again. "Vern, where are we?"

I spoke the place's name in my native tongue, enjoying the hisses that emulated the flowing winds. I could have added the wing flap, but I wasn't going to antagonize my injuries.

It didn't matter; the subtleties were lost on my gobsmacked friend. "The Sahara? How did we end up in Africa?"

"No, the Shehehra. About where your Libya is, but in my dimension. In my territory, in fact."

"We're in Faerie? How? What are we doing here?"

"Reenacting my battle with Saint George. Just like you'd wished."

"Saint George?" He spun around, looking for the saint, I guess. Then his brain caught up with the conversation. "Wait. That was a real genie's lamp? There are real Faerie genies?"

"Yep, wish-granting genies, just like in Arab stories, with even more conniving deviousness. Fortunately, they are few and far between. Just our 'luck' that we'd find one." When we got back, I was going to have a serious talk with that shop-keeper.

Father pulled at his pristine white garments that covered his mithril chainmail shirt. "If I'm replacing Saint George, why am I not in full armor? This... This is my D&D character's outfit." He furled his cloak around him in emphasis, then winced as his own injuries made themselves known.

"Yes, it is, in all its glorious impracticalities," I said. "Fortunately, I came to my senses and gave up before I did you any real damage. You're welcome."

"'Real damage'? I think my ribs are cracked!"

"You've got a deep gash on your arm, too," I replied amiably. "There should be some bandages in Bernice's saddlebag."

"Bernice?"

"St. George's valiant steed. Also known as Bubu. You're getting the full wish-fulfillment treatment, you lucky boy."

Father gave me a dirty look and went to the warsteed, moving slowly because the adrenalin was wearing off and he was feeling every one of the not-really-real damages that I'd inflicted on him. I was starting to feel it, too. Aches and nausea. I think I'd shrunk again as we were talking and my body converted mass into healing magic. I glanced at the sea. The cool water would wash my wounds. That would help some.

In a couple of minutes. Right now, it just felt good to be still.

I watched as Father approached Bernice, who'd been surveilling us with big eyes and tense ears.

Father interposed himself between me and her, speaking calmly but confidently. "Hey, Bernice. You okay? Did the big, bad dragon scare you?"

"Hey!" I protested.

Bernice jerked her head, in fear or maybe agreement. Father took her reins and shook them, then eased her head so she had to shift position.

He praised her and rubbed her nose and cheek. He moved around her, talking, rubbing, directing her to move until she released some of the tension. Then, he ran his hands over her, checking for injuries. Only after he was satisfied that she was unharmed and calmer did he reach into the pack and search its contents.

"Where'd you learn to do that?" I asked as he pulled out a waterproof sack with bandage rolls and other medicines. He also found a wineskin.

"I wasn't always a priest, you know. I grew up on a ranch. I had dreams of professional rodeo. I was going to ride broncs a few years, then go back and help Dad with the ranch."

"What happened?"

He popped the cork on the wineskin and sniffed it, then did the same with some of the ointments from the kit. "A horse named Plan Wrecker. I drew him at the Colorado State Fair, and he threw me seven seconds in. I woke up in the hospital with broken bones, a concussion, and the complete conviction that I was meant to be a priest. Any of these antibiotics?" he asked, holding one jar in my direction.

"Doubtful."

"This is going to hurt." He took a large swig from the wineskin, grit his teeth, then poured the contents over his wound. He cussed more like a cowboy than a priest. Bernice stood steady. This, apparently, was something she was used to seeing.

Father breathed out quickly through pursed lips. "Lord, I give my pain in sacrifice for those in Purgatory—and for a friend who's entering chemotherapy," he said, then took one more calming breath. "All right. Which one of these do I put on now?"

I pointed out the right ointment, then helped him tie a bandage on his bicep. Bernice watched warily.

"I thought you and she were friends," Father commented.

"We were, but not at first. It took a few days, maybe a week, and I was the size of a lizard then."

"I don't want to be here that long! Besides, my wish came true. What are we still doing here? You didn't make a wish."

"The others did." I finished the knot, tightening it as gently as I could. Father still hissed with pain, but my words bothered him more.

"What? So, they're here somewhere, too? How are we going to find them? Faerie is huge—just as big as the Mundane."

"Bigger. We have entire civilizations underground, too, remember? But don't worry. I have the feeling we're all supposed to meet up for some great adventure." I paused as a wave of pain and dizziness washed over me. I'd forgotten how much this fight had hurt. I could have done without the reminder.

"That's a nasty wound," Father said, noticing my injuries at last.

"Yeah. If I had wished, it would have been to not get sliced by a demon-tainted lance."

Father nodded. He knew the story of how St. George had appeared through a portal, riding Bernice at full charge. He'd run a demon through with his lance and went after me without even stopping. It had been the first score in a battle that had ended with my becoming little more than a sapient lizard. I'd lost my magic, my size, my flight, even my fire.

But not this time. I'd quit while I was ahead. I could feel the sweetly familiar chemical processes grumbling in the special sac behind my stomach.

"I have an idea," he said. He moved his hand near my wound, then pulled back. "That's not going to poison me or anything?"

I shook my head. "It should be fine."

"Okay, well, bow your head."

I obliged, and he set one hand between my horns and the other lightly over the wound. Then he murmured a prayer of healing.

At first, I felt a pleasant warmth. Then, the demon taint inside me battled with the power of his prayer. I gritted my teeth and sucked in a breath as a whole different kind of fire raced through my veins. Dragons don't shed tears, but that didn't mean I didn't want to cry.

After a moment that seemed like an eternity— and as an immortal being, I don't use that term lightly—Father pulled away. He was as sweaty and out of breath as he had been in our battle. "I'm sorry. I think that's all I'm up to for now," he said.

"Yeah," I said, more a grunt than an agreement. "I think that's about all I can stand." I shivered and took shuddering breaths until I was able to draw and release one more calmly. When I could, I found I did feel better. I let Father know.

"It still looks pretty nasty," he said. "I don't have enough wine to wash it off."

Now that I felt stronger, the sea looked cool and inviting. "I'll go wash off."

"Okay, good. Take your time. I have another idea."

The water soothed my wounds, but as the buoyancy lifted my wings, I felt every break with exquisite intensity. I've heard humans see stars, but I saw pixies. Dozens of little pixies flying around my head, squealing and cooing.

"Won't you play with us, Vurnerrah?"

"You're a mess, Vurnerrah."

"Did you see that storm, Vurnerrah?"

Wait. Those were actual pixies. I roared, and they scattered, leaving me to stand, half-submerged and grimacing in the water.

When the pain had morphed into a bearable blur, mermaids appeared. They swam around me, all questions and exclamations about the storm:

"Won't you play with us, Vurnerrah?"

"Did you see that storm, Vurnerrah?"

"I was so scared, Vurnerrah! Were you scared?"

"Poseidon was so mad. He had planned a party."

"I was going to wear my new shells."

"Will you come to the party with us, Vurner-rah?"

"They canceled the party, Liis! Poseidon was furious!"

"It was because of the storm. Did you see the storm, Vurnerrah?"

One accidentally brushed against my wing and I yipped.

"Vurnerrah, you're hurt!" several exclaimed.

Then they all started crying. One tried to throw her arms around me, but a snap of my teeth disabused her of the idea that I'd find that comforting. Instead, they worked as one to gently carry me deeper into the sea, some supporting me from below while others stroked my hide with their tails and used their hair to floss the sand from between my scales. Despite their gentleness, it was distinctly uncomfortable, but I knew I'd be better off for it.

As they carried me back to shore, one caught sight of Father Rich. "Who is that?"

Father was making a large rectangular pile of sand. He had pulled off his outer tunic and the chainmail shirt and had draped them over Bernice's saddle.

"He's so handsome!"

"Will he come play with us?"

"What is he doing?" one asked, and I had no good answer. Curious, the mermaids watched silently. I watched, too. It was a rare occasion when something could make a mermaid stay quiet, much less a whole pod. I didn't want to spoil it.

Once he had a sandpile about the height of his knees and the breadth of his shoulders, he dusted himself off and went back to Bernice. He put the tunic back on, making my fishy friends sigh with disappointment, then dug through Bernice's packs. He draped a blanket over his sand table, then set a dish and the wine on it.

"Is he hungry?" one of the mermaids asked. "I'll get him some food!"

"No, me!" another said. "Let me!"

"Me, me!" they all started insisting, with shoves and tail flaps as they fought over who would have the honor of tempting the handsome human stranger with food. Father still hadn't noticed. They were speaking in their native language, which sounded more like squeaks and burbles.

Then one cried out, "Look!"

Seemingly from nowhere, a raven swooped toward Father, a loaf of flatbread in its claws. It dropped the bread on the table, cawed once, and flew away, vanishing from view before Father had time to register his surprise.

Father turned the loaf over in his hands, then looked to the sky. "That is so awesome!" he shouted.

The mermaids giggled, then went quiet once again as he reverently began a blessing over the bread, the wine, the water. I realized it wasn't a table he'd set, but an altar.

"He's a priest," one of my companions murmured with disappointment, then brightened. "Vurnerrah, do you think he'll bless us?"

"I'll ask when he's done," I promised. He had other priorities at the moment, like praying for our friends, wherever in this wish-world they might be. While he was at it, he'd better pray for some direction, because I had no idea where to start.

Chapter Three: Welcome to the Wish-World

I sunned myself on the warm, firm sand as I watched Father say a final blessing over the mermaids. It had felt good to rest for a while and let him be useful. He'd not only prayed over each mermaid's head but also coaxed Bernice to the water so they could coo over her.

Before that he spent time working with the warhorse to get her used to me. That would help a lot. In my real past, George had reduced me to the size of a large lizard, but even then, Bubu took days to get comfortable with me. Plus, plenty of other creatures had startled her. More than once, we'd been thrown off her back as she'd reacted with surprise, fear, and aggression. Now, she followed Father docilely as he returned to where I reclined.

Moving slowly in deference to his sore muscles, Father sat next to me. "So, despite everything, I'm kind of having fun," he said.

"Glad to hear it," I said wryly. I was feeling better after Communion myself, but not enough to make up for being stabbed again by a tainted lance. The one time with George had been enough for any dragon's lifetime. It was not my idea of fun to relive that just to make a priest's dream come true.

If Father noticed the ire in my voice, he ignored it. "I mean, even living as close to the Gap as we do, I will probably never get to the Faerie Mediterranean, much less get to meet mermaids. To say Mass for mermaids, no less! So, why are they wearing seashells?"

"Blame the Fae. There have always been small, temporary gaps that open and close between our worlds. The Fae know how to find them. That's how you get legends about fairy folk, plus random sightings of other creatures."

"Like Sasquatch?"

"Yep—and the Loch Ness Monster. That's one of my kin, as a matter of fact. Levvy likes to play peek-a-boo with the gaps. We never cross, however. It's verboten to dragons."

I paused, as the realization of what I'd said struck me. How had I not remembered that until now? Had I known it before? I must have—pre-George, anyway. It was a basic tenant of all dragons—written into our DNA, as Mundanes might say. And I'd forgotten. Even worse, I'd crossed the Gap. I lived among Mundanes—the one thing dragons were never supposed to do.

But God had Called me to go.

Hadn't He?

One of the mermaids summoned Father back to the shore, so he didn't notice my confused silence. As he spoke to the mermaids and accepted their gifts, I racked my brains for details. I came up empty. All I could remember was that God had forbidden dragons to cross the Gap. It was, in a sense, our version of the Forbidden Fruit.

And I'd "eaten" of it.

By the time Father had returned, I had pushed back my confusion as something to ponder later, and put on a neutral, bemused expression as he showed me his gifts: A jug of drink, some fish wrapped in seaweed, a decorative hairpiece—for

Bernice's mane, I assumed. They'd gushed over his pretty warhorsie.

"Anyway, the seashells?" he prompted.

I was glad to get back to such a mundane topic. "Yeah, so you know the Little Mermaid toys? One of the Fae returned from a visit to your world with one and gave it to Poseidon's youngest daughter. Seashell bras have been all the rage ever since. They didn't use to wear anything."

Father blushed a little at the thought but laughed anyway.

"Priest!" the mermaids called out and made drinking motions.

He grinned and held up the jug to show that he was going to drink.

"Is it wine?" he asked me as he pulled the stopper and raised it to his lips.

"It's a specialty of their species," I replied blandly as he took a swallow.

Father choked and gagged.

"Fermented seaweed."

Hacking and gagging, he still managed to wave to the mermaids. I gave him points for that and for not tossing the amphora aside. However, I wasn't going to take the chance he might ditch it at the next convenient opportunity. I snagged it from him and emptied the contents into my gullet. I could use the pain-numbing effects of the alcohol. With my tail, I flung the empty container to them.

I belched. "Hm. Just a touch of sea urchin," I said, smacking my lips.

Father sputtered. "Seriously? You could have warned me!"

"Why should you be having all the fun?"

He turned his face to the heavens, asking for patience, I'm sure. "All right, then, now what? Do you have any ideas on how to find the others, or maybe we should recreate your journey with Saint George?"

"Was that your wish?"

He paused to consider, then said sheepishly. "No, not really. I just wanted to beat the tar out of you. No offense."

"None taken. I'm just glad we quit while I still have my fire." I blew a thin flame into the air. The mermaids squealed their approval at my display.

"Impressive," Father said.

I preened a little, and not just from the praise. I'd forgotten how good it felt to breathe fire.

Beyond the sheer joy of regaining a core dragon ability—something St. George had taken from me over eight centuries ago—it had a physically healing effect. My stomach settled, and the headache I'd been trying to ignore receded. Even beyond that, it was part of a dragon's identity. Fire was not just a weapon to us. It was art. It was communication.

Once this adventure was over, would I get to keep my fire-breathing ability? It was almost too much to hope for, the way my luck ran, so I replied with seriousness. "I'm sending a message. If any of my kin are around, they'll know I need their help. If we can set up a network, we'll have dragons around the world looking for our friends.

"There are other dragons?" Father asked.

"Of course, there are. You thought I was the only one?"

"You never mention them, is all."

I frowned. That's because my kind had abandoned me after my fight with George, and I never knew why. It was a mystery I hadn't been able to solve in over 800 years.

"They're not around anymore," I said. "They've gone into hibernation. But if my kin exist in this wish-world, I just sent out a signal one of them will notice. If they are here, they span the world—and they have contacts. They'll help us find the others, no matter where on or under the earth they may be."

I stood and stretched carefully. "In the mean-time, let's check with some of my contacts."

"Shouldn't we wait here?"

"If my kin are around, they'll find me. We won't be moving that fast. Besides, my wings are broken, and I'd really like to find a healer."

"What? Vern, I'm sorry! That's not what I intended when I wished..."

"That was the storm, not you." The words were out of my mouth before I realized I'd said them. Was that what had happened? Why had I been flying in the storm—or rather, why was I flying so carelessly in a storm that I'd break my wings? Was I chasing someone? Being chased?

"Vern?" Father asked.

"What do you remember from before our fight?" I asked.

"Sitting at the picnic table at the renfest talking about wishes. There was a flash, and then we were in the fight of our lives."

I growled with frustration. That's about what I remembered, too. Figured his wish would start *in medias res*. Why then did I feel so certain that I broke my wings in the storm and not the fight? "There's something weird about this wish-world."

Father snorted. "I'll take your word for it. But that's all the more reason to find the others, and that means a tavern. That is where most adventures begin."

I looked around. "If the wish-world is following Faerie format, we'll find one about two hours west."

Father groaned. "That's a lot of walking. I should have imagined my character with better shoes." He kicked out a foot to show the long, narrow peak of armor that made an impressive display and added to his armor class but were heavy, hot, and uncomfortable.

"What are you complaining about? You get to ride Bubu."

"Boo-boo?"

"That's what George called Bernice when he was feeling cuddly."

Father turned to the saint's warhorse. "Bubu?"

Bernice nodded her head, then rubbed her cheek against his. He laughed and stroked her neck, then mounted. "All right, lead the way."

We walked along the cool, wet sand, the mermaids pacing us, calling to us, asking for more blessings or a chance to pet pretty Bernice. Father tried to ask them about the rest of our group, but they didn't know anything. I hadn't expected them to. Mermaids were a gossipy group, but very little stayed in their minds for long. They might remember long enough to report our presence and injuries to Poseidon if he was interested and patient enough to ask questions. Otherwise, they'd forget the details of our visit. That was the fun thing about mermaids, though. Every encounter had the excitement of a first time for them.

Father chuckled. "I can't believe this is happening."

I grunted. Sure, he could laugh about it. He got to ride the horse. I was getting footsore and my injuries were starting to ache again. "Your ribs aren't proof enough?"

"Yeah, true. How are you doing?"

I moved my jaw back and forth. It was still sore. "I could use some more of that wine. You know, you have a mean right cross. Too bad you didn't use it when Quanz took you hostage."

"They had guns, remember?"

"How can I forget? They shot me. Twice. Or was it three times?"

"Is that story going to get bigger with each telling?"

"Will this one?"

"Probably. Why do the mermaids call you Vyoonrurrah?" He ended with a throat hacking that would have shamed an Arab speaker.

I winced. "Vurnerrah. It's my real name. Pope Pius shortened it to Vern because humans don't have the right vocal cords to pronounce it correctly." I didn't mind having my name mangled, much, as long as real effort was put in. They were only human after all. Plus, we didn't often have occasion for humans to call us by our names, anyway. But when George had reduced me to essentially nothing but a beautiful and intelligent reptile, he'd also consigned me to obedience to the human Church until God returned to me all my dragon abilities.

I had to wonder if he had understood that I would be stuck among humans for centuries, if not millennia. Pope Pius had seen it, though. Hence, my christened name. I might have appreciated it more if he hadn't added "the Wyvern," thinking he was clever.

As generations passed, more and more species forgot my true name—even the High Elves with their long memories. Only the nymphs and the empyrie remembered, anymore. After five or so centuries, I'd stopped noticing.

But here in this wish-world, I was Vurnerrah again. I supposed I should enjoy it while it lasted, but thinking about what I'd lost reopened old wounds I'd forgotten I'd had. I was ready to find the rest of our team and be done with this adventure.

"Maybe I should have wished for something. I could have wished for a long nap in one of my caves. Or maybe to reenact that scene in Lord of the Rings where Smaug is engulfed in molten gold."

Father looked at me as if I were crazy. "Gold melts at like 2000 degrees!"

"I haven't been that warm in millennia." That was it. The next time I had the chance, I was going to make some inconsequential wish for my own comfort. Why should humans have all the fun? "A dragon spa day. Yeah. A hot metal soak, a thorough scale flossing, a massage…"

"A massage? Really?"

"Dragons have muscles, too. Oh, and before all that, a field of sheep where I can select and catch my dinner, with a barrel of Summer Court wine. None of that cheap Exxon rotgut."

"I still can't believe you like gasoline. How did you even figure that out?"

I shrugged. "Don't judge my taste buds just because they are more varied than yours. I stopped a robbery at the gas station on my corner, and the guy gave me a couple of gallons in reward. I drop by now and then, show people I've taken a special interest, and he tosses me some spare food and a gallon or two." I grimaced. "I could use some Premium right now."

As if awaiting a cue, the mermaids started calling, "Fatherpriest! Vurnerrah!"

They'd forgotten that they'd given us gifts, so we were treated to another hairpiece for Bernice and a new amphora of seaweed wine for each of us. This time, Father only pretended to drink before asking to keep the rest.

"We should share this with the others," he said, tying the jug to the saddle.

I grinned. "Now, you're thinking."

We heard a chuckle and looked to see a fairy reclining on a boulder that hadn't been there a minute ago. He wore leather pants, a bowler hat, and nothing else, and his hair was slicked back as if he'd been swimming recently. His wings were dripping slightly. Yet his hat was dry.

He gave us a smile full of mischief. He jumped off the rock and strode toward Father. "A well-meaning joke played in good humor among friends always warms my heart, it does. Robin Goodfellow as your service, my dear paladin."

"Otherwise known as Puck—yes, like from Shakespeare," I told Father, then added, "What are you doing here?"

He spread his hands innocently. "I'm merely about my mistress's business when I decided to take a short respite among these most enchanting mermaids." (At this the mermaids giggled and preened.) "And what great fortune it be, for had I not, I would not have been here to discover you in your time of need. Friend dragon, you do not look your best."

"Thanks for noticing," I grumbled.

Father asked, "Can you help him? Heal his wounds?"

"I can do better! Let me take you to my mistress, Titania, Queen of the Summer Court. Her hospitality is famed among the tribes of sapients and not lightly refused. She can heal you, equip you, and help you find these friends you seek, I'm sure."

"At a price," I warned Father. However, Titania and I went back a long way. I had witnessed her springing forth from the rosebud. I was there when her parents promised her and her sister Mab in marriage to Oberon. I'd counseled her...

Why was I remembering this now?

Whatever. At least my memories told me that while there was more to this than a friendly offer of help—which should have been obvious, given the source—we would not be in any immediate danger. Besides, hadn't I just wished for Faerie wine?

Fortunately, Robin Goodfellow mistook my pause for suspicion. He feigned indignance. "But Vurnerrah, are you not the favorite of my Queen and Court? You, who have played in our pranks, counseled us to peace, ensured harmony between the sisters and their husband."

"You overstep, Puck," I said on reflex. No fairy should comment publicly on the relationship troubles of their king and queens. I'd told their parents it was a bad idea to marry the twins to the same husband. And why was I remembering that now?

Puck bowed. "No disrespect meant, your grandeur. I only wished to emphasize that you are welcome among us, always—and especially now. Not that we believe the rumors, of course."

"What rumors?" Father asked, sparing me the need.

But Puck waved his hand as if it were of no consequence. "Please. You are weary and sore, and hungry, I'd wager. Let me bring you home."

Father looked at me.

Puck was right. I was tired and sore. And hungrier than I wanted to let on. My body was expending a lot of energy—physical and magical—to mend my wounds. I was either going to start sacrificing my size again or I was going to have to eat a large meal, like bovine-large. The thought of walking another hour and a half did not appeal to me.

I bowed my head regally. "If it makes you happy. I would be glad to see Titania, anyway."

Puck bounced on his toes and clapped. "Wonderful! Wonderful. Now if you would just make room..." He took Father by the elbow and led him and Bernice away from the boulder and to my side.

Puck put his back to us, squared his stance, then, with thumb and forefinger in the "OK" sign, crossed his wrists. Then he moved one hand in circles. It looked remarkably familiar, but nothing I've seen a fairy do. In fact, it reminded me of a certain human who took it from a movie.

"What are you doing?" I asked.

"Fascinating, is it not? It helps to focus the magic. One of our young fighters developed the technique. Now, silence, if you would, your greatness."

Father and I exchanged glances. Samwise!

The portal opened, and we stepped through.

Chapter Four: Side Quest of the Summer Court

We arrived at Titania's palace to a party in full swing, and I meant that literally; the dancers swayed and twisted each other back and forth at a furious rate while the human band struggled to keep up. Drums kept time. The piano pounded out the chords. Two horns played backup while the saxophone player ran up and down scales as if the key to sanity lay in the right combination of sound. I caught a lot of missed notes. I cut them some slack; they were in a fugue state, after all.

The Faerie didn't care, either, as long as the music continued, and the band wasn't about to stop. To do so would forfeit their lives.

The band wasn't the only thing they'd stolen from the Mundane. Everyone wore Mundane clothing, ripped in the back to let their wings though. The women wore flapper dresses with jewels and tassels, most cut above the knee, though some as long as the ankles. They had jeweled headbands with feathers or half-shell hats perched atop short, bobbed haircuts. The males wore loose suits with wide ties. I liked their hats. Others just had their hair slicked back with some kind of grease. The shoes looked like nothing I'd seen among the Seelie before, and the women had rows of beads around their necks and nylons with seams up the backs of their legs.

There were humans among the revelers, too, drinking, dancing, laughing. Several had a manic, haunted look in their eyes.

Father gaped. "It's like the Roaring 20s met a rave."

I snickered. "Traditionally, they borrow from an era in the Mundane for the theme for the party."

"Have you ever seen one from our future?"

"Remember the bar scene in Raumpatrouille?" I asked just to mess with him. The German sci-fi from the 1960s has laughable, highly choreographed dance scenes that my friends loved to mock.

The horn in the band let out a high-pitched squeal that made us wince, then darted over the notes in a frenzy as if chased. My heart caught the excitement of the notes and beat just a bit faster. I liked it.

Father let out a low whistle. "He's good. Who is he?"

"Probably no one. Now, concentrate. See the female fairy on the divan? That's Titania, Queen of the Summer Court. We need her help, so you need to stay calm and polite and nonjudgmental, got it?"

At the far end of the ballroom on a dais, Titania lounged in the arms of a human. Their actions alone could give this party an R+ rating. Father said, "She's not acting like any royal I've ever heard of. The man beside her. That's not Oberon, is it?"

"No, and you're not going to comment, got it?"

"Okay, okay," Father said. "He's human, isn't he? In fact, many of them are."

Suddenly, one of the humans noticed us—or rather, noticed me. It was enough to break her from her spell. She screamed.

The revelers all turned toward us. The band stopped two beats later, shushed by a courtier who was in charge of them. They let their arms drop.

One closed his eyes in relief. Another braced his hands on his knees and panted. He muttered something about "going dry" and got a quick lash by the courtier.

One of the fairies shouted, "Puck!"

Soon, they were all chanting, "Puck, Puck!" as the crowd split to make a walkway for us. Puck took the lead, waving and bowing and soaking in the adulation. I expected that. What I didn't expect was how they were looking at me: with hesitation, suspicion, and distrust.

What had I done that I didn't remember, and why was it reflecting into the wish-world?

Father seemed to be picking up the vibes, too. "You're sure you can trust Titania?"

"I can handle her. I've known her since she could sleep in a rosebud."

"Yeah?" Father muttered. "How much do you remember?"

I ignored him and concentrated on looking as regal as I could, considering I was small, wounded, and aching with every step. I was an Eighth Day Creation, after all. Father, ever the paladin, moved with dignified steps, holding Bernice's reins. He managed to keep his expression from being too judgmental, but when his gaze came upon the tear-streaked face of a human girl, his hand tightened on the hilt of his sword.

I flicked my tail, smacking his calf to draw his focus to our more pressing matters. My authority only went so far. If he drew steel here, he would not leave alive.

Queen Titania had her entire attention on the man she was kissing. So, she and Oberon had fought again. Good. I didn't like Oberon, and the feeling was mutual. Did that predate my fight with George? Father was right; I didn't remember a lot about the fairy from before then. Yet I did remember that Titania at this age was vain and emotional, and Oberon had way too much fun pushing her buttons.

The Herald of the Winter Court stepped in our path as we reached the throne. While Titania disengaged herself from the embrace of her new toy, he gave the accepted greeting for a dragon party crasher. Of the 2,315 greetings, there is only one, and he delivered it with casual perfection as if he needed to use it every day. Even so, he didn't sound very welcoming.

Titania, for her part, ignored me. Instead, she smiled at Puck. "My faithful servant!"

He gave her a deep, theatrical bow. "It is my duty and joy to fulfill your commands."

"And so you have. You have the favor of this court—but for now, enjoy yourself. We shall speak of your reward later. But first! The paladin?"

She turned her nose at Father as if smelling something foul.

Puck bowed even more deeply as he shrugged. "Vurnerrah's new pet, I assumed. He insisted they come together. I had no choice."

I rolled my eyes. Like he'd even asked.

She smiled sympathetically, but I saw the falseness in her eyes. She spoke with sweet venom. "Yet you did choose to parade him—a paladin— through our festivities, no doubt thinking only of turning the focus to your victory. That was in extremely poor taste, my dear, theatrical Puck."

"Yes, my queen." He cringed.

She pursed her lips thoughtfully. "So, then, perhaps recognition is reward enough?"

"Yes, my queen." Puck sighed.

Now her smile brightened into her eyes. "Then so be it! Let it be known throughout all the

Summer Court that Robin Goodfellow, loyal and clever, through wit and cunning, was the first to find and bring to me the dragon Vurnerrah!"

Everyone applauded and the band played a fanfare. Puck turned and accepted the congratulations graciously, but his grin was more of a grimace.

"Now, go! I've no more need of you," Titania said, and Puck melted into the crowd.

That bit of business done, she turned her attention at last to me.

"Vurnerrah," she purred, and it sent a thrill along my spine. Next to dragons, no other species came close to pronouncing our names as well, and the Titania had a special flare. She stepped off the dais, arms flowing in time to the sway of her hips. She unfolded her wings in a luxurious show. I felt the heat of the room rise and pulses increase as the males reacted to her.

All except her human plaything, that is. He had passed out on her divan. He snored, but his fairy handler was too engrossed in the queen to discipline him.

She circled me, looking me over. "You are a mess."

So much for sweet talk. "It's been a tough week."

"So I've heard." She caressed my cheek crests with the back of her hand. I fought the urge to purr, myself. I did love getting scratched behind the cheek crests. I had a flash of memory: Griss and me visiting when she and her sister Mab were just children. They'd insisted we sit with them and let them rub our scales and, with nothing better to do, we'd indulged them. It was a pleasant afternoon that lasted six years.

Griss. Grislakeh. I had a sudden flash of a dragon with scales the color of sunset and eyes that sparkled with mischief and intellect. Who was she, and why would I remember her now?

And what had Titania heard?

Titania stepped up close to Father. She did not rise to meet his eyes, but tilted her head, her lips not quite brushing his chin. He stared ahead and feigned disinterest. "Where did you find so strapping a human? So broad of shoulder..."

"It's a long story."

She chuckled. "So it would seem." She set a hand on his shoulder then trailed it down his chest. When she got to his broken ribs, she pressed hard. He flinched.

"You're a mess, too, paladin," she said in perfect Latin.

"It has been a tough week," he said.

It was the perfect reply. Titania stepped away, laughing. She stepped back, arms and wings gracefully spread wide to indicate her court. She'd always been graceful, even as a child. Then, she clapped her hands imperiously. Several of her attendants ran to her, half bent in obeisance while they awaited her commands.

Titania said, "I want healers tending the paladin. Feed him stout food. He will not be rejoining the festivities, I'm sure. And do have a human farrier remove those offensive iron shoes from his beautiful mount and replace them with something more suitable. In fact, outfit her. So magnificent a warrior as this should have a properly equipped horse."

"Some food and a place to rest and pray will be just fine," he said. Father was no fool. He'd heard enough fairy tales about the dangers of becoming beholden to fairies.

But the Summer Court Queen's eyes flared. Literally. They went flame red, then yellow. It was a thing of beauty—to a dragon. Humans and Seelie alike quailed at the sight. Again, the room fell silent.

"You will accept my gifts, and you will like them!"

He glanced at me. I gave a brief nod. Titania wasn't doing this for kindness or to incur an obligation. In D&D terms, she was leveling up Father—but for what? And why was Titania searching for me, in particular? This wish-world had more plans for us.

Father gave her his most courteous bow. "Forgive my impertinence, Your Highness. I am grateful for any kindness you show me and my faithful warhorse, Bernice. You are as generous as you are beautiful."

She smirked. Her eyes cleared to the sunny blue of a midmorning sky. "Better. Now, go. *Nunc vade.* The rest of you, dance! Frolic! Love! We are the Golden Ones, and ours is the right to pleasure!"

Cheers rose from the crowd and they toasted her with martini glasses complete with olives on toothpicks.

Father and Bernice were led away by three dapper fairies in suspenders. The band, rested from the break and fortified by faerie drink, played with renewed vigor. Couples took each other's hands and began to strut and sway. With lithe grace that was a dance in itself, Titania led me to the exit behind her throne. Beyond it was her private garden, where we could have a conversation away from the noise of the revelry and safe from spying ears. As we passed her divan, she paused to stroke the cheek of the human sprawled on it. "Ah, dear Gwaelod."

The human let out a loud snore.

She glared at him in disgust. "He brays like an ass! Oh, I was bored with him, anyway. Guards, expel him from our realm. Leave him where a portal may open. But first!"

She plucked a jeweled pin from her hair and wove it into his. Then as if the act had returned her to childhood, she flounced to the door, crooking her finger at me to follow.

The enchanted door closed, cutting off the chaotic chorusing of the musicians and leaving us with the gentle sounds of leaves rustling in a soft breeze. Although we'd arrived around sunset, the sun hung high in the sky. Time here was fluid and under her command. Servants waited just inside the entrance. They flew to us, asking our pleasure, but she waved them away with an imperious flick of her hand.

She led me down an enchanted trail. The path widened to accommodate both of us. We would meander along it for as long as our conversation needed before reaching the destination she'd decided upon. I hoped it wasn't long. Despite the shortcut thanks to Puck, I was tired and achy. I hoped she just wanted to play or complain about her husband.

No such luck.

"My people tell me of dragons in the Mundane," she opened.

I shrugged. "Yes, and?"

She stopped to gape at me with an impressive combination of fury, astonishment, and fear. I realized I'd spoken as present-day me, who had for the past year been subjected to the Mundane legends and misinformation of the creatures they called dragons. Old me, even after George, had lived in blissful ignorance.

I feigned annoyance to hide my mistake. "Legends! Tales. It's not us."

"Are you so sure?" she asked, and something about how she said it made my scales crawl. But she turned back to the trail and our walk as she continued. "My scouts say otherwise. Your kind have no place in the Mundane. You belong here. Long have I searched for you and your twin to warn you or scold you as you so often scolded my sister and me."

Twin? Again, a flash of memory made my heartbeat accelerate. Again, I hid my reaction. "I prefer to call it 'advising.'"

"Then take my advice, Vurnerrah: Find your twin, figure out what your kin are up to, and convince them to return to their rightful places before their actions damage this world in ways no one can repair."

I followed her through a shade-dappled trail to a knoll where a great elm spread its branches wider than I was long. Her great-grandfather had planted that tree when he established the kingdom.

She dropped all queenly pretense when she reached the security of the tree. Settling under the shade of its branches, she patted the ground next to her. I lay down, and she ran her fingers over my wings and ribs, frowning as she counted the fractures. "You are a mess. Why did the paladin challenge you? Did you burn his village?"

"What? No! He's a Mundane. I told you..." My voice trailed off lest I lie and say I had never been to the Mundane. "I haven't burned a village in ages," I added. That was true enough.

She sighed. "No, of course not. You didn't do anything. None of your kind are doing anything it seems. Monsters are running rampant in the lands, and you are playing with holy knights? Where have you been?"

That question begged a longer answer than I wanted to give at the moment, so I skirted the issue. "Playing? I've been locked in combat for way too long with a particularly stubborn paladin who had God on his side. The only reason I'm not reduced to a sapient lizard is because I called a draw. Tell me about these monsters."

"I have had my knights scouring the earth in search of you and your twin to give you vital intelligence about your own kind. And now, you presume to ask me for information about the happenings in your own territories?"

"I just want to compare notes," I replied mildly. I could not afford to let her get suspicious. Even a wish-world Titania could be a dangerous thing, and I'd rather have her on my side of this adventure. "You always hear the best stuff. Knowledge makes it easier for me to defend my turf."

She tickled me behind my cheek crests. "Now, you presume to flatter me. Not this time. I must get back to the festivities. Besides, you'll find out soon enough, but you're in no shape to defend anything. Stay still and I will heal you, and you will listen to my important concerns. I'm sure then you'll know how to repay me for my generosity."

I wanted to protest that that generosity didn't work that way, but not only was that a losing argument, but neither of us was in the mood to enjoy the debate. I gave myself to her ministrations. I gritted my teeth against the stabs and prickles as my delicate wing bones knitted and the tears in the membranes fused. For all that Titania had publicly declared me "a mess," no one had to know the extent of my weakness.

"Oberon is a selfish turd," she opened.

"This argument again? There are other play-things."

"Oh, but this one was adorable, with skin the color of copper and soft curly stubble on his chin. And his accent! Mundanes have the most delectable accents. All I wanted was for him to read to me while I bathed. Just read. But that's too much to ask, it seems. Why are males so possessive?"

"You're asking a dragon about possessiveness?"

She chuckled, and I felt an increase in her power. Titania always found strength in happiness, which is why when her parents split the rule of the Fae, they gave her the warm seasons. Mab, being fond of reason and cool thought, took winter. Then, to unite the kingdom, they married both to Oberon.

Fae logic gets mighty twisted when it comes to affairs d'heart.

"I share everything—my reign, my people, my husband. Not that he is much of a husband. I share everything except my bath, especially not with a hairy human! Oberon knows this, yet he can't even share with me the pleasure of a voice! Then he left. With the Midsummer celebrations only weeks away, he left. No explanation. Poof."

She made a little cloud of pixie dust to emphasize her point.

"He's not with Mab?"

"Ha! Of course, he's with Mab. They are making mischief, and they've left me out!"

"How rude!"

"She has only gotten more rude over the years. Her whole court has gone mad. Do you know what their idea of fun is? They found some Mundane device that lets them manipulate images on a screen. Now, they sit with their backs to each other, pushing buttons and talking through devices on their heads. They are handsbreaths from each other, but they talk through these devices. And that is fun for them! They are getting fat and slow, and she does not care. Mab is mad. Mad Mab. Mabbie the Mad. Mad Mab MabbieMad Mad Mab..."

She continued to sing-song her sister's insanity as she worked my wings, her magic getting clumsier until I snapped my teeth at her.

"Are you such a tender thing, then? Just a minute more," she scolded, but worked more gently as she continued her conversation. "Yes, but when Oberon came up with some fun new game, did he invite me? No, he abandoned me—abandoned the whole Summer Court in the height of our season—to run off and play games with my fat, rude, mad twin.

"So, I am alone on this, our celebration of love, making do with a braying human, yet you, my dear Vurnerrah, have interrupted even that."

I butted her leg with my cheek. "I'm better company than some silly mortal."

She scratched behind my cheek crests. "Maybe. Under different circumstances. But tonight, I am vexed and unsatisfied and undyingly curious."

That was my cue. "Perhaps I can at least assuage that. What if I found out what Oberon was up to and the role Mab plays in it? Because you're my favorite, of course," I said.

It was a game I played with the twins from when they were tiny, declaring each my favorite then coming up with some convoluted conditions and excuses that let them both imagine themselves in the top slot of my affection.

This time, however, I meant it. Mab knew better than to deny Titania the attention of their husband on this night. And I did feel much better.

Titania whispered a spell, and I felt a dusting of warmth and comfort settle over me as the last of her healing magic settled in under my scales. Then she patted my shoulder.

"Stay, rest. I will make accommodations for your paladin so that he shall not be corrupted by our celebrations. You may remain here. I know you no longer approve of our ways."

Where my shoddy memory had failed me about my kind, I remembered why I disapproved of her "ways." The celebrations were more than parties, they were key to the fairies' survival; a time to drink in magical power when it was best attuned to their physiology. Once, they had been full of love, innocence, and joy; then came the Proscribed Prank, played by Queen and King against each other and breaking the trust of their union. It tore the kingdom and sullied the celebrations. Festivities soured into debauchery and indulgence as they more desperately tried to recapture an intimacy that had been lost.

That had happened long before my actual fight with George. In the years since, I'd seen the influence of the fae on the Mundane world wane. The parties borrowed less and less from that other universe, and the fairies' power diminished as well.

Had we dragons tried to warn them? I could not remember, but I was getting a distinct feeling that we were failing in our responsibilities. I apparently had, it seemed, if monsters were running wild in my territory. If—Titania was a fairy; she'd twist the truth to best suit her mood and purpose.

Regardless, I had a responsibility to my Mundane friends to find them and get them out of here, and somehow, a monster-infested part of my own lands seemed a fitting place to start looking.

Fairies came into the glen bearing food and soft cloths. They fawned over me, tsking over the sad state of my hide. Two lithe fairies took a paw each and began to clean my nails. Others used magic and gentle scrubbing to wash my scales and polish my horns. A few strong males massaged my muscles. Sensing I wasn't interested in talking, they took turns telling me stories and court gossip.

I put aside my brooding. This was the wish-world, I told myself. Nothing I do here makes a difference to anyone but me and my friends. I may not have made a wish, but nothing said I couldn't enjoy a little pampering. After all, hadn't I said something about wanting a spa day?

Chapter Five:
Thunderpaws, Dire Corgi!

I stood upon a mountain crag in the Himalayas, the air biting into my scales. I was uncomfortable. I was furious. But I was not alone. All around the rocky mountainside were my kin, a bright patchwork of colors against the stark terrain. The sight of it would have filled me with joy if not for the reason for our gathering. The King and Queen of the Fairy Court had done the unthinkable. They had broken their covenant with each other and with God. Durrehkeh had called us to inflict punishment upon them.

"We should eat them." His voice bounced off the rock and echoed with power. He blew an arch of yellow fire that lit the dim sky. "Flame them. Destroy them all until the entire species is gone. God can begin again with a species more suited to obedience."

I saw his face, sharp and dark as slate, indignant and enraged on behalf of our Creator. Durrehkeh was the first of our kind, the eldestkin, and in those moments we all felt his power and authority. The others cowered before his fierce determination, but my twin Grislakeh and I argued him down. How long had it taken us? What had we said that finally brought him around? I heard myself arguing, felt the language flow from my mouth and body, but I could not make out what I was saying.

Nor could I bring up the face of my twin.

I slept fitfully and awoke with dreams I did not remember but which left me edgy and disturbed. At least I was healed. In fact, I was in better shape than I'd been in before we started on this cockamamie wish adventure. I shook myself, bathed in Titania's pond for the sheer joy of feeling the enchanted waters, then demanded that my pet paladin be brought to join me for breakfast.

Titania had been true to her promise. Father came in looking rested, content, and leveled up. His mithril chainmail glowed with fairy magic, and they'd added some magical upgrades to his blade as well. They also gave him new boots of enchanted leather that were stronger than his metal ones but far better suited for walking and riding. His clothes were cleaner than any dry cleaner in the Mundane could make them, and his hair...

He caught my eye and pulled at the wavy shoulder-length locks self-consciously. "I can't explain the hair, and I figure it's best if I don't try."

But even better, he'd found Samwise!

Sam wore the garb of a Summerfae cavalryman—light armor in sunflower colors, riding boots, a spot on his belt for a scabbard and short sword. His hair was pulled back into a topknot. And yes, he had wings—graceful curls of membrane in iridescent browns and gold. He kept his original height, but he'd slimmed some to better match his new species and vocation. My dragon sight also took in the aura of magic that flowed through him. Overall, not a bad look for our usually shy friend.

"So?" I asked our fairy warrior as everyone took seats at the table Titania's servants had set for us. "How are you enjoying living the life of a Summerfae?"

He looked around, but I'd already made sure we were alone. "It's been interesting. I mean, I really enjoy working magic and it actually, you know, working. Wait! Watch this!"

He stood up and walked over to a charred and brittle branch of the grandfather tree. He cupped his hands around it and whispered some words. At once, the branch grew smooth and supple. A bud formed at its tip.

He turned to us, and I thought he was going to cry with joy. "How freaking awesome is that?"

"The most freaking awesome," I agreed. "Enjoy it while you can, because as soon as we find the others and get that lamp, we're back to the real world."

"What's the rush?" he grumped as he sat down. "Aren't you enjoying yourself? I mean, isn't this a lot like home for you?"

I nodded. "Too much. The fight with George. The mermaids. Robin Goodfellow. The Summer Court. This..." I waved a paw, taking in not just the garden, but all of Faerie. "This is all playing out from my memories but adding information I didn't know. Or maybe I did, and I forgot. I don't know."

"So?" Sam asked, stuffing a pastry shell with a sweet cream that my swiss-cheese memory now reminded me was made from milking beetles.

"So, why from my memories, when I didn't make a wish? Why not from one of Ray's worlds? Surely, he'd have gotten a kick out of that. You never said anything about being a fighter in Titania's Court."

"But I did wish to be Saint George," Father said.

"No," I corrected. "You said you wished you knew how George handled me, and I made it more specific by saying you wished you could smack me like George did and have God approve."

He thought back. "Yeah, you're right."

Sam chewed thoughtfully. If he kept eating like that, he'd go back to his original girth, species considerations notwithstanding. "Still, that doesn't mean any of this is real, though. This could just be an elaborate fantasy. Wish fulfillment to the extreme."

Father said, "Extreme, is right. This wish-fulfillment broke two of my ribs."

That got Sam's attention. "If we hadn't healed you, would you have kept those injuries after the wish was done?"

A fairy herald entered the room, sparing me from speculating. We all jumped back into character—or rather, they did. I got to play myself. A good thing, too, considering I usually played a halfling thief.

The herald bowed deeply to me—something I would have missed as a halfling, for certain—and bade us join Titania in her court. I was glad to see he used the proper show of respect and the correct phrasing—not that I actually remembered all the invitations applying to dragons, mind you, but instinct told me it felt right. We stood from the table, Sam stuffing a couple of treats into his pockets. Father picked up an apple he said was for Bubu.

You'd have never known the Great Hall had hosted an even greater party. The tables of food and drink were gone, the mess cleared. Now, it had the beauty and harmony of a mountain meadow at the beginning of summer; the colors reminiscent of wildflowers giving their last, best blossoms before succumbing to the heat, the walls green then gold then the purplish-blue of distant mountains. They gave way to curved ceilings with such subtlety that humans would have a hard time discerning where the room ended and field and sky began. The ceiling mimicked the sky outside, and despite it being cloudless, the light nonetheless seemed to focus on the brilliant gold throne on which Titania sat, posture regal, eyes languid, sated with magics and pleased with herself once again.

A forget-me-not grew from the seat of Oberon's throne.

The humans had been sent home, save two. Her snoring lover Gwaelod had been returned to her but wearing the head of a donkey and manacles on his ankles. He reclined at her feet, quiet and still except for the occasional mournful bray as he touched his nose with human hands.

"Hey, like in..." Father whispered, and Sam promptly elbowed him.

The other, one of the band members, was begging to remain. He stood before Titania, supported on each side by two Summerfae still in their frilled Mundane dresses. Even though he was squinting from the hangover and the brilliance of Titania's glory, he offered her the pleasure of his saxophone.

"I ain't never played like I played last night," he said. "I can't go back. Let me stay and I will make my sax sing for you. I will make it wail. My baby and I don't need no band. I'll compose a song, just for you. Just give me a shot. I ain't never played like I did last night..."

Her smirk became a smile at his impassioned plea. She did love being told she brought out the best in someone. Lazily, she waved her hand to dismiss them. "We were much pleased with your performance yesterday, though it was three of your human days, not one night."

"Three days," he whispered, and as if his body suddenly understood, his knees buckled, nearly toppling his companions as well. Even so, he did not lose his grip on his horn. I wasn't sure he could let it go if he tried.

"Oh, do you hurt now, my talented pet?"

He looked up, the hope of relief in his eyes. "Help me? Please?"

She stepped down and caressed his bristly cheek. Her touch was tender, but I sensed no healing magic in it. Her voice was a velvety counterpoint to the brutality of her refusal. "No. Excellence comes at a price, my pet, even here, and Art is a harsh mistress."

"Worth it," he whispered.

His reaction pleased She Who Burned with Summer's Intensity. She returned to her throne. "Take him away. Find him quarters. But do not heal him. Let him fully appreciate the price of excellence in our court."

His companions had to drag him out, but he muttered thanks and hummed to himself as he passed by.

I stepped to the center as if it were always my place to do so—which, considering I'm a dragon, it was.

Gwaelod let out a huge "heehaw!" of surprise and fear.

"Your doing?" I asked Titania. I managed not to laugh. I shouldn't have found it funny. I know. But still.

She reached down and fondled his long, velvety ears. "No, though it does amuse me. Tierdan felt it necessary to make up for his inattention to his charge last night."

"You'll need to fix him before you return him," I pointed out, more for the sake of my friends and Titania's unlucky victim. Doubtless, he was envisioning a future with a mule's head.

She sighed with mild petulance. "I know. The spell will wear off soon. Unfortunately, he panicked and ran through a gap and we had to retrieve him. But not before he startled some poor playwright who had fallen asleep over his manuscript. No matter. You are rested, Magnificent One? And you, friend priest, did you find your accommodations to your liking?"

Father stepped forward and bowed. "Very suitable, thank you, your highness. I appreciated the privacy and the chance to pray."

She raised a brow at me as if to say, *See? I do know how to treat a paladin.* "I believe I felt your prayers last night. The roses bloomed. They don't often during the festival. Perhaps next year, I should invite more priests and fewer playthings."

Her courtiers chuckled, and her languid gaze hardened. "It was not a joke."

The sky filled with roiling clouds. The room darkened. Her court went very still. Then, point made, she relaxed, and the sky cleared once again.

She returned her attention to me. "So, Vurner-rah, Innocent Among His Kind. We are in agreement as to what must be done?"

Never was I so glad for an indeterminate phrasing. I nodded my head in agreement. Beside me, I could feel Father tense with unasked questions, but wisely, he kept them unasked.

Titania smiled with satisfaction, though something in her eyes told me she might be satisfied, but not necessarily happy. For some reason, that made me feel better. However, all she said was, "Excellent. We have indeed found the friends Father Paladin described. They are in a tavern in the human kingdom of Farrayway. I see one of my guardsmen stands at your side."

Sam hastened forward and bowed deeply. "Forgive my forwardness, She of Brilliant Light. I met Father Paladin in passing, and he invited me to break fast with them."

She tilted her head toward Father. "You have a liking for our Gedarrin?"

"I learned from Robin Goodfellow that Gedarrin is a gifted mage as well as a capable fighter," Father said. Truthful, yet, not completely accurate. Puck was not going to be happy when he found out.

But at least it worked in our favor. Titania nodded. "Then, please, take him on your quest, Vurnerrah. Consider him the eyes and ears and strong arm of the Summer Court."

Which meant, she didn't trust me to complete our deal. Understandable, since I was more interested in finding our friends and leaving than in finding her deadbeat husband and playing marriage counselor. Good thing Sam was exactly the fighter I wanted.

I made a show of barely hidden petulance. "You're too kind, Your Majesty."

She preened. "I know. We have anticipated your needs. Take them to the stables. You'll find all you need there. And give Gedarrin his war hound."

"Thunderpaws?" Sam exclaimed.

She flicked an annoyed look. "Do you think I would give you another hound? That beast is annoyingly loyal to you. Now go, before I change my mind."

More bows, and we were led away. I could see both Father and Sam fight to keep composure as we made the long walk down the Great Hall, but all eyes were upon us. In fact, I saw more than a few female eyes turning our way. Now, of course, I knew I looked good. I was still small for a dragon, but I was buffed—as in shiny scales, buffed—and I felt stronger than I had in centuries. And Father, of course, was resplendent in pure white and gold paladin's robes with shining mithril peeking out of the gaps and flowing dark hair. But it was Samwise—Gedarrin—that was the actual center of attention.

Instinct and a keen sense of smell told me where the stables were, so I dismissed our attendants as soon as we were out of the palace. Once we were over a small hill and out of sight, Sam launched himself in the air and did a couple of fancy twists and spins. "Thud's here! And did you see how those girls were looking at me? It was like that all night last night. But I could hardly enjoy it because I was worried about Thunderpaws. What if we'd disappeared and he was alone?"

"I don't think any time is going to pass in our world," I assured him. "Besides, I recall someone making a wish on his behalf as well—and it was the two of you that got us into this mess."

"Oh, come on, Vern. This is the best day ever! Do you think they made him little fairy armor?"

"I don't think 'little' describes it," Father said. He pointed to the fenced field where a white warhorse was being chased by a horse-sized corgi.

"Thud! No, bad dog!" Sam yelled and flew toward them. We ran after him.

Bernice was running full out around the perimeter of the field, Thunderpaws bounding behind her, yapping and oblivious to Sam's commands. Suddenly, Bernice reared and spun, hooves flashing.

"Bernice, stop!" Father yelled.

Thunderpaws flopped onto his back, waving his stubby paws. His tongue lolled. Bernice lowered her hooves safely to the ground and bumped him with her nose.

Then they were off again.

Sam stopped midair to watch. We caught up with him. He landed and rejoined us.

"Aw, man. I don't have my cell phone to record this," he moaned.

Thud passed Bernice and cut her off, then ran circles around her. She spun in place to keep her eyes on him.

Sam whistled through his teeth. "Thud, sploot!"

Thunderpaws, six feet of fluff and joy, fell flat on his belly. Bernice paused, backed up, and nosed him. He obligingly rolled onto his back.

At this point, Sam couldn't take it any longer. He flew over the fence to cuddle his dog. Father joined him.

Behind us, I heard a fairy heave a longsuffering sigh. Three others were with him, loaded with supplies and armor for our valiant dire corgi.

"Your battle steed is wagging his tail," I observed. "The paladin is rubbing his belly."

"It's embarrassing, I know. It is only this breed. I have begged my lady to reduce their size and release them to the humans."

"You're such a Fluffy Thuddy!" Sam called out, joining Father in giving belly rubs and telling Thunderpaws that he was a good battle doggie, oh, yes, he was.

"Not to mention the effect they have on their riders. Perhaps we should send them through a portal to the Mundane," the fairy continued.

Father pulled Bernice aside and was checking her tack. She, too, had been given the royal treatment. Her mane and tail were combed and braided. Her shoes, as promised, had been replaced with a faerie metal far superior to the iron she'd worn (and far safer to the Magical species of Faerie like myself). Her gray coat had been brushed smooth. Someone had cleaned and repaired her tack and added a finely woven yet durable saddle blanket with silver tassels. Her reins were also adorned with silver ribbon and more tassels. Overall, Bernice looked more suited for a princess than a warrior. Someone was having a little fun with Father. Still, for all its prettiness, I could tell her tack had been upgraded as well. Father removed the bells from her bridle but otherwise appeared satisfied.

The Master of Steeds ordered the other fairies to equip us and saddle Thud. One took Sam aside, to brief him on his mission, most likely. Then, they all wished us luck and retreated. They may have had their magic renewed, but everyone was tired after the party.

I waited until I was sure we were alone, then said, "All right, Gedarrin. Let's see how good that magic is. Can you open a portal to Farrayway?"

He grinned. "You mean like this?" He did a fancy hand waving reminiscent of Dr. Strange, and a portal appeared. We saw a tropical island, then a wintery landscape, then a quaint farmland with a castle in the background. Then it faded. "I can take us almost anywhere. I can't get us home, though. I did try."

"Do you think that's how we end the quest?" Father asked. "We find the Gap?"

"I doubt it," I replied. "The Gap doesn't open for another 800 or more years in the real world."

Sam blanched. "But this is a wish-world, right? There has to be a way home?"

I shrugged. "One thing at a time. First, let's find our friends."

Chapter Six: Victim of Bad Press

The Kingdom of Farrayway was nestled in a wide but cozy valley in our equivalent of the Pyrenees mountains. Castle Farrayway snugged up against a great cliff but near the valley, so that it overlooked the lands on both sides of the river. The woods had been cleared during the war for a league around the castle to prevent enemies from sneaking up on them, but during the long time of peace, it had regrown lush and full of deer. The fields would be green with ripening crops, and the animals sunning themselves while munching on grass. The portal opened in the newer forest. We stepped through, and I led the way toward the castle.

For some reason, one of the things I did remember was my time in the kingdom of Farrayway, and I shared the story as we walked. That was in the day when battling a dragon had been the vogue for courtships. After the first couple of times of eating the annoying offender and then listening to the potential bride cry, I'd decided to make a scheme of it. I offered my services to the maiden's family: I'd kidnap her, hold her hostage in some out-of-the-way but not impossible-to-reach location, and let her be rescued by a suitor of her choice. Eligible men came to do battle, usually with swords and lances, but sometimes with their wits. I'm not above a good workout, but I did enjoy the brainy types. I and the suitor would spar, and if he was skilled and brave enough and the maiden was suitably impressed, I would retreat and he would rush to her, just as she swooned into his arms.

Now and then, I'd prepare a special lair for the occasion, stocking it with some valuables, and they could even grab a trinket or two as they fled. I charged extra for that, of course.

Later, as the happy couple was celebrating their nuptials, a servant would meet me in a designated spot with whatever payment I and Daddy had agreed upon.

Queen Arlene and King Geoffrey were the last ones to take part in my little scheme. Arlene's kingdom, Farr, was at war with Geoffrey's, Ayway, and King Daddy refused to give his baby girl in marriage to the enemy until after he'd defeated them soundly. Thus, the kids arranged the kidnap-and-rescue without their families' knowledge. That had made for some incidents which I found funny, but the King Daddies had not. I had agreed to wait until the angry fathers had died and the kingdom was united before taking my payment, but I got busy and forgot about it. Time to collect.

I could almost taste the fat, lazy bovine that would be mine. Slow-roasted sounded good.

Father grinned as I related the tale. "Interesting as some seedy tavern might be, I don't think any of us would mind dining with royalty."

I heard the twang of a bow from the woods. I skipped to the side and an arrow pierced the ground where I'd been standing. Instinctively, I arched my back and roared. Bernice reared back, though whether in reaction to me or whoever was shooting us, I didn't know. I had an impressive roar, of course, but with no bulk to back it up, it felt like pitiful posturing.

Nonetheless, it was enough to rattle the archer. Three more arrows followed the first in quick succession, but each easily missed me and my companions.

Sam spun Thud in a circle, searching the woods for our foe. "Show yourselves, cowards!" he called out. "By the name of my Queen, Titania of the Summer Sun, I command you!"

For a wonder, they obeyed. Six men approached on foot, swords and war axes drawn. "Get away from that beast!" the squat one in a shining breastplate reminiscent of Geoffrey's called out. "Unless you have brought it as tribute so we may inflict the punishment he deserves."

You'd think by now, I'd stop being surprised by anything mortals said, but that made two races in 24 hours that wanted to punish my kind. Unlike with Titania, I did not need to negotiate with them. "Get out of our way, humans. We've come to see Queen Arlene and King Geoffrey. They owe me."

"My grandfather is dead, my grandmother frail, and the only thing anyone here owes you, you vile kidnapper, is the taste of our steel!"

He charged toward me and I readied myself for his attack. I hoped Farrayway had other heirs because this idiot was going to be lunch.

Father leaped between us, his blade blocking grandson's before I could chomp down on it and yank it out of my attacker's hands. I almost bit Father's arm. I thought I felt something knock my snout away just in time. His guardian angel, probably.

Sam and Thud moved on the others. Thunderpaws growled, his teeth bared. He may have been a fuzzy-wuzzy corgi, but at 14 hands, he was a formidable foe.

"Wait! We have come here as guests and friends of the queen. Explain yourself," Father demanded.

My attacker snarled and pushed against Father's sword, but the paladin held firm. Finally, with a grunt, he shoved away. "That? A friend of the queen? Is that what that...thing...has been telling you?" he asked, but at least he lowered his sword.

Father Rich took a step back, still keeping himself between us. I could see him hiding relief that he hadn't had to engage in combat. Glad as he was to give me a good thwacking, he was more reticent about damaging fellow humans.

"That's right—and who are you to question his word?"

The man spoke slowly as if Father was an idiot. "I am Derek, son of Andrew and Elise, grandson of Geoffrey and Arlene, Prince and heir of Farrayway. Prince Derek, understand? That dragon attacked my kingdom and kidnapped my grandmother. And now, it and its kind are terrorizing the lands—but they shall not have mine!"

I groaned. "Human, you have your facts wrong." This wasn't the first time that humans had twisted the facts and it'd come back to bite me—which is why I'd given up the scam, fun as it was at the time. Of course, the unamused King Daddies, backed into a corner by their rebellious children, had taken out their ire on me by spreading lies about the innocent dragon who was just trying to help.

"Do not attempt to fool me with your falsehoods!" Prince Derelict spat out. "All know you, the wretched beast swept across our kingdom, darkening the skies with its shadow."

"Aye," one of his guards said thoughtfully, "I always thought you'd be bigger."

I shrugged, hiding my embarrassment behind indifference. I had been at the height of my glory—and size. I had been an awesome and beautiful thing to behold then.

Derek continued his accusations, spitting the consonants in his rage. "You breathed your terrible flame upon the fields, causing destruction and weakening our armies."

"One field! And it was fallow."

"You blew it up! My great-grandfather showed me the crater."

I started to snicker, but Father smacked my flank.

"Crater?" Father repeated, scowling at me.

I scowled back. "I chose that field because it didn't have any crops. It's not my fault one of his great-grandfathers was using it to hide explosives."

Derek ignored my facts. "You stole our livestock so that famine threatened our lands."

I rolled my eyes. "Please! I took two sheep—an advance on my payment."

Nothing I said was getting in the way of his narrative. He turned to Father to continue the tale. "Then, when my brave grandmother, Princess Arlene, went to confront the beast, it savagely snatched her and imprisoned her in its lair."

"You mean the cave she picked out for us? The one that was far from the fighting but close enough that her 'Geoffreypoo' wouldn't strain himself getting to us?

"Listen, Prince," I said. "If it weren't for me, your grandparents would never have gotten together. Their two kingdoms would not have forged a peace, and you might not even exist. Now, take us to Queen Arlene so we can straighten all this out."

Prince Derek looked me over with a curled lip and a calculating eye. I didn't need him to articulate what he saw. I was undersized and at least one of my companions was clearly hesitant. His friends stepped forward.

I did quick calculations of my own. The archer had stayed behind to provide covering fire. If he was smart, he'd take out Bernice first. How many could Father take? Or would he? In my peripheral vision, I saw him watching me, doubtfully. The easiest thing would be for me to make a hasty retreat and hide until they found our friends. Most likely, Sam could bluff them out of the situation. He was good at that when we gamed, and I had a feeling this wish-world wanted us together again, anyway. Still, I hated running away, especially from such a stubborn, misinformed, little turd.

Fortunately, the fight got preempted by the pounding of hooves and a woman's voice yelling for everyone to hold. Queen Arlene crashed through the woods with her own guard at her heels. She stopped her horse between her grandson and me. Her hair had gone silver and lines etched her face, but she still had that regal posture I remembered from her youth. She didn't look frail. She seemed energetically riled.

"Derek, stop this, now!"

"Grandmother, stay out of this. I will protect the kingdom from this beast!" Derek said. He drew his sword for emphasis.

"Put that down before you take an eye out. Vurnerrah is not our enemy!" She butchered my name but got closer to it than Father had. I remembered that she had insisted on practicing it while waiting for Geoffrey. I'd liked that about her. Too bad her progeny was such an idiot.

Prince Derek the Dunce was gaping at her. "What? But Grandmother—"

"It was a falsehood designed to convince my father that Geoffrey was a noble man and his father that I and my kingdom were no threat. It was the only way we could marry."

"Told you!" I crowed.

She looked at him pleadingly. "Please, Derek."

"No! Your mind is addled, Grandmother."

At this, Arlene drew herself tall, the strength of her birthright reinforced by her years of experience. "Derek Geoffrey, son of Andrew, Prince of Farrayway, you forget yourself! I am your queen. Now sheathe that sword before I treat you as any other subject who disobeys my commands!"

When he had done so with the sullen expression of any teenager of a humanish species, she dismounted and approached me, arms outstretched. I accepted her hug, giving her grandson a smug look over her shoulder. Then I introduced her to my friends and their mounts. She was too much a queen to fall into goo at Thunderpaws' bright smile and puppy bow, but she graced him with a small grin and rubbed between his perky corgi ears.

"Vurnerrah, dear friend. It has been so long! Our scouts sighted you entering our lands. I would have been here sooner, but everything takes me longer these days."

"The curse of mortality. I understand. As you can see, I'm somewhat slower myself, though I have a more immediate cause." I flicked my gaze toward Father, who struggled to look dignified and paladiny instead of rolling his eyes at me or making a snarky reply as I knew he longed to do. He didn't quite manage to hide his self-satisfied smirk, however.

"I apologize for the behavior of my grandson. I'm afraid our fathers' version of the tale continues to hold sway among many of the people. I regret now that we did not work harder to educate our people about the truth. If you have come to seek retribution for the stain to your reputation..."

"We're here to gather a party of adventurers," I replied, way too aware that I sounded like one of Ray's non-player characters. "We're only looking to find our friends and go. I have no quarrel with Farrayway, your parents notwithstanding. You are in my territory and have always been under my protection. You need only signal me." I wasn't sure why I said that, but it seemed to reassure her.

"I thank you for that, dear friend, but the years have been kind. We've seen great peace and prosperity for two generations."

"Your protection?" Derek scoffed incredulously.

She cut him off with an angry look. "The word of a dragon still means something, young prince, no matter what the circumstances. You would do well to remember that."

He bowed his head and muttered, "Yes, grandmother," without real conviction.

It was enough. She returned her attention to me. "That said, Vurnerrah; I cannot offer you the hospitality of the castle. Our deception, you see, has taken a life of its own. You are welcome in our kingdom, and I shall command that no one harass you during your time here, but I must ask that only your companions go into town to seek these adventurers. There is too much fear and mistrust. It would only distress you and my people at best, and at worst... I am sorry."

I bit back a sigh, but I'd expected as much. "Do you remember the lair where I took you?"

She nodded, a slight grin on her face. "Geoffrey and I often returned to it to celebrate our anniversary."

How romantic. Which version of the story did they celebrate, I wondered. "I'll be there. My friends will need an escort into town."

She motioned to one of her guards. "Easily done. And I shall have a meal brought to you."

Queen Arlene curtsied low to me. The men around her stirred uneasily, and I saw the momentary narrowing of the prince's eyes.

As the queen ordered one of her servants ahead to prepare the feast, Father stepped toward me. "Vern, are you sure about this?" he asked quietly.

I nodded. "You should be fine. No sense stirring up the locals with my presence, though. Go find the others. See that series of low caves? When you've found them, head there, and then tell Thud to find me. He should be able to lead you to the cave. Right, Thuddy, boy?"

Thunderpaws wagged his tail so hard, his whole behind shook. He circled once in doggie excitement.

"And what will you do?" Father asked.

"Eat. Sleep. Don't worry about me."

Behind him, the queen cleared her throat. He nodded, and with easy movement worthy of a hero, he leaped into Bernice's saddle, and they and Sam and Thunderpaws rode off with the queen and the others.

I was alone to wrestle with my thoughts.

Chapter Seven:
Adventurers, Assemble!

The "lair" where I had held Arlene while she awaited rescue by the charming Prince Geoffrey was really nothing more than a small cave. At least, it was small when I'd been my true size. Miniaturized as I was, it seemed spacious. And empty. For the scam, I had scattered enough gold and jewels to make it look like I was moving in, but all that had come from the royal treasury and been enhanced by a clever illusion. Now, the cave was nothing more than a carved-out hole in the hill with dirt, stones, and the discarded remnants of some human romantic tryst: a thick rug, a dirt-covered goblet, a silver candlestick tarnished with age... Arlene and Geoffrey must have left them.

The sun had set, and a chill had started to seep under my scales. I dragged a rolled-up carpet from where it leaned in a nook of the cave, spread it out not far from a large, round boulder, and brushed off the dust. Apparently, the queen and king had had it bespelled, for no vermin had made their home in its fibers and the dirt came away with ease, leaving it almost new. I spread it out, and settled on it, enjoying the cushioning of the thick fibers. Quality stuff.

I breathed a long steady stream of superheated flame onto the boulder until it glowed. Then, alone at last, I laughed for the sheer joy of being able to breathe fire.

My true fight with Saint George had left me unable to breathe flame, and I'd not regained the ability in the 857 years since. Fire is more than being able to warm some rocks, although in the chill of the evening, I appreciated the ability. It was defense, communication, expression. It made us dragons. I'd always wondered if losing my fire had caused my kind to abandon me, although some instinct had told me that couldn't be true. I had vague recollections of swarming to the aid of my kin when one or another had been injured beyond the ability to care for itself, including the loss of flaming breath.

I made three circles around the carpet, just because I could, then flopped down in the perfect position to take in the warmth while I worked through my thoughts. Was this adventure or part of it some fulfillment of a secret wish of mine? And if so, what, exactly? I had longed for so many things in the past eight-plus centuries: to find my kind, to know what happened to them, to understand why I, of all dragons, had been left behind. To know what God expected of me.

Titania had said a dragon or dragons had flown to the Mundane and were using their powers there. Was it true or just rumormongering based on tall tales told by unwary Mundanes who sighted one of us through a portal? If true, it would explain the legends of dragons among Mundanes.

No. It could not be true. Not my kind. Not the Eighth Day Creations. We were forbidden from creating portals into the next dimension, and the Gap, the permanent portal between our two universes, had not happened yet. That one had resulted from a combination of a magical mishap in Faerie fueled by a nuclear explosion in the Mundane. A once-in-a-lifetime combination of mistakes, and I'm talking a dragon's lifetime, which is without end.

But before that Gap, had dragons entered the Mundane through portals of their own? It would be the Unconscionable Flight—the Original Sin of dragonkind.

A fruit, a song, a metal... Every species had one prohibition. For dragons, it was the other worlds. A rhyme said by mortal children and inscribed in the dragon heart suddenly returned to me.

The world is yours, its creatures you reign.
But only this world is the dragon's domain.
In this world shall dragons remain.

I shivered. We'd seen what happened to the species as one by one, they fell from Grace. The dwarves grew increasingly focused on tunnels and riches until they lost their taste for the world aboveground. The sirens' voices twisted until their songs became a beacon of death to mortals who heard them. The pixies' pranks grew cruel, the sense of innocence lost from their fun. If one or more of my own had brought the downfall of dragonkind, what had we lost?

I looked around at the once-too-small, dark, cold cave, and thought about my home in the Mundane: a leaky warehouse in the bad side of town whose one redeeming feature was it attracted rats I could snack on. And I knew what we'd lost. With a sickening twist in my heart, I knew. Glory. Some or all of my kin had traded the eternal grandeur of dragonkind for the fleeting diversion of interdimensional travel. And they had doomed us all.

No. I would not believe it. There had to be another explanation.

A rustling of footsteps and the grunting of humans carrying something heavy broke me from my reverie. I straightened myself into a more regal position. Even if we had lost our splendor, I did not have to advertise the fact. Besides, I smelled spiced meat, a pleasant surprise. I'd expected them to tie a sheep to a tree and make me do the work.

"D-dragon?" a voice called from just outside the cave entrance. "Great one? We've brought your dinner."

"Bring it in here."

I listened to the two men argue. It appeared that no one had enlightened them to the fact that I was not some savage bloodthirsty beast. Why had I dreamed up that scheme, anyway? That's right. I didn't. Not this one, anyway. I'd let Arlene and Geoffrey handle the details. I should have known better than to delegate.

I was about to remind them of the consequences of keeping a hungry bloodthirsty beast waiting, when one started to mention the prince. I shut my mouth and listened, but his partner silenced him with a hiss, and they entered with my meal.

The side of beef hung on a pole they carried, a metal roasting spit, but not iron. So far, so good. The beef had indeed been roasting. My mouth watered in anticipation of the warm meat and juices. I could smell pepper, garlic, and curry. They set it down as close to the entrance as they could without being rude, gave quick bows, and started to back out.

I didn't like how eager they were to leave. Maybe if they had to stay a bit, they might give away something. Besides, my rock was already starting to cool.

"Wait," I said. "I have one more request. Build me a fire."

"I, uh. Can't dragons make fires?" The one who spoke looked at the rock, which had turned gray again, but still emitted some heat.

"Dragons can breathe fire," I said. "But I want you to build me a fire. Bring some wood and stack it properly for a nice long fire, there."

I pointed to the fire pit someone had dug to one side of the cave.

"Why?"

"Because I like atmosphere." I grinned wide, showing my teeth.

They took the hint. In short order, they had a fair-sized pile of wood well-arranged within the stone circle. I treated them to a showy display of my flaming talent, pleased that I could remember how to make my flame curl. As the fire burned merrily, they silently gathered more wood so I could continue feeding it. They asked permission to leave and I granted it with a regality that would put any emperor to shame.

One paused at the entrance. "Thank you for not killing us. I didn't know dragons could be merciful."

"Your education about my species has been in error. You also apparently didn't know we sometimes play matchmaker. Now you have learned two truths about the splendor of dragonkind. You seem clever. Put them together, and you may figure out the truth of your country's past. Or you could ask the queen."

He looked from me to the food and to the fire. He opened his mouth again to speak, but his friend shouted for him, and with a flustered apology, he left.

I waited until their footsteps had receded down the hill, then sniffed at my meal tentatively.

Something about the way the servant had looked at the meat triggered my instincts. Instead of laying into my meal like the hungry dragon I was, I took a small bite and chewed slowly. Pepper, curry, onion, garlic...poppy...and lotus. Lots of lotus. Enough to knock out an elephant. I sighed. Did the prince think I was that stupid? Maybe one of the Fates was toying with me. I wondered if the other world knew how lucky it was to have gotten rid of those troublemakers.

At any rate, I took a couple of bites, because it'd been a tough week and I felt a headache coming on. Then, because I was feeling snarky, I went outside and set up a few surprises in case Prince Drek really thought I was stupid enough to take his bait.

I settled by the fire, facing the door, and dozed while I waited for whatever the universe, Fates, the prince, or God had in store for me next.

It didn't take long before I heard stealthy footsteps followed by twangs and not so stealthy yelps of surprise. Snickering, I rose and ambled out to greet my 'visitors.'

Prince Dreadly and three of his buddies hung upside down from the trees, their feet caught in vines, arms flailing in a combination of surprise, panic, and fury. Their shouting at each other did even less to free them. Their swords lay on the ground. I paused to watch them struggle, savoring their surprise. You'd think mortals would not underestimate the creativity of dragons, but no, it works every time.

When they'd calmed down and were just about to come up with a concrete plan to get out of their mess, I stepped out of the shadows.

"Oh, look, the cunning hunters, caught in a snare. How ironic," I said.

"You?" the prince asked. "Why would you set snares?"

"Why didn't you watch where you're stepping? For that matter, why would you drug my dinner?

Aside from your being cowardly, I thought the queen had straightened all this out."

"I don't know what dark magic you or your companion used on my grandmother, but she's obviously under your spell. You won't get away with this. I will kill you and free this kingdom of your tyranny!"

Dragons using dark magic? It was almost as laughable as dragons wanting to rule over humans, as a tyrant or otherwise. Yet the hate in the prince's eyes said he believed what he had said. His companions as well. This was more than a courtship story getting exaggerated. Someone had been telling lies about my kind, and with enough consistency to convince them.

I dearly wanted to talk to him about that, but something else he said demanded my immediate attention. "What did you do with Father Rich and the fairy?" I demanded.

The prince spat at me, missing the mark. In return, I blew at him. I wasn't going to distress the queen by burning her heir, but that didn't mean I couldn't put my lungs to good use. He started swaying anew.

"I'm not in an especially good mood, and since you poisoned my dinner, I'm hungry as well. However, I don't particularly care for human flesh; plus, I'm lazy and I've had a rough week. I'd rather we cooperate. Let's start with, 'What did you do with the paladin?'"

"'Paladin?' You think we believed your lies? My grandmother's men took him to the tavern as requested. My men are watching him while I have come to eradicate the real villain. If your death breaks him of his spell, then he will be free to go his way—and grateful to me, no doubt. If not— hey!"

The prince's monologue ended in a yelp as I blew hard enough to send them all swinging. "I told you. Lazy. Bad week. I don't have the patience for obstinacy. Maybe I'll eat one of your horses. You left them down the hill, right? Enjoy your evening."

I turned my back on them and started toward where my nose told me three horses were loosely tied to trees. I grumbled every step of the way. Damsels and knights! Would the night get any worse?

I should know not to ask such questions.

Bernice crashed through the trees in front of me, skidding to a halt just before we collided. Bernice reared up in surprise, nearly unseating Linda who rode behind Father. On his heels were Sam and Thunderpaws, Ray riding behind him and strumming a lute. He was dressed in bright clothes more suiting the stage at the Los Lagos RenFest than a rough ride through the Faerie woods. Owen came panting beside them with a dwarf in tow.

"Hey! You found the gang! Who's the dwarf?" I said.

"Never mind that now," Father replied. "Vern, run! They're after us!"

"Oh, I know. I took care of the ringleaders. The prince and two of his lackeys are swinging from trees." I grinned. I felt kind of good about that.

"The prince? What are you talking about?"

"Yeah, he thought he could drug me and–"

"Vern! Shut up and use your ears!" Linda cried.

Her panicked plea got through to me. I paused, listened, and heard a small rumble of hundreds of clicks and rustles as a great many something came our way. Suddenly, horses started screaming.

Oh, right. Monsters. In my territory. Dang it, Titania. That was information I could have used.

"This way!" I spun and ran back the way I'd come. Beatrice paced beside me as the trail allowed.

"Is going deeper into the forest a good idea?" Sam asked. He ducked yet another branch.

"No, but necessary. As we go by, cut them free," I said.

"Who?"

"You'll see!"

When we entered the clearing, I didn't hesitate but launched myself at the vine holding the prince, mouth wide.

The prince screamed like a ninny.

My teeth slashed his bonds cleanly. As he hit the ground with a thump, I landed beside him and set my feet on his shoulders so he could not ignore me. With my tail, I loosened the vines on his feet while I said, "Listen to me. Giant spiders are attacking."

"You vile–!"

From down the hill, the screams of horses had finally stopped.

"It wasn't me, you idiot!"

Linda jumped off the horse and approached the prince. Somehow, she managed to look humble and subservient, even though she was looking down at his prone figure. "Your Highness, sir, we've been following rumors of colossal spiders for some time, and now they are invading your kingdom. We've done our best to lead them out of the town, while your troops defend the citizens."

"Yes," Ray added from Thud's back. "You should return and lead them in glorious battle against these most foul beasts."

The others, freed by Father, had pulled off their snares. I stepped off the prince. For a wonder, he didn't protest or call me names but made a dramatic gesture toward the town. Wisely, he pointed to a path that would go around the horde heading our way. Just in time, too. Our delay had given the spiders time to catch up despite stopping for a snack. A dozen poured out of the trees.

Mottled black and brown, they blended with the bark and the gaining night. Their sizes varied from small dog to pony, but their thin legs stretched far enough to double their reach. Their myriad eyes reflected whatever light touched them. So did the venom of their fangs. They chittered amongst each other, rapid exclamations of excitement at the chase and anticipation of a fight.

Fine by me. I was ready to play. I had my favorite toy back.

I bounded in front of everyone and let go with a wide stream of flame. It caught three of the spiders and all but incinerated them. Two others behind them caught flame and staggered away, shrieking in pitches beyond human hearing.

Bernice sped by me on the left, Father astride. He held his sword high and called upon Saint Michael's protection. Thunderpaws loped beside him, Sam shouting the name of Titania, Queen of the Summerfae.

"Vern! You got your fire back!" Linda's delighted exclamation was punctuated by grunts as she fought a spider on my right. She swung her broadsword with the strength and grace of her D&D character. She kept her guard high, protecting her upper body, which made sense, considering she was clad in a chain-mail bikini top. A spider slashed at her leg. She swung low, cut off its claw at the joint, then kicked it between the eyes with a high-heeled boot. She let out a triumphant laugh.

Owen, taller and broader than even his usual large self and dressed more appropriately as an orc ready for battle, protected her exposed back. The dwarf fought beside him, holding his own but hollering that we didn't stand a chance here. "They'll be surrounding us at any moment!"

I was getting tired of this game. "Head toward the cliff. I'm going to set fire to the whole forest and let them all burn." Through the swish of tail and clicking of my claws against a stone, I telegraphed my intention in spidertongue as well.

"Vern!" Father protested.

I took a deep breath.

A spidery voice called out, "Wait!"

The spiders backed away, taking station in the trees. They remained far enough to not pose an immediate threat while still staying close enough to jump into the fray.

"Vern?" Father asked nervously. He scanned the trees.

I smirked at the spiders and spoke in spidertongue. "Wise choice. Let my pets leave and we won't kill any more of you."

To my friends, I said in Klingon: "There's a cave in the cliffs. Follow the path to your right. Move calmly—no sudden moves. I'll stall."

"qalobrup. Q'plah!" Owen replied and motioned the others to follow.

"What the dirt kind of orcish was that?" the dwarf asked.

"Warrior talk. My people." Owen grunted.

One spider, larger than the rest and bearing an open wound it chose to ignore, stepped toward me, his lieutenant a pace behind. "We were told the dragons would not interfere, yet you are here."

For a moment, I had the urge to say, "I am altering the deal. Pray I don't alter it any further," but this was my one chance to get some information. I put as much sneer into my tail and claws as I could as I said, "You'd dare think that applied to my playmates?" I added a curled lip for emphasis, glad that with six eyes, he'd see it in triplicate.

The spider paused, weighing its reply. He looked like he might take a while. The descendants of Anansi didn't often inherit the empyrie's wit. I feigned at being magnanimous with my patience. Meanwhile, I reached out with my other senses to get the lay of the land while I counted spiders within my 270-degree field of vision. There were at least 15 I could see but further toward the town I could hear far more. Legions more. Once they killed or cocooned all the humans for later, they'd be heading or way. We were not going to fight our way out of this one.

"The humans were ours to hunt," the spider leader said at last. "Our queen said the dragons would not interfere."

"Fools, all of you!" I blew fire in the air to emphasize my rage. The spiders skittered. Some backed up. I heard a message telegraph its way back to the township: *Wait! Everyone, just stop a minute!*

I stepped forward, oozing menace. I had to keep them all on the defensive. "We are the Eighth Day Creations, little arachnid. Whatever your queen may have told you, you need to understand this: You are in my territory. These are my mortals. And nobody messes with them but me."

The spider's back two legs shifted backward, but the rest stood firm. "No. We are legion! What can one dragon do aga—"

I blew a white-hot stream of fire that incinerated his head before he could finish his sentence.

Then I flung out my tail, I slammed his lieutenant to the ground. I leaned in close. "You are in my territory."

"These are your mortals. Nobody messes with your pets. I got it!" he chittered.

Wow. I might get us out of this yet. I let him up slowly. "I'm glad we understand each other. Now send a message to your brethren..."

That's when I heard a scream, a bark, and a battle cry. And I knew all my hard work had just been ruined.

The spiders turned as one and rushed in the direction my friends had gone. I roared for them to stop, but I didn't expect any of them to obey. I could hear the clashing of steel, barking, neighing, the dwarf yelling, "Are ye all daft? There're too many of them!"

The only thing I could do was put on more speed and plow through any spiders stupid enough to get in my way. I trampled one, then sent another flying, but it did a neat flip and landed on six of its eight legs. The whole time I cursed. We were so close! Why didn't they leave the spiders alone?

Then I entered a clearing and saw Sam standing over a dead spider and pulling spider silk off the face of a cocooned woman while the others protected them. A damsel in distress. Figured.

The dire corgi continued to growl and snap at the spiders lunging at him, but he maintained his position while his master got their still-wrapped damsel secure. Meanwhile, the others were swinging and hacking for all they were worth. Even Ray had abandoned his lute for his weapon. He stood as close to Thud as he could and fired arrows above everyone's head.

I spun to dodge one spider, and struck out with my jaw and bit off the leg of another. It gave a high-pitched screech but tried to bite my flank. It got the angle wrong and its fangs raked harmlessly against my scales.

"They're coming! Dump her on Thud's back and let's go!" I shouted. A spider launched itself at me. I batted it away with my tail. It slammed against a tree and went still.

Sam took my advice and with apologies to the gasping and crying girl, flopped her onto Thunderpaws' back.

Then Sam shouted out in Seelie—actual Summer Court Seelie—and a shield extended around himself, Thud, and the others.

I, however, was outside its range.

"Vern!" Linda yelled as spiders bounced ineffectively off a dome of magic they did not see but certainly felt.

"Go!" I hollered back, then put my breath to fire. If I had to go down, I was taking spiders and the whole dang forest with me.

I heard the clomp of hooves, and Bernice was at my flank. She made furious horsey shrieks as she spun and reared, kicking out with her hooves. On her back, Father hung on for all he was worth while slashing on the opposite side at anything stupid enough to come at them. One got under their guard, but Bernice stomped hard and smashed its thorax with enchanted horseshoes. Gore exploded from her victim.

"Good horse!" I yelled as Father tried to both swing his sword and vomit.

In my moment of distraction, a spider wrapped its legs around my tail and started gnawing on my tail spikes.

"Vern!" Father yelled.

He held his sword high, and I swung my tail to meet it. Together we decapitated the spider.

Suddenly, Father screamed.

Old Seven-Legs had leaped in and bit Father's calf. I chomped down on the spider's head, digging my teeth into its eyes. It released Father as it tried to twist and defend itself. Too late. My jaws closed, and my incisors pierced its brain. I spat it out quickly and dashed after the others, yelling for Father to follow.

The sun had fully set, and the moon had not yet risen. Nevertheless, we ran through the dark forest, dodging trees, taking the most direct route to the cave. If the others missed it, I'd get Father inside and go back for them. Someone had better have a healing potion.

Behind me, I heard a thump. Bernice whinnied in distress.

Father lay on the ground, moaning.

"Damsels and knights!"

I ran back to him and nudged him hard. "Get on that horse!"

"I don't think I can. Dizzy. Go save the others. Take Bernice."

Like that was going to happen. A well-trained warhorse, she was not leaving her knight helpless. She'd taken station between Father and the on-coming spiders, and I knew she'd fight until he was back in the saddle or she was dead.

She'd better have the sense to follow me. There was a break in the trees above us. If I was careful, I could squeeze us through it. I spread my wings—and realized only then that they'd been shredded by spider claws.

Father blinked at the sight, as shocked as I was. "Just go."

"Get up! You're annoying enough as a paladin and a priest. I will not spend eternity hearing the tales of how you martyred yourself for me. I al-ready have one saint haunting me."

I grabbed his cloak with my teeth and tried to pull him onto my back, all the while knowing I could not run fast enough. The spiders were upon us.

Then a six-foot streak of fluff passed by. I saw a floofy heart-shaped butt. Owen came pounding up beside us. He was panting hard, but he didn't hesitate as he lugged Father over a shoulder.

"Being orc fun!" he grunted. I couldn't tell if he was sincere or sarcastic. He grabbed Bernice's reins and started back to the others while we covered his six.

The next wave of spiders broke through the trees.

Sam yelled, "Thud! Shed attack."

We shielded our faces as Thud began to shake for all he was worth. Fine hairs went flying, sending a cloud of fluff. I blew a long breath and sent the fur fluttering right at the oncoming rush of spiders.

They all stopped and clawed at their many eyes, giving us enough time to rush to the cave.

We dashed in to find the others safely inside, weapons on the ground but handy. Linda and Ray were pulling sticky spider silk off a buxom blonde maiden as quickly and carefully as they could. She had her hands free and was tearing at the stuff with much less care. When they saw Father, Linda and Ray left her to help him.

"Got them!" Owen said. "Q'plah!"

"No victory yet," I said. "We slowed them, but we've pissed them off. And I think we killed the one I gave my Malcolm Reynold's speech to."

"The 'pretty bonnet' speech?" Ray asked.

"No, the 'take this message to your boss' speech. What a waste."

"I shall include it in the Ballad of Vernerd the Dragon."

"What are ye going on about?" the dwarf asked.

"Never mind. We have to seal this cave. Sam, Ray, we need an illusion and a shield. And please tell me someone has something for spider venom or a healing spell for Father." I was feeling nauseous myself, but Father was pale and shaking and had thrown up twice on the way.

Linda was cleaning Father's wound, and Ray had his hands on either side. I could feel magic, but very faint. "You're out of juice?" I exclaimed.

"Hey!" Ray retorted, "We were fighting long before we ran into you."

Sam, likewise, was near the end of his capabilities. He'd managed a shield, but it was transparent and shimmery. The first spiders had seen us and were throwing themselves against it. It sparked with magic energy but that didn't discourage them.

"Saddlebags," Sam said through gritted teeth. "Healing potions."

Linda leaped to Bernice and pawed through her bags, pulling out several meticulously crafted bottles with fairy carvings. "I can't read these."

Leaving Sam, I snagged the phials from her hands, then passed them one by one. "Make him drink this one. Pour this one on the wound and then bandage it tight."

Our troublesome damsel let out a scream and pointed.

The spiders had been joined by a fresh wave of their swarm and emboldened, were climbing over each other to pound at the shield.

"Vern!" Sam cried out. "I can't..."

With a shout of frustration, the dwarf shoved past us. "Back of the cave, the lot of you!"

Ignoring the spiders scrabbling mere inches from his face, he rubbed his hands and planted his feet. "Hold it just a minute more, fae," he said.

"Hurry, Colvert!" Sam grunted.

With a dwarfish mutter about not rushing an artist, Colvert smacked the flats of his hands against the rock. Immediately, the cave wall began to tremble.

"What are you doing?" Ray demanded as dust fell on us. Bernice added her own complaint, while

Thud alternated between cowering and yapping at the spiders who now completely blocked the entrance of the cave.

Above and outside us, I heard the crumbling of rock and boulders sliding and crashing over dirt. "Cover your heads." I spread my wings over Father and the girl.

Then with a roar, a landslide fell upon us and the spiders.

Chapter Eight: Al'Beah Genie Wish Artist

The rock thunder quieted. The only sound was our breathing and coughing in the settling dust. The cave dimmed, but the fire still crackled bravely, and the ceiling began to glow with magical phosphorescence. The queen must have added mood lighting after our adventure. Gingerly, I refolded my wings and looked around.

The entrance was blocked by a semi-solid wall of rock and dirt. Sam had fallen to his knees, exhausted and covered in a thick layer of dust. Linda and Ray had taken cover under the rug and now peeked out of it tentatively. They ducked back under as Thud shook himself, sending more dirt flying.

The dwarf backed up, looked over the earthy barricade, then dusted off his hands, although he was completely clean.

"That should hold them for a bit," he said.

And that's when Bernice decided to panic.

She reared and screamed, almost smacking Owen in the face, then dashed toward the entrance as if she could barrel through it.

"Bubu, no!" Father called. He tried to get up, but the spider venom wasn't done with him. He buckled over. "Vern, do something!" he gasped between retches. "You know her."

Oh, I did. I knew well enough not to get near George's little war horsie when she was in a tizzy. I just wished I'd remembered she was claustrophobic before I suggested we hole up in a cave.

I folded my wings tight and backed up to the wall, dragging Father and the girl with me. My roasted cow lay there, narcotized, dusty, and forgotten. At least it could serve as cover. I pushed my humans behind it and told them not to eat it. Just the idea made Father turn green, and the girl was more interested in cowering behind it while watching the unfolding chaos with wide eyes.

Owen moseyed beside us and leaned against the wall.

Linda, however, decided to take initiative. Shouting Bernice's name, she ran toward her, having no idea how to calm a claustrophobic charger. Bernice was now spinning, looking for a way out without actually looking. The dwarf grabbed Linda by the waist and pulled her aside just in time to avoid getting kicked.

At this point, something clicked inside our dire Corgi's brain, and Thunderpaws remembered it was descended from a proud line of herding dogs. He bounded in between the struggling Linda and the shrieking warhorse and put on his best doggie warface.

Bernice headbutted him.

Thud yelped, but went right back at her, yapping and nipping at her heels, trying to herd her into a corner but instead giving her more reason to dash around the room.

The girl broke from our relative safety to throw herself over Sam, who had curled into a ball to protect himself. Her actions spurred him to bravery. He grabbed her hand and pulled her into a corner, yelling at his dog to calm down.

"Stop it!" Ray shouted from where he'd perched atop a boulder to avoid the chaos. "You're using up the air! Gah! The fire!" He threw the rug over it and started stomping energetically. Bernice raced by, narrowly missing him. Thud, in hot pursuit and focused only on proving he was a good herding doggie, knocked Ray onto his butt.

Owen snickered and sat next to the roasted heifer I'd abandoned. He sliced off a chunk.

"Don't eat that," I told him. "The prince drugged it."

"What?" Owen stabbed the carcass. "No fair! Owen Hangry!" With tantrum-like roars, he drove his knife into the corrupted carcass again and again.

More screeching as Bernice broke past Thunderpaws and nearly trampled Sam and the girl on her way to the other side of the cave.

"Peace be with you!" Father's voice boomed in the small space.

Everything calmed. Bernice stilled and lowered her head as if ashamed. Thud splooted and watched us, panting and smiling and not the least bit embarrassed. Ray sat on a rock, his head in his hands. Owen pocketed his knife with a mumbled apology.

The rest of us murmured, "And with your spirit."

The peace, spiritual and emotional, descended upon Father, too. He let out a shaky cleansing breath. "Thank you."

"What kind of seasoned adventurers are ye lot, anyway?" the dwarf demanded.

Linda sank to the ground and started to cry. "I'm sorry. This is all my fault. I shouldn't have been pushing everyone to make wishes."

The dwarf went pale. "Wishes? You made wishes?"

She sniffled, trying hard not to break out into full sobs. "It was just talk. I didn't know about the lamp."

"A genie's lamp. Ah. That explains it." The dwarf sat beside her and rubbed her back. "It's all right, lassie. Don't blame yerself."

His contrite nature said more than his words. "You wished on a lamp, too?" I asked.

"What?" Owen asked. "Are you really a dwarf, then?"

The dwarf, Colvert, gave him a dirty, confused look. "Do you have water where yer brains should be? 'Am I a dwarf?' Are you really an orc, then?"

Owen wisely kept quiet.

Then the girl spoke up. "No. This is all my fault."

She stepped away from the nook where she and Sam had been cowering and holding each other protectively. Standing where all could see us, she reached into her bodice and pulled out a necklace. The charm was a small genie's lamp.

Linda blinked. "Betts?"

Sam gasped. "From the shop?" His face went beet red when he realized he'd just had his arms around an actual, real girl from the actual, real world.

"I'm so sorry," she said. "This didn't go at all like I'd planned…"

"Never mind that!" Ray exclaimed. "Rub the dang thing. Let's end this."

She glanced at Sam, but he had his head buried in his crossed arms. Anyone who knew him would understand that he was embarrassed beyond his ability to cope, but it was obvious from how the light dimmed in her eyes that she misunderstood. However, she settled the lamp on the palm of her left hand while with her right index finger, she gently rubbed it.

The lamp grew to its normal size. Smoke billowed from the spout, thickened, and resolved itself into the form of a human. Dark skin, bald head, black goatee, biceps as thick as Owen's thighs, with a bare chest to match. He wore an undersized black vest and gold bracers. Someone had been streaming Disney inside his lamp. At belt level, the form faded into a trail of thick smoke.

He glanced around, his expression changing as he realized we all knew about each other, then decided to play innocent, anyway. "I am Al'Beah, genie of the lamp. Who has summoned me?"

"Knock it off!" Ray said. "We know what you did."

Linda cut him off with a sharp gesture, then stepped forward. "Powerful genie, we appreciate that you've granted us our wish. It's been...um...more than we hoped for, truly. But my friends and I are ready to go home now, please."

His eyes grew wide with delight, and he tilted his head. "Oh! I don't think I've had anyone ask me anything so nicely in centuries! Alas, I can't accommodate you. I wish I could say I was sorry, but..."

"Can't what?" Linda asked. From across the cave, Thud growled low and Bernice's ears flicked back.

He spoke gently as he handed her a tissue he conjured from thin—and thinning—air. "I didn't mean for this to make you cry, yet wishes do take on a life of their own, don't they? And, as for ending them... It's not that simple. You see, this is bigger than your wishes alone."

"I don't understand," Linda said in a small voice. She wiped her cheeks and looked up at him with soulful eyes. I heard shuffling as my friends subtly prepared to grab weapons. Linda had played this part in many a D&D game, and when it worked, she got her way; when it didn't, we got a fight.

Of course, there were no charisma checks here, and our genie was no NPC. Without looking away from Linda, he said, "Please. There's no need for violence—not against me, at any rate. I have simply arranged the pieces on the board. It is your choice to move or not move until all wishes have been granted and the adventure plays out in full."

"Are you saying you're a DM?" Ray exclaimed. He sounded so insulted.

A forgotten piece of knowledge popped into my mind. "No," I answered, "he's a wish artist."

The genie, however, shrugged humbly. "I try."

Beside me, Father sighed. He'd finally stopped throwing up at some point in the chaos, but he was still pale and sweating. His paladin's spell of peace had taken a lot out of him. He didn't even try to sit straighter and look paladiny as he said, "Okay, I'll bite. What's a wish artist?"

Al'Beah tried to feign humility and give me a chance to answer, but I glared at him until he dropped the act. "All right, fine. Wish art is the combining of more than one wish into a grand tapestry of cause-and-effect."

"But you had a bunch of wishes with us!" Ray said. "And we're done now. Seriously done. We didn't ask you to drag other people into this."

"Does the tile ask to be part of the mosaic? No, you must understand: This is bigger than even everyone in this room. You are my Masterpiece!"

Sam, who had moved past his embarrassment to pay attention to the conversation, now groaned. "Great. I'm going to die for someone else's 'art.' Now I know how my characters feel."

Father pressed his fist against his mouth. I imagined he was wondering why someone's masterpiece would have to include vomit. "Okay. Fine. We have to play this out. But you're in this game or play or whatever kind of art this is, too. So, help us."

Al'Beah's dark skin got a little blue, the genie equivalent of embarrassment. "Oh, no. I simply set events into motion. I'm the artist. I'm outside the work. I..."

"No," I said, musing. "Father may have something here. Just imagine if you were a participant in your own art." I glanced meaningfully at my friends.

"It'd be groundbreaking," Linda wheedled. "Visionary, even."

"Very meta," Owen added.

"No," the genie said, his smoke tail shortening as he started to back into his lamp. "I couldn't, really."

He wasn't going to fall for it. I gritted my teeth into a grin. "Oh, but you must. I wish it."

"You—" Al'Beah called me the nastiest word in the genie language, but I grinned a real smile this time. It was a small victory, but I'd won it.

He threw up his hands. "Fine. I join your merry band of adventurers. But don't expect to wish your way out of trouble. That would ruin everything! You have to do this yourself."

"Agreed. You're a tool," I said, causing my friends to snicker.

Ray said, "Can you teleport us out of this cave before we run out of air?"

Al'Beah shook his head. "No deus ex djinni."

I grimaced, in part because I hadn't thought to say it first. "Besides, the spiders will get in before the air gets unbreathable. We need another way out."

"Aye, I'm on it," the dwarf grumbled and moved toward the back of the cave, muttering to himself. "And what the frack does 'meta' mean?" He gave Bernice a wide berth, but she still side-stepped nervously. Thunderpaws gave her a warning snarl.

"We have to do something with Bernice," Father said. "She's not going to be able to deal with this much longer."

"What if we put her in the lamp?" the girl— Betts—answered. "Surely you could create an illusion of fields for her to run in. That wouldn't be too much interfering, would it?"

"She's an NPC," Ray added. It was a good point—as a non-player-character, she didn't have any wishes to influence his work.

The genie answered by snapping his fingers. Bernice disappeared. Thunderpaws yelped and jumped to his feet. He circled where she'd just stood, sniffing and whining until Sam called him over and ordered him to sit. Soon his distress at losing his herd was forgotten in light of ear rubs and sweet cooings from the pretty girl who thought he was a good doggie and cute and smart.

"Thank you," Father said, then grimaced and rubbed his stomach. "That healing potion wasn't so great."

"That healing potion saved your life," I corrected him. "That spider was biting to kill, and its venom is necrotic. Be thankful you're just queasy and not rotting out from the inside."

Father turned away from me to heave, but his unrotting stomach was empty. I heard him whispering the name of his parishioner with cancer as he offered his suffering for him. Owen.

Owen? I glanced at our friend, but if he'd heard Father, he gave no indication. All right, then; he didn't want us to know. I'd play the part for now.

Linda caught the genie's arm and pointed to Father. "Please, can't you heal him?"

When he shook his head, Ray said, "All right. Look, we wished for a D&D adventure. We just had a huge battle and killed a boatload of monsters. How about you level us up and grant us a long rest? Can you work that into your tapestry?"

The genie grinned. "Now, you begin to understand!"

A shimmering light flowed from his outstretched hands. It drifted upwards to the ceiling, then spread and rained down on all of us gamers. For a minute, we all sparkled, then the leveling up was absorbed.

"Whoa," Sam whispered. He looked at his hands, turning them from palm to backs and palm again as if he could see the magical energies flowing over his skin. Beside him, Thud leaped to his feet, nearly spilling Betts, who made a small but delighted shriek. He floofed his fur and danced on his front paws. I had no idea what he gained, but he enjoyed it.

Owen thumped his chest. "Owen like!"

Ray giggled like he'd been snacking off my cow. He reached for his mandolin and played a riff worthy of Santana.

Linda felt the biggest change. She leaped to her feet, laughing, tears forgotten. "This is awesome!" She pulled out her sword and dagger and started to move through a crazy routine as if she'd been doing it all her life.

I turned to Father. He looked stronger and more grounded, but still pale and sick.

He, in turn, inspected me. My wings were still shredded, and I certainly hadn't gotten any bigger or more majestic. "You don't look any different."

"I didn't wish. Besides, I play a halfling thief. My pickpocket skills are probably improved. You?"

He gave me a wan grin. "I don't think a genie magic is going to replace real rest or actual prayers."

Linda was now swinging and spinning in time to Ray's song.

"Both will probably help. Sit back and pray. We have a little breathing room still."

Father smirked. "So to speak?"

"Or not, if Ray gets his way. Though he seems content for the moment."

Suddenly, Linda whirled and flung her dagger at the rock-filled entryway. A spider scream rent the air, and ichor seeped down the rock from where she'd cut off a probing claw.

"Vern! They're breaking through."

Sam stood and started to chant a spell. The area just in front of the rock barrier started to glow. However, behind it, more rocks started moving away as the spiders dug through.

"So much for breathing room," I grumbled to Father. "Time to go, people. Owen, Linda, we cover them. Back of the cave, everyone else. Take your stuff. Sam, tie that spell down and help Father. And someone tell the dwarf to hurry."

"I heard ye! It's a small cave. I found the path."

"Get on it."

A growl of dwarf and rock answered me.

A spider leg pushed through the hole, followed closely by the head. It braced two, then four legs on the rocks around it and pushed forward, trying to squeeze itself through the hole. I made ready with my fire. Flanking me, Linda spun her sword over her wrist, a nervous rather than showy gesture. Owen pulled his ax from his back holster.

The spider smacked the barrier with its head. Lightning flashed and magical energy crackled. It didn't even squeal as it folded over, dead, its abdomen blocking the hole.

Owen snickered. "Well, that was anticlimactic."

Then, its body yanked back, and like pulling the right block from a Jenga tower, the rest of our barrier crumbled.

"You had to say it," I snapped.

"Sorry!"

Spiders started pouring over the top, too numerous and crowded together to count. The shield glowed and sparkled so much, I didn't know why we didn't go blind. It must have been part of the spell. Spiders shrieked and died, but this time, their brethren were more ruthlessly smart—or maybe just focused on getting to us, I didn't know. At any rate, they didn't try to clear the bodies, but instead pressed them harder against the shield, letting the dead take the damage.

"Get behind me," I told my companions. "Back up as I do. Watch the ceiling. Don't let any get past."

Behind us, I heard a thunderous earthy groan and then our friends cheering. About time. I inhaled deeply.

The barrier shimmered once more, then broke.

I let loose with a wide spray of fire.

There were so many spiders coming that the first flaming row tumbled forward and was almost immediately trampled by the crowd behind it. I stopped only long enough to take a breath and flamed the next wave of arachnids. I noticed a few trying to escape by climbing to the ceiling, but it was too low to afford any real safety. Owen and Linda made short work of the stragglers, Linda shrieking as the pieces rained down on us.

"Guys! Come on!" Ray hollered.

"Go!" I said and breathed in until I thought my lungs would burst. Some of the six-eyed monstrosities noticed, or maybe there weren't as many behind them pushing forward. The surge of spiders hesitated.

I let forth an inferno worthy of a dragon five times my size. The vermin in the front didn't so much burn as melt, and the blaze tore through the ranks. The rocks around the entrance glowed, and the heat like from Nebuchadnezzar's furnace rebounded toward us. I didn't even need to add my voice. The shouts of my friends and the shrieks of the fleeing spiders sounded distant and dim from the roar of my flame.

I didn't stop until my breath ran out, leaving me lightheaded. I ignored the dizziness and dashed to the back of the cave.

Colvert had used his magical skills to forge a new tunnel toward the back. He was good, too. In the time I'd spent sparking spiders, he'd already pushed aside enough rock and dirt to lead the rest in and down. As I cleared the entrance, the rock reformed behind me. This was no pile of boulders, either, but a natural wall. The spiders would never know where we'd gone unless one saw me, and even then, they would not be able to dig in without equipment or magic. We'd gotten lucky that the team had come across a professional-level tunneler.

Or had we? What exactly did Colvert wish for?

The tunnels were just large enough for everyone to walk single file. Sam had created a mage light; a basketball-sized glowing light floated just above Thud's back, but with the push of bodies, it did little to light the area. Everyone was quiet except for panting, some with effort, a couple with pain. I could smell the sweat and fear coming off my friends. It was a good thing we had a place to hold Bernice.

I caught up to the end of the line. "How are we doing?" I whispered.

"I'm not even sure what we're doing," Linda replied, her voice shaky.

"Trust the dwarf," I said. "Tunnels are their lives. If he's leading us this way, then there's something on the other side. He'll get us there."

"Unless we run out of air first."

I kept my voice light. "Nah. Oxygen creation is part of the tunneling magic. They couldn't dig deep otherwise. He looks like he knows what he's doing."

"Okay." She gave a small gasp. "I think you 'sunburned' my back. I'd better get a nice tan out of this."

"Shh!" Colvert hissed loud enough for all to hear. "We're coming to a natural cave. I feel vibrations."

"Spiders?" Sam asked.

"Nah, but life. Hold on."

He grunted loudly with effort, and the walls around us expanded until we had a small but more comfortable dome of space. The mage light floated to the top, and the makeshift room filled with cool light. Everyone sat down.

I wove my way to the dwarf and pressed my ear against the stone. I heard faint shuffling, muffled through tons of rock. I glanced at the dwarf, impressed that he'd pick them up at all. "More than one," I said.

He nodded, "Big."

"Not humanoid."

"'Humanoid'? What kind of word is that? But aye—creatures of some sort. But the mountain is riddled with tunnels from here for quite a ways. Tunneling around would take days."

We glanced back at our weary adventurers. Betts had huddled up against Sam again. He had an arm wrapped around her, but I could see he was ready to jump out of his own skin. Father leaned against Thunderpaws and had shut his eyes. Thud whined softly and licked the sweat off the priest's forehead. Ray was purposely taking shallow breaths. Owen had dug into a pack for some salve and was applying it to Linda's back. His face, I noticed, was pink from a burn as well. The genie hovered in a corner, unfazed but ready to move on.

"They can't do this for days," I said, and he nodded. "Let's move on, come out somewhere behind the creatures and reconnoiter."

"All right, but not you. We're going to need stealth in case there are more lurking outside earshot. Besides, I think this lot looks to you for leadership, anyway. I'll take the fairy and his dog. If we get into trouble, he can spirit you a message."

We told the others our plan. Seeing how Betts clutched at Sam's arm, Linda offered to go, but the Colvert said, "This is a job for magic, lass, not muscle."

Sam gently pulled Bett's hand from his bicep, kissed her fingers gallantly, then stood and called for Thud to heel.

I took the corgi's place supporting Father.

"You okay?" I asked him as the trio moved off to the rumble of moving rock. He looked awful and leaned against me with worrying heaviness.

Bad as spider venom was, fairy healing potions should have been up to the task.

"I'll be fine," he said, not bothering to open his eyes. "I understand what's going on." He grinned a small, pleased smile.

In the corner, Al'Beah returned his expression.

Chapter Nine: Thuddy and the Hell Hounds

We spent the next twenty minutes in silence. Father was right: Genie magic could not replace real rest. Despite the tension of our situation and the less-than-optimal surroundings, my human companions slept. I also dozed, but lightly, eyes half-open and ears alert for any signs of trouble coming from tunnels or our genie tool. When I heard Colvert hustling up the tunnel, I had the others up and ready to move before he got to us.

He looked us over and nodded once with approval. "We've come into a dungeon, looks like," he told us. "It's guarded, but we think we can get past if we're quick and stealthy. The dog is distracting them."

"How?" Ray asked. "Belly rubs?"

"Hey, Tool," Ray said to the genie, "I can cast Zone of Silence, but it's only got a range of five feet. Can you extend it over all of us?"

"I don't know," he mocked. "Can I?"

He wasn't making fun of my friend's grammar. Fortunately for us, he was dealing with a dungeon master with decades of experience and what I (until now) would have called an unhealthy obsession with the game. "Ilsidore Expansion Set for large parties, Volume 4. It'll cut the effective time proportionally to the size, so let's say range 20 feet, duration 15 minutes."

"Wait, really?" Father asked. That spell could have saved our in-game bacon more than once.

"Google it. Ready?"

The genie rubbed his hands together. I wondered if he was getting into the idea of being part of his art, or if he was just waiting for a chance to repay us for tricking him into participating. But Ray sang a quick ditty, and Al'Beah clapped along. Suddenly, we were enveloped in a dome that we couldn't see but sense. It felt still.

"We've got fifteen minutes, so let's get moving."

Colvert shook his head. "'Google?' 'Expansion sets?' What arcane dialect are all of ye speaking?" Without waiting for an answer, he led the way.

Sam met us just past where the tunnel opened into a larger cave. As if they had done it all their lives and not just around a table with dice and miniatures, Linda and Owen quickly moved to cover our rear. Sam stepped into the spell area.

"Good idea," he said, but still kept a hushed tone. "OK, listen. There are guards around the corner. They haven't seen me yet. Thunderpaws is keeping them busy, but he can't do it for much longer. Stick close and move quick."

He pulled us to the tunnel wall then led us to the intersection, where Thud's saddle and bags sat against the wall on our side. He pulled out a mirror and eased it around the corner. We all crowded in to see the reflection. Around me, everyone struggled to hold back gasps and laughter. It made for a lot of muffled squeaks.

Six dogs sat around a circular stone table, cards in their paws and piles of bones before them. Not just ordinary dogs, mind you. We were in a dungeon in Faerie, after all.

Cerberus, Guardian Dog of the Underworld, had apparently dealt a new hand. He was most noticeable, with his three heads towering over the rest yet all focused on his hand with poker-faced intensity.

Pesanta's expression was direr. It looked like the spirit who invaded homes to suffocate people and cause nightmares was having a nightmare of his own.

Tiangou, Eater of the Sun, was pondering his hand as if he had all the time in the world. In a way, he did; at least until the next solar eclipse.

Panhu sat to Thunderpaws's right. Guess the missus let him have the night off. His human hands made it easier to hold the cards. A Far Eastern spirit with a dog head and human body, he was called dragon-dog, but there's nothing dragon about him. He just puts on airs because he married a princess.

Barghest, Omen of Death Who Roams the North, must have folded immediately and was laying across the threshold. Not a good sign.

"Are they...? How does Thuddy know how to play poker?" Father stammered.

"He watches when I play it online," Sam said. "And now he's a fairy dog. See why we have to hurry?"

"You're afraid Thunderpaws will lose?" Linda asked.

Sam sighed. "That would be the least of our troubles. Thunderpaws has all the qualities of a fae-trained warhound who was born and bred in the Summer Court."

"He's cheating." If dragons smacked their foreheads, I would have done so.

As we watched, Pesanta tossed down his cards and left the table. He tried to sit on Barghest's chest and was promptly snapped at. Just because Barghest had lost a round didn't mean he wanted the demon dog to steal his breath, too.

Pesanta chose a spot in the corner and started licking himself. Thud used that moment to casually bring his paw to his ear. He had an Ace of Spades "pawlmed" in it. When he brought his foot down, the card was gone, hidden in his neck floof. If we hadn't been watching from our angle in the mirror, we would never have seen it.

Of course, there was something else in the mirror I saw—and it wouldn't be long before one of the dogs noticed, too.

I turned to the others and intoned, "Brace yourselves. Chaos is coming."

"Why is that funny?" the dwarf demanded as everyone else started snickering. Finally, he shook his head in resignation. "Daft, the lot of ye."

Sam scooped up Thud's saddle. Owen tossed the saddlebags over his shoulder.

The game had heated up. The pile of bones in the middle had grown, and Thud had just raised the ante again. Where he'd gotten the bones to start was anyone's guess, but he commanded a fine bankroll of them now. Cerberus was dealing out replacement cards when what I expected happened.

It wasn't obvious, I'll give them that. Panhu gave Pesanta a casual glance. Pesanta, while seemingly interested in his hygiene, raised his leg just a bit higher. Easy to miss if you didn't know to look for it.

Or if you only had one set of eyes. Cerberus put down his cards and growled. He rose from the table. He was taller and bulkier than me and had three sets of sharp teeth. He towered over the others. I was glad not to be a part of that game. Two heads focused on Panhu, who raised human arms in an expression of innocence. Pesanta was not so smooth. When Cerberus's third head turned to him, he immediately tucked his tail between his legs and wet himself.

"Go!" I told our group. Then everything happened at once.

Tiangou caught the fear and guilt in Pesanta's scent and figured out what was happening. He also stood, growling.

Thunderpaws tilted his head in friendly confusion, but when he backed away from the table, he toppled it with a crash. Of course, he knocked it in Cerberus's direction and in such a way that it looked like Panhu had done it.

Cerberus lunged at Panhu while Tiangou took Pesanta. Barghest watched with interest until he couldn't take not being part of the fun and jumped in on Taingou's side.

Thud yipped excitedly, a combination of "What's happening?" and "Sic 'em!" I had no idea acting was part of warhound training. He dashed back and forth between the two fights, snapping and barking, adding to the chaos without getting physically involved.

We ran across the gap.

"Thud, come!" Sam called quietly.

Thud spun and ran. Panhu reached out to grab Thunderpaws but missed the tiny knob corgis called a tail. Cerberus, more intent on the cheater before him, grabbed Panhu's arm in his teeth and yanked him back.

I bounded into the lead, senses stretched out to detect anyone else in the corridor, ignoring the sounds of barking, scratching, and breaking furniture behind us. I took turns at random until we got to what seemed, for the moment, a safe area. We ducked into an empty room and shut the door. Owen stood by it, ax at the ready.

"How much longer on that silence spell?" Ray asked.

"About three minutes," the genie answered.

"Perfect!" Ray buckled over laughing.

"Good dog," Linda said, shuffling and scratching at his floofy cheeks while Sam got his dire corgi geared up again. "Who's a clever doggie? Is it you? Is it?"

Thud wiggled and panted through the huge bone he held between his teeth. He scratched his shoulder and a smaller bone fell out of his fur.

"That was amazing. Those dogs were playing cards." Father shook his head, his grin almost as wide as Thud's. He seemed to feel better. Guess laughter was good medicine.

"Those dogs were cheating at cards," I corrected, which made them all laugh harder. "I wonder if Panhu and Pesanta got together before this game or if it's a regular thing for them."

"It's not, anymore," Sam said. He pulled yet another small bone out of Thunderpaws's fur and placed it in a saddlebag. Thud licked his hand.

"Hush, the lot of ye!" the dwarf snapped. He was sitting hunched in the middle of the room, hands flat on the ground, concentrating. I realized now he was humming, deep and low, beyond human hearing. I hushed the others, too. Our time was about to end, anyway.

"Well?" I asked when he sat up.

"This dungeon is a maze of corridors, and we're practically smack in the middle of it," he said. "To make things worse, the halls are moving."

"Any treasure?" I asked. After all, I was the party thief.

"I'm a tunneler, not a soothsayer. My talent is for knowing the depth of stone, not the contents of open space." He drew a quick map on the dirt floor.

Ray whistled appreciatively. I could see him longing for a map he could use later in a future campaign.

"Aye," the Colvert said. "'Tis some expensive magic, but old. I can feel mechanisms breaking down. I think our best bet is to burrow through, crossing corridors as we come to them."

I heard growling and the scrabbling of claws heading our way. Thud's canine gambling buddies had noticed some of their loot was missing along with their newest player. Whether they had made up or were still angry at each other, they certainly wouldn't let a strange dog make off with their spoils, no matter who should have won. "Let's get moving."

"Stay close. I'll seal the entrance behind us," the dwarf said. He went to the side wall, pressed his hands against it, and shoved. Earth gave way, compressing at a molecular level, creating a smooth, arched cranny. He stepped forward, and the tunnel lengthened in his response. The dimensions were perfect, the pauses between steps barely noticeable. He started out slowly, but as the ground around us warmed, figuratively, to his presence, things sped up. As soon as Owen crossed the threshold, the ground sealed itself. Dragons can't whistle, but I would have in appreciation. It'd been a long time since I'd seen a tunneler in action, much less a master. This guy was world-class.

Once again, we moved in a single file, a mage light casting just enough brightness to keep us from bumping into each other. This time, I took point behind the dwarf. We made our slow way forward. My friends would say we inched along, but burrowers measured in tons. Just enough room for our party probably took 18 tons. The best tunnelers I could remember, both in my spotty memory pre-George and my far-better memory of the 850+ years afterward, could handle three, four hundred tons in a day. I hadn't been counting, but at a guess, Colvert had already doubled that and was just starting to sweat. He seemed to be enjoying his workout, too.

He paused and hissed for my attention. "Tunnel ahead. I was going to bust through, but there's something in it. Can't tell what."

"Go around?"

"No." Now that we'd stopped, he was panting. "This area's unstable enough. I make this tunnel much wider, much less change direction, it'll collapse on us."

I glanced behind me. Our genie was following us, floating reclined. He acted like he didn't have a care in the world, but I didn't trust the amused grin on his face. What did I expect? You can't have a D&D adventure without a dungeon crawl. I doubled my head back along my own neck, a nice stretch that worked out some kinks from moving so hunched up, and addressed Linda behind me. "Corridor. Unknown danger. Be ready."

As she passed it on, I told our tunneler to make an entrance then flatten himself against the wall on our side. "We'll clear the path, then call for you and Betts. When we do—"

"I'll pull the lass across with me and find the next best exit. Good luck getting the girl to leave the fairy's side. I'd have thought he'd bespelled her except he looks as besotted as she does."

I remembered Linda's wish for Sam and held back a groan. "You really want to gossip right now?"

It took a dragon's vision to see the mirth just creasing the lines of his eyes. "Be ready."

A grunt of effort, and the way before us exploded open with a shower of stone. I poked my head out and looked both ways. The others crowded behind us.

A man in a leather jacket and a very cool hat was running our way, yelling unintelligibly. Behind him rolled a giant boulder.

"Get back!" I yelled.

The crowd behind us bumped and shuffled, those in the back not understanding why the others were retreating. I waited until the guy passed, then snapped out, caught the scruff of his jacket in my teeth, and pulled him in with us. The boulder rolled past, bumping over the debris we'd spilled.

I released the guy. He paused to catch his breath, then checked the bag of whatever treasure he'd stolen. I peeked over his shoulder. Hey! A Chachapoyan fertility idol. I didn't have one of those...that I remembered, anyway.

"Thanks. I owe you my life," the guy said. He turned around, saw me, and blanched.

"I'll take your trinket as payment."

"But I..." He sighed and handed me the bag. I tossed it to Sam to store in Thud's saddlebags. Father glared at me as if to remind me that poverty was part of my agreement with the Church. I didn't care. This was the wish-world, right? It's not like I'd be keeping it after we were done. Besides, he never had a problem with my snagging treasure during a real campaign.

"You'll find another one, I'm sure," I told the treasure hunter. "Next time, replace the weight with something so you don't trigger the trap." It might work better for him than Indiana Jones. Who knows?

He smirked, bemused. "Good tip. Thanks. Hey, aren't you a little small to be a dragon?"

I roared and sent him running. Meanwhile, our dwarf had crossed the empty tunnel and pressed his hands against the stone, reaching out and muttering something about shale. He shuffled up the path recently cleared for us by the boulder. Everyone took stations before and after, protecting him and Betts, who had the good sense to keep in their protective circle, albeit on the side occupied by Sam. I was kind of impressed with my friends. Aside from recent events, the most danger any of them had ever seen was when we were all attacked by enchanted chili pepper plants, but they moved together like the well-trained, experienced team they played in our weekly D&D games.

We moved as a unit, adjusting our speed to Colvert's. His mutterings had turned to growls. "This whole area's a mess," he said. "Cheap construction. Substandard interior terrain. Some kind of fancy spell is keeping this whole mountain from collapsing in on itself."

"I hate every word you just said," Ray told him. I could hear the suppressed whimper in his voice. Apparently, he'd discovered that being a dungeon master was more fun than being a dungeon crawler.

"Ah, keep yer lute tuned," Colvert griped at him. "The corridors are too small. We need a large room with high ceilings and no adjoining hallways. That will give me room to forge an exit of our own."

"Owen see door," Owen grunted, back into character. He pointed his ax toward a heavy wooden door just peeking around a curve.

"Isn't that convenient?" I mused, turning my gaze toward our genie.

Al'Beah spread his hands, the picture of innocence. "Don't look at me. I'm just the tool."

From down the corridor, we heard a familiar rumbling followed by equally familiar yelling. Looked like my advice didn't work, after all.

They were growing louder fast.

"No debate!" Owen said, and he kicked down the door.

We automatically fanned out in our standard pattern—except for me. As the thief, I usually hung back and started looting whatever shinies were within reach. Now, I played the responsible tank and jumped ahead, ready to flame anything that looked, felt, or smelled wrong, with Owen and Linda flanking me, and Father and the Samwise/Thunderpaws team flanking each of them. Bets hung back. Colvert shut the door behind us, cutting off a thin wail of "Waaaaiiiit!"

Chapter Ten: Trouble with Trolls

Nothing came out of the woodwork—or stone-work, for that matter. We stood in a rough-hewn cavern, about 20 feet in diameter, the ceilings even higher. The far wall had a huge door, held tight with spells and locking mechanism. That was only for show; the locks bore marks of corrosion, and the wood had rotted. My thief persona grumbled that there wasn't anything worth looting. Poor workmanship, really; cheap locks that had probably looked impressive but were set up for show while the spells did all the work. A complex web of cabling lined much of the walls and climbed the ceiling. For some reason, the whole setup was filling me with déjà vu.

In the center of the room, an old man lay stretched across a narrow table, wrists and ankles held by shackles that tied him to the cabling.

"Wha?" he called out when the door closed with a heavy thud. "Wassat? Somebody here? What are you waiting for? Get me outta this cockamamie thing."

Linda promptly forgot any hard-earned lesson Ray had tried to teach her in the years of gaming together and rushed to the old man, sword high to cut the ropes binding the man.

I wrapped my tail around her wrists and pulled her up short.

"Vern!" she shouted in consternation.

"Hey!" the genie interjected. "I just got it! Vern the Wyvern." He flew up to a corner of the dungeon and watched, chuckling.

I ignored him. Obviously, that was about the only insight he intended to give us here. "How about we assess the situation first? Do we know why he's stuck there?"

"Shoot. You're right. Amateur mistake. Sorry." Linda relaxed and I released her. She pointed at the man. "Okay. He's on a rack. It seems quite clear to me that the poor man is being tortured. Detect spells?"

"Oh, they're everywhere," Sam said, "but give me a minute to look closer."

He made a point of leaving Betts under Thunderpaws' protection before cautiously approaching the man on the table. Thunderpaws pressed against Betts the way he liked to do with his favorite people, but with his new size, he almost toppled her to the ground. She clung to his fur and peeked around him to watch Sam intently. The others started to spread out, looking for traps, magic, loot. Whatever. I paused in the middle of the room, turning slowly, trying to figure out why this place seemed so familiar. Ray looked as cautious and baffled as the others, so this wasn't a recreation of one of his dungeons. So, where could I be remembering it from?

"It was supposed to be a temporary thing, ya know," the torturee offered from his reclining position. "I think they forgot me or got killed or something. Ain't been so bad, 'cepting the boredom and my back. My back is killing me! Please get me outta here."

Sam examined the cables. "Good thing you stopped, Linda. There's a spell running through them. A containment spell of some sort. Odd that it's in the ropes, though, and not the manacles. It's ridiculously entangled. Whoever set it was quite an artist." He said that last with a slur, and he curled his lip in Al'Beah's direction. The genie pretended not to notice.

There was something fishy about this setup. Familiarly fishy. "We shouldn't break the cords. It might release the spell."

"That's good, isn't it?" Betts asked from where she peeked over Thud's saddle. He'd obliged by laying down. At his size, even his stubby legs were sizable.

Sam ran a hand along the cable that led to the man's feet. "Probably not. A spell this powerful might backlash. No telling what it would do."

"Oh, that'd be bad, fer cert, it would," the prisoner agreed. He stopped and cried out in sudden pain.

"Lever!" he managed to gasp out. Sure enough, there was a lever on the wall nearest his head. It, too, looked corroded and useless. Below it, however, was a very well-made spindle-like those used for drawbridges and raising and lowering gates. It held the same cord that was pulling the man tight. Linda ran for it, but then stopped, unsure what to do. She waved her hands as if begging the universe for direction.

By now the man was crying out and hissing in an effort to control his pain. "Oh, Procrustes! This is a bad one."

"What? What is it?" Father asked.

"Back spasm! Oh, this stopped being funny so long ago!"

"Funny?" I said, and once again, the feeling that I should be remembering something struck me.

"What do we do?" Linda asked, flustered by the old man's agony.

Sam followed the lines and examined the wheel below the man's feet. "I think we can release him, but..."

He pointed to the wood stop jammed in the gear. I could feel the magic coursing through it was well. Why was everything tied to this spell?

Father looked it over, frowning. "Sir, we can release you, but we'll have to tighten your bonds first."

"Yes, anything! Get me outta this, please!"

"It'll hurt. Gird yourself!"

"Do it!"

George and Sam grabbed the handle of the wheel and turned it counterclockwise. The ropes pulled taught, making the pulleys shriek with unfamiliar stress. The man howled. Linda grabbed the wooden stopper and flung it out of the way. "Good! Let go!"

The boys gingerly released the lever. The bonds loosened.

The man sighed.

Linda and Sam hurried to the man's head. Each took hold of an arm, gently grasping wrists and supporting elbows as they helped him ease his still-bound arms down. It took effort, with his muscles stiff from being so long suspended past his head. Rather than lay at his side, however, they seemed to naturally move to cross at his chest.

I didn't like that, and apparently, neither did Father. He set his hands on the man's wrists and whispered a healing prayer. Then, he made the sign of the cross on the man's forehead.

"Whew. Thank ye. Thank ye all. Wow. Worst fraternity prank ever. I've gotta be in now."

"Fraternity?" Whatever I should be remembering, it was making my scales flatten.

"Phi Iota Tau Sigma, at Hermes Magical University. This has to be some record for longest prank. Maybe my name will go in the books. Whadya think? Me in the annals of PITS..."

As he spoke, his voice grew fainter, and his breathing slowed. As his eyes glazed over, he said, "Ya know, my back hasn't felt this good since..."

And then he was dead.

Thunderpaws began to whine. Betts rubbed his chest and tried to soothe him, but he was not distressed by the strange man's death. Rather, he was facing the wall where a tangle of ropes and pulleys made a design that had more to do with art than engineering.

No, not art. Spellwork. Rather badly, done, too, like a bunch of talented amateurs did it after too much ale...

And the memory at last kicked in.

Thud started to growl.

The body on the table began to disintegrate, and it was my turn to panic. "No, no, no! Quick, tie the cords together. The spell wasn't to hold him. It was *running through* him. We broke the spell!"

I leaped forward to grab the manacles in my teeth, but before the others could react, the cuffs on their end flung away as the trap released. As the ropes retreated, they loosened what was a cleverly hidden door. It cracked open. The fog, like solidified stench, wafted out of it.

Everyone gagged and made sounds of disgust, but before Ray could make a bathroom joke, Colvert shouted, "Troll!"

Everyone gaped at the crack in the door, which towered twenty feet tall and was wide enough to let a semi through.

Colvert raced across the room and started his magic. Owen grabbed up Betts and tossed her onto Thunderpaws' back. "Follow dwarf. Good dog!" Ray dashed after them saying something about "singing support." Owen guarded their retreat.

Cords loosened in a complex array that, I now realized, wasn't the result of drunken spellcraft, but drunken, sophomoric humor, and spellcraft. The stone doors opened with dramatic slowness. The magic changed, causing parts of the ropes to glow. As we got to our escape tunnel, the light coalesced into four letters: $\pi \ \iota \ \tau \ \Sigma$.

And a new memory clicked, along with the sinking feeling that every stupid thing I'd ever done pre-George was somehow going to come back and bite me in the haunches. I was stuck with biting back; even the most controlled flame would set the troll-stenched air afire.

"Go!" I yelled. "Crowd into that hole and tell Colvert to close it fast behind us."

Sam cast a shield spell, but I could see the magic get absorbed by the ropes. Only a thin veil was left. With his fairy eyes, Sam saw that, too.

"It won't last," he said. "Run!"

They all retreated. I backed quickly, an awkward move for a dragon, really. We don't generally give ground, much less retreat. Still, I kept everyone covered. I heard the jostling as they crowded in, trying to make enough room for me.

The troll, impatient with the spell's dramatics, bashed the doors open the rest of the way. They topped into the shield, which shredded like tissue. The troll pushed past and stood to full height, his greasy hair leaving a stain on the vaulted ceiling. He looked remarkably hale and well-fed, energetic, and very angry.

And wouldn't you know, he recognized me despite my diminished form.

"Vurnerrah!" he said, and despite the menace in his voice, I had to appreciate how well he pronounced my name.

"I can explain!" I said though I'd already decided I didn't want to. I spun and made an undignified dive into the tunnel. Even before my tail had cleared the threshold, the wall started to reform.

The Troll—Gurlurk, my swiss-cheese memory supplied with its usual stellar timing—reached in, unheeding of the rock growing toward his arm. He grabbed me by the tail and yanked me out. My spikes scraped backward against the stone. I howled.

Linda, the last one in the crowd, grabbed my paws and pulled. Father managed to reach behind her and grabbed my wrist. Owen could not reach past, so he grabbed them both by the belts. Together they pulled, and I moved toward them enough to stop my spike from digging into my back like a fingernail bending backward.

Then Gurlurk smashed his fist through the still-developing wall. Oh, this was so not good.

"This isn't tug-of-war!" I told them. "Go on. I'll catch up."

"No! We can't split the party!" Linda wailed, but the troll pulled me right out of their grasps.

I caught a glimpse of Linda's horrified expression before the wall closed, cutting off her scream.

And then I was swinging in the air, roughly eye level to one big, ugly, stupid-looking troll.

"Gurlurk," I said with as much dignity as I could muster in the circumstances. It wasn't much but more than most sapients. "Let me down and let's talk."

"Me trapped!" he said. His voice shook the rafters—or would have if we'd installed any—but he didn't whip me about or toss me against a wall. Apparently, his time out had calmed him some.

Because, I'd remembered about 30 seconds too late to do any good, I was the one who'd stuck him behind that door in a slowed time spell in order to trap him for however long it took for his tribe to come to get him.

"You did bad," I replied in the guttural language of his people. "You eat people!"

"They mean! Say I no..." He paused to think, then concluded. "No go into PITS."

"No join Phi Iota Tau Sigma." I corrected, though I didn't know why I bothered. He'd tried to join the fraternity, was rebuffed, and decided to "voice" his complaint by destroying the campus. Some ambitious frat brothers had come to me to stop him. If I remembered right, they'd wanted me to eat him, but I'd refused. I think I'd had a big lunch that day. Or maybe, people-eating aside, I thought it was funny that a troll was having a tantrum because he couldn't be a frat brother.

What had they paid me to imprison him? Anyhow, they'd designed the trap and I'd put him in it. Now, he's out, and I'm the one who has to deal with it. Again.

Gurlurk said, "Like Pie! No like trapped."

"PITS no like dying! You do bad. You get trap."

"Want go into PITS!"

"Can't join PITS. Pits for mages. PITS for learn magic. Trolls no do magic!" Why was I arguing? We'd already had this conversation back when he was destroying buildings and shouting, "I do magic! I believe in me." He hadn't been listening to anyone, but since at that time, I was full size and outmuscled him by a factor of ten, he'd had no choice but to deal with me. We'd had this same conversation while I had held him suspended by his ankles—and yes, I saw the irony of my current situation. What I didn't see was why I was discussing it again. Maybe the blood was pooling in my brain.

"You go home," I said. "Smash rocks. Find girl. Make babies."

"No! I do magic. Can learn! Will learn!"

"Trolls not mages!"

"Can do! Believe in self!"

"Who say?" Not every species could tap the magic that fueled the Faerie world, and even of those species that could, not every child was born with the talent. Most understood that, but here I was, victim to the one troll who got convinced that if he believed in himself hard enough, he could rewrite his own biology. "Who say that?"

"Ted say! Ted say, 'Believe. Can be anything want!'"

Great. A Ted talk. Figured; only a Mundane would be so clueless as to think a troll could "believe" himself into magical talent. "Where Ted?"

"Ate him!"

"Ted want eaten?"

Gurlurk paused. "No."

"Ted believe safe? Ted believe stay uneaten?"

"Maybe."

"Ted wrong! Ted wrong about Ted. Ted wrong about you and magic."

Apparently, my logic was too much for him. He hollered and stomped, then flung me hard. I hit the far wall with teeth-rattling force and plopped to the ground, dazed. He snagged me up again before I could recover my wits to run and shook me for good measure.

"Hunnerd years! Me stuck hunnerd years." he said. His shouting was like a punch to my now-aching head. I didn't think it'd been a hundred years, but in addition to being unable to do magic, he wasn't much with math, either. Still, I had to credit him for knowing the number 100. Trolls counted in terms of "many."

"Not my fault! Told trolls. They come." After I'd put him in the prison, I had found Gurlurk's people and told them where to fetch him. Then I took my reward, whatever it was, and went home, confident that the lesser sapients would handle it from there.

Why they hadn't, however, I didn't know. And yet, somehow, it didn't seem completely unexpected.

Why was it when someone else failed their obligation, I had to pay the price? That seemed typical of my life, too.

"No come. No come, no one. Hunnerd years!"

"You free now. Put me down. Go trolls."

"No! Go HMU. Be mage. Pledge PITS. Me do. Me believe."

The trollish language had very few words, but thanks to George, I wasn't fluent any longer. I was surprised, given my current inadequate abilities, that I had managed as much as I had. I did not have the vocabulary to explain genetics and the nature of magic to an angry stubborn troll. Come to think of it, even fluent, I couldn't make him understand. That's why I had to lock him up in the first place.

"You know, you could wish for him to have magical powers," a voice said in draconic. That smug, trouble-making genie had followed me out—just to watch!

"Or, you know, he could wish it himself," Al'Beah added.

No. More than to watch. To tempt me into a wish. Al'Beah obviously had been following the conversation. Maybe he was more fluent than I was. He couldn't tell the troll to wish for magic; that was against the rules. He had to suggest it or better yet, lead the troll to the idea. Right. There was no way I was going to let the violent, people-eating, dragon-smashing troll get even more power.

Fortunately, trolls were very direct and generally did not change their mind once convinced of something. Gurlurk, especially. And I was going to use that to my advantage.

I said to the troll. "Not my fault. Genie's fault. Genie say no."

"What?" Troll and genie shouted together.

Before Al'Beah could contradict me, I added, "Genie tell humans. Genie tell dragon. No HMU for Gurlurk. No PITS for Gurlurk. Troll no mage, never."

Gurlurk, for all that he was a slow thinker, had quick aggressive reflexes. He again threw me, this time in the direction of the genie. Then he charged.

I had anticipated the throw, and while my torn wings would no longer let me fly, I could at least fall with style. As soon as I had cleared his grasp, I unfurled my wings and directed my descent to a spot out of his way. Al'Beah, taken by surprise, reacted like any intelligent being when confronted by an angry troll. He yelped and fled.

Forgotten, I hugged the wall as the troll rushed by me and down the corridor, leaving a troll-sized hole in the doorway without even slowing down. As the troll's angry shouting and the genie's epithets about me faded, I did a quick body check to make sure I hadn't broken anything this time.

I heard a rumble. At first, I thought Gurlurk's damage to the doorway had shattered the foundation. But a gaping maw opened in the wall where he had yanked me out of the tunnel. I saw Colvert smash himself flat against the wall, then Owen charged out, yelling an Orcish-ish battle cry and swinging his ax. He slowed to a confused stop when he found the room empty but for me. The others poured through after.

"Um...?" Owen asked.

I shrugged. "You just have to know how to handle these things. Shall we?"

I moseyed to the opening. Colvert gave me a confused look, then shrugged and headed down the tunnel he'd already started. Guess he decided he was better off sticking to what he knew and understood.

I flicked the kinks out of my tail as I took point. The others hurried to catch up.

Chapter Eleven: Kobolds and Keggers

For the next few tons, as the tunneler travels, we moved in silence. This time, Colvert was digging a roundabout path. We moved up, down, left, right, as we avoided corridors and other hazards only he could sense. The others started to complain about the weaving, but I had to admire his skill.

Unfortunately, even the most skilled dwarves had limits, and we'd pushed Colvert to his. In trying to go over a tunnel, he nearly intersected a room above us before noticing and angling down. Its weakened floor gave way and something dropped on top of Betts. She screeched and slapped at her head, but the creature grabbed hold of her hair with ferocity and held tight, making angry snarling sounds. The others tried to drag him off but only succeeded in pulling Betts's hair.

"Kobold!" Sam said. He swung his sword and cut the nasty goblin-like creature from her hair. Owen hefted it down the way we'd come, grunting in disgust.

Two other heads looked down the hole in their floor. They hissed and spat.

"Quick, seal that hole," Ray told Colvert.

"I can't. Kobold magic's keeping it open."

"Then burrow faster."

"This is a tight area. It takes precision."

Linda yelled from the back, "They're coming!"

"Aargh!"

Colvert pushed on, trying to move us away from the floor above without sending us through the roof below. Behind us, we heard Linda and Father swinging at the horde while trying not to hurt each other. Sam hollered a spell while Ray sang... Was he singing "Diggy Diggy Hole?" Whatever, it seemed to be helping.

At least until we heard a rustling above us, and dust rained on our heads.

"Not me!" Colvert shouted, against any false accusations even as he started moving to the left. He wasn't fast enough. A new hole opened, half the size it probably would have been had he not turned, but enough for a kobold to spill through. And another. And then three more before I could poke my head into the hole and breathe random fire until the angry shrieks told me the vermin had backed off.

I held them off with snaps and snarls. Below me, people were shuffling and bumping into me as they were alternately fighting kobolds and trying to get past me. I could only hope the ones who could not fight were squeezing past while the others held back the tide.

Owen had decided to break character to join Ray in song; even Linda was managing a few words in between grunts, and Betts was joining the chorus. It wasn't hard; there are only 13 words, and the tune is catchy.

Then I felt someone smack my flank as he brushed past.

"Vern!" Father yelled, "let's move!"

I breathed another round of fire, driving the kobolds back, but most had retreated, probably to go through the first hole. Then I ducked down. Behind me, Owen swung his sword and Thud snapped at kobolds while Sam cast another spell.

"Go!" Owen said, "Colvert broke through. Thud can't get past you!"

I roared at the horde of nasties, and they fell back. The momentary respite gave Sam time to cast a stronger shield spell, which in turn gave us a head start.

We burst through the corridor, but the kobolds were almost on our heels. I pushed past everyone, "Follow me!"

Once again, we were running down tunnels.

"Do you have any idea where you're going, or are you taking turns at random?" Father panted. He was running, but the leg with the spider bite dragged and he winced with each pace.

"It's coming to me," I said, and the layout was— along with what I'd gotten in return for imprisoning Gurlurk. "We're in the Labyrinth of Chamenos."

"The Maze of the Lost?" Father translated. "Are you out of your mind?"

"Nope. I'm an honorary Piota."

I took a hard left, then a right, the others scrambling to keep up. Linda screamed, and I chanced a glance behind me. The kobold swarm had grown into a wave as the faster creatures climbed over their slower companions in their excitement to grab us, pull us apart, and eat us alive.

Now atop Thud with Betts riding behind him, Sam looked as well. "Vern, how about some fire support?"

"We can't slow down. Almost there!"

I'd found the room I was looking for. I fumbled at the door with oversized paws I was no longer used to as I said, "When we get in, go left and right, not straight. Hug the wall!"

As I remembered, the sides held short, wide platforms for standing on, just enough to hold our party—or a party of drunken frat boys if they crowded in. Years of neglect had caused the edges to crumble. Railings sprouted from the walls at one end of the platform and lined the edge only partway before they bent and drooped over the pit.

Fortunately, everyone did as I said, and soon we had lined the nearest walls of the pit trap that yawned before us. The kobolds, however, were running top speed and focused only on overtaking us. They burst past the threshold, sometimes three wide and two or more piled atop each other, and were still running even after their feet no longer touched the floor. They hit the ground with plops and cries of surprise and fury. I counted as they poured through: 10, 25, 40, 61...

At 83, the final kobold was groaning and cursing from the bottom of the pit.

"They're alive?" Ray asked. "How far did they fall?"

He leaned forward to look. The ground gave way under his feet.

Before anyone could react, he managed to grab hold of a lever conveniently placed near where he'd stood. A fortunate thing for him.

Less fortunate for us, it was the lever to the door.

"No!" I said, but too late.

The lever swung down but stopped when it was horizontal to the ground, just like it was made to do. And, just like it was made to do, it closed the door on our side while opening the door on the opposite side of the pit.

"Great!" I said as Owen, braced by Linda, grabbed Ray by the wrists and pulled him to their side of the new gap. Thunderpaws danced on his paws, wanting to get in on the excitement, but unable to reach his friend. "The ramp to that door won't extend until we close the one on the other side."

Linda cried, "Our door! It's gone!"

"Mmm, hmm." I sighed. Best laid plans of drakes and men. Below us, kobolds were scratching at the walls, trying to climb over each other to get at us or just get out. They wouldn't have much luck with either.

Colvert leaned against the wall, and the words coming from his mouth were not fit to repeat. I thought I knew why.

"We're not burrowing outta here," he announced once Ray was safely on the ledge. "There's a spell on the rock. I can't push through it."

"I'll fly across and open the door from the other side," Sam volunteered.

"You can't," I said, and to prove my point, I found a loose rock from the new gouge Ray had created in the already decrepit room and lobbed it. About 20 feet over the pit, it stopped as if hitting sludge, then dropped. A kobold let out a howl and a curse.

Ray groaned. "Well, that's just great. Where's Al'Beah? About time he stopped watching us perform like some ridiculous parody play and made himself useful."

"He's keeping the troll distracted."

Linda, calmer now, examined the lever, though she didn't make any move to touch it. She was learning. "Come on, Vern, you're the party thief. Are you certain we can't open the door from this end? If we return the lever to its original position...?"

I shook my head. "Then we lock both doors. It's a trap. Unfortunately, the key is down there." If only I could remember what the key was.

"With the kobolds?"

"Yes."

Sam added, "The ones you tricked into falling into the hole? So that, to escape this trap, we have to jump in the pit, anyway, and fight all the kobolds we were running from that led us to this trap, and then find the key in order to escape this trap?"

"Yep. The Phi Iotas had been especially proud of this room." Even more so after they'd blocked all the potential escapes and workarounds that I had pointed out.

Father had sat down with his back against the wall. He looked pale as if he'd been running in the dungeon for years rather than minutes. "Much as I appreciate the respite from the kobolds, what did you think we were going to do next?" His voice was thready.

I shrugged. "I intended for us to run back out the door, not lock ourselves in."

"Right." He sighed. From Thud's back, Betts reached into a saddlebag and handed him a skin of water. He thanked her and took a meager sip, waited to see if it would stay down, then took a longer drink.

Linda was peering over the edge. "It's hard to see, but it looks like they're rolling something against the walls. Can they climb out?"

"We're missing something," Father said. He swallowed hard, then continued. "Vern, how did you even know this room was here?"

"I told you. I'm an honorary Phi Iota Tau Sigma."

"You're a what?" Colvert sounded surprised, disgusted, and disappointed all at once. Quite an emotional range for a dwarf.

I replied with a little more pride in my voice. "I'm a Phi Iota Tau Sigma."

At my declaration, a light lit up the pit. We saw the kobolds, some milling, some poking the barrels, and long hooks strewn around the floor. Others, however, had started to climb over each other on our side of the pit.

"Guys..." Linda said as she unsheathed her sword.

Owen, also peering over, ax at the ready, noticed something else. "None hurt. Why fall not kill some?"

"Well, they didn't want to kill their candidates," I said.

They all turned to gape at me.

"This is a hazing dungeon?" Ray exclaimed.

"Weelllll..."

"All right, honorary frat dragon," Father said. With effort, he heaved himself to standing. "If this is an initiation test, what's the answer?"

I racked my brains. Had I ever been to an initiation? I was an honorary Piota, but I'd never really done anything with the fraternity. They accepted me after the troll job. They had liked the idea of having a dragon on their rolls and I had wanted the pin because it was pretty, with a dragon stone chip surrounded by emerald. I certainly would not have subjected myself to the humiliations of being hazed in, but if I remembered this room, I must have had a tour, and they probably would have... Oh.

Right.

Fewmets. There was one thing, but it was going to be humiliating after all.

A little black hand with thick claws clamped down on Linda's foot and she sliced it off with her sword. "Vern!"

Fine. We didn't have time to think of anything else. But I was going to hate this. Dragons can't sing, but I gave it the old college try:

Phi Iota Tau Sigma, to the world we're an enigma

We plunge the depths to reach new heights

In Phi Iota Tau Sigma

The pit walls glowed with a strong steady light. Owen kicked a kobold who was just clearing the ledge. I started the chorus again, warbling and off-key; then, to everyone's surprise, the kobolds picked up the tune.

Phi Iota Tau Sigma, May our magic live foreva

May our friendship long endure

For magic, friendship is!
Together, we can all excel
We plunge the depths of every spell
Phi Iota Tau Sigma, may our magic carry on.

Suddenly, one of the kobolds let out a cheer. "Beer!"

The barrels had sprouted taps. Eighty-three taps, in fact. The kobolds abandoned their quest to destroy us and flocked to the kegs. After some jostling and pushing, they each found a spout, opened it, and started suckling at it like furless, slick-skinned puppies. Soon the cavern was filled with happy slurping sounds.

"What?" Sam exclaimed.

Then the barrels began to rise. A couple of the imbibers, caught by surprise, fell to the floor, but the rest sunk their claws into the kegs, gently as to not pierce the wood, and hung on. The ones on the ground shrieked in anger. A few jumped, and one used a nearby hook to pull a keg down so he could latch on again.

Of course!

"Quick!" I told the others, "we have to line those barrels up to make a bridge."

I reached out with my tail and pulled the closest one to me. The creatures attached to it didn't notice, so intent were they on their drink. Using spells and my tail, we soon had a reasonably straight line of hovering, kobold-barnacled kegs.

Owen pulled a rope out of his pack, and the party tied themselves together. Linda, laughing like this was an amusement park game, took the lead, hopping lightly from barrel to barrel. Ray followed, then the others, alternating the strongest and most sure with those needing help. Sam had to lead Thunderpaws, but once the dire corgi got the rhythm, he pounced from barrel to barrel with joyful ease, his tongue lolling out his mouth. I brought up the rear.

Just as Linda cleared the barrels to step onto the platform beyond, one of the kobolds paused to belch. His barrel started to drop, surprising Father. He slipped but grabbed hold of the barrel in front of his. Colvert and Owen pulled at the rope as Father struggled to climb onto the barrel. One of his legs smacked a kobold, who paused to swipe at it. That barrel started to sink, too.

"Drink!" I commanded, using the kobold word, "chuugg."

"Chuugg!" Colvert yelled. "Chuugg, chuugg!" The others took up the chant.

Thus encouraged, the two kobolds went back to their taps in earnest. We hurried across, everyone taking extra care to be sure of their footing before moving on, in case any other drinkers paused for a burp.

Linda and Ray were pulling the lever, but it didn't budge. I shouted out the Phi-Iota song again, and taking the hint, they did their best to sing along. The door responded then stopped half-way at the end of the first verse, enough, perhaps, to let Linda and possibly Ray squeeze through, but not the rest of us—certainly not Thud or me.

I racked my brains.

Phi Iota Tau Sigma, may our magic live foreva

Mumble knowledge, um something well

Mumble uh ponies?

Um, something study and good wine.

We plunge the depths of every spell

Phi Iota Tau Sigma, our brotherhood carries on.

The door moved with aching slowness, but apparently, the brotherhood of Phi Iota was used to people forgetting the second verse and gave points for effort. Thunderpaws had to step to the side and wait while it got wide enough, but everyone slipped through. Colvert was already hurrying to find the best place to start a new tunnel.

"How do we shut this door?" Father asked when Thunderpaws squeezed through.

Colvert stopped his humming and cracked his knuckles. "Allow me."

The once was an elf from Endota
Who needed a frat on his rota
He'd nary a brain
And his spellwork was lame
And so he became a Piota.

The door slammed shut.

Colvert spat on it for good measure. Then he smirked at me.

"Envy's such an ugly thing," I quipped because, after all, I did have the Phi Iota pin.

Chapter Twelve: Should've Watched Season Two

Everyone learned to stop asking Colvert how much longer until the surface. In fact, after we heard the snarling and claw-scratching of one or the other hell beast scrabbling at the walls as we passed by a corridor, we forged ahead in silence, broken only by the dwarf's heavy breathing as he pushed his way through the stone. I'd known a lot of tunnelers in my life and had seen several competitions. Colvert was putting forth an effort worthy of an Olympian—an Olympian being chased by kobolds and hellhounds and trolls, in fact. Never underestimate the power of proper motivation.

His efforts let us bypass several traps and who-knows-what other nasty creatures. The Piotas had not been policing their labyrinth very well. If I weren't so busy fighting for our lives, I'd be embarrassed.

Ray was finally adapting to the closed quarters, or else the dangers of the more open corridors had finally convinced his subconscious that the narrow dark tunnel crowded with friends was a Good Thing. Betts and Sam walked together, holding hands and occasionally trading shy glances. Behind them, Linda and Owen made mocking googly eyes at each other and suppressed their laughter. I said nothing. I knew they were happy for their friend.

Besides, I was more concerned about Father. I'd offered to guard our rear so I could keep pace with him. He trudged along, not quite falling behind, but with an increasing gap growing between us and the rest of the party. With no one but me to see, he limped visibly. He tried to hide how hard he was struggling for breath. I didn't have to touch him to know his skin was as clammy as he was pale. He'd managed to hold down the water, but I felt it was by stubborn effort.

He whispered prayers under his breath, and not just any prayers. Prayers for suffering.

I moved closer so I could speak quietly. "What did you mean when you said you understood what was happening?"

He paused to take another cautious sip of water, then poured a little on his hand to wipe his face. "When I first joined the priesthood, I wanted to be a missionary, did I ever tell you that? I wanted the toughest, most desperate mission I could get. I thought the experience would make me a better priest. The Bishop said no. I'm 'good enough,' and we didn't have enough native-born priests as it was. Every year, I'd make my request. Every year, the diocese refused me. Then, the Gap opened."

"And I'm the ultimate tough mission?" I teased, but then I realized. It wasn't about the preaching. "Father, you didn't wish...?"

"I live a pampered life, Vern. Aside from the injuries that sparked my vocation, I've never known suffering. No, I never said anything aloud, but what priest doesn't wish for the opportunity to unite in suffering with Christ? Besides, there's someone who... He needs these prayers."

Owen. I wanted to ask more, but it was none of my business. As far as I knew, no one in our party except Father knew he was ill. I don't know; maybe with everyone going their own ways (if we survived this wish-world), he didn't want to bring anyone down on our last days together.

Father paused to cough, then to catch his breath. "Didn't quite expect this, though. But I'll be fine," he assured me. "Or not, according to God's will. Even in the Wish World, I'm sure He's still in control."

"Spoken like a true paladin," I said, and he laughed.

Colvert shushed us. "Cavern ahead. Feels small. I'm going to push us through."

I was in the rear, and there was no way I could move past Thunderpaws. Everyone steeled themselves for a fight, and Colvert busted into the room. There was a moment's silence.

"Come on, then," Colvert called. "There's nothing but a daft old man muttering about spells and burning paper."

We crowded into the small room. There was indeed a man at a desk, writing and muttering. He ignored us completely.

Colvert went to the walls and hummed, using his magic to find the best way out. Meanwhile, everyone took advantage of the rest. Sam checked over the gashes Thunderpaws had gotten from the couple of kobolds that had managed to scratch at his nose, healing them with magic while Betts caressed the corgi's ears to keep him still. Linda found some liniment and tended Owen's wounds, sans ear rubs.

Ray, the only one unscathed from the battle, was watching the "daft old man" with interest.

"What's he saying?"

The man, who was more disheveled and emaciated than aged, had risen from the desk and tossed a paper into a fire that burned with green flame. Then he paced back to the desk with methodical steps. He muttered in Greek.

I translated.

"Ninety-six seconds, write the spell. One hundred and eight seconds, burn the spell. One hundred and nine seconds, spell resets. Can't forget. Must save the world. Fifteen, sixteen, seventeen... Now he's counting."

"Sounds crazy."

"But familiar?" Father said, his voice turned up in a not-quite-question question.

Colvert tapped a stone and grunted with approval. "Not much farther 'till we're out of this mountain. This way." Without waiting for an answer, Colvert started to burrow.

The others started behind him, but Ray went to the man. Father hung back, too.

"Excuse me, sir. You seem in distress."

"Thirty-one, thirty-two...Leave me alone. At 96, I write the spell." He shrugged off Ray's grasp and continued his pacing.

"What spell?"

"Forty-four... Spell that preserves the world. Keeps it safe. Forty-seven..."

I shrugged. "The world is safe—or not—regardless of any influence of a spell here."

But Father's face bore an odd, pensive expression. One like I was fairly sure I'd worn more than once in this cockamamie adventure. "Father?"

The old man was shaking his head. "No, if I stop, if I hesitate, it all ends. The world crashes. Must keep the spell going until the others come, fix things. The HMU will bring others. Fix things. Sixty-eight..."

"How long have you been here?" Father asked. "Doing this over and over?"

"Can't think numbers! Seventy-three...only count and at ninety-six write the spell. Go away!"

"Come on, guys," I said. "Look what happened the last time we tried to save a random stranger instead of making our way out of here."

"But you said it yourself," Ray protested. "The world won't end if he doesn't keep up the spell."

"The world? No, no not the world. The..." The man stopped, confused. "I... Who? No, no. Have to do the spell. At ninety-six, write the spell. At one hundred eight, burn the spell. One hundred nine, the spell resets. Ninety-two..." He pulled out the chair and readied his quill.

In the distance, I heard Colvert saying they were close. "Guys, let's go."

Father had a half bemused, half-torn look in his eyes. "Yeah, Ray. I think..."

But Ray had grabbed the man's writing arm by the wrist. "Listen to me! You do not need to remain a prisoner here!"

"Let me go. Must stay until they come. One hundred one..." He yanked and fought to write, but Ray held firm.

"Ray!" Father said. "Let him finish! It's *Lost*."

Ray missed the reference. "No one is coming. You will remain here until you die! The world will keep going, but you'll continue to not enjoy it. Come with us."

"One hundred and seven... Aargh! Too late." He threw down his quill in disgust.

At one hundred and eight, he was not ready with a spell to drop into the flames. At one hundred and nine, the flames puffed bright, then went out. For a moment, there was an eerie silence.

Then I heard a distant rumble.

The spell wasn't to hold the world together, but to keep the labyrinth intact!

Father hadn't meant the cause was lost. He meant the script was *Lost*—the part of the TV show where they thought they had to keep restarting some program or the island was going to get destroyed.

And in this case, the script was playing true.

"Run!"

We dashed into the tunnel, Ray dragging the man along as Father explained his suspicions, too late. The man was counting again, but this time backward. I did some quick calculations.

"Colvert, we have three minutes and ten seconds to get out of this cave!" I yelled as I entered the tunnel.

"Aye, I feel the rock. What daft thing did you do this time?"

Father said, "It wasn't me. I tried to warn him."

Ray shot back, "I gave up on that show after Season One."

Colvert gave a growl of frustration. "What are ye saying? Never mind. We're close to the surface. Another break. Feels like a tunnel."

Without waiting he burst through. We all poured out. Here, where the rock had already been hewn and—I now realized—supported magically by the spell the old man had had to renew every four minutes, everything rumbled and shook just enough to feel it but not enough to upset our balance. The lower levels, however, were crumbling, and the rest would not be far behind.

Speaking of behind, shouting and howling of creatures in flight were heading our way. They sounded frightened, angry, and familiar.

I didn't need to tell people to run.

I took the lead. Dragons know tunnels. I could have led us out of the labyrinth on my own if we had wanted to waste time dealing with more creatures than we already had. Now, of course, we had them all coming our way, fleeing the destruction of the shoddily constructed caves. The kobolds were in the lead, but only because they had been closer. I could hear the slurring and tripping and belching. They were drunk, and kobolds were mean drunks. Behind them and coming up fast were the hellhounds, including our poker-playing friends. I hoped Thunderpaws had hidden his ill-gotten goods well.

I hurried on, letting instincts tell me the turns to take. I could hear the others puffing behind me. We were close enough to the surface that I felt the breeze against my cheek crests.

The cave suddenly opened to the outside. I saw a glimpse of a beautifully forested mountain and blue sky, but instead of a clear path leading to a sunshiny meadow, we found our escape plugged by a troll.

"Don't stop!" I yelled to my friends, then to Gurlurk, I shouted, "Run, you fool!"

"No pass!" Gurlurk yelled at me. "You no pass. Me smash."

"No stop me!"

"Ha! Gurlurk big. Dragon puny!"

"Dragon dragging kobolds!"

He looked behind me and his face went from smug to terrified. He turned to run, which gave us enough room to the right to dash past him and cut right toward the side of an adjoining hill. We leaned against the scraggly slope, panting and watching.

Gurlurk managed to retreat two steps when a cloud of small, dark, angry, drunk kobolds vomited out of the cave entrance and swarmed over him. He toppled and landed face-first in the dirt, but they didn't stop. Instead, they continued down the hill, tromping over the unlucky troll who could only cover his head and make "oof" sounds. Now that we were in the open and free of the echoes of the cave, I could tell the kobolds weren't just shouting randomly in anger. They had been chanting.

Phi Iota Tau Sigma! You're not much of an enigma

We drank yer kegs to the dregs

And we're coming down for more!

Soon they were all gone but for one inebriated female who staggered to a tree and started throwing up. One of the others paused, ran back, and held her hair out of her face while crooning, "It's okay. Just let it out. You're beautiful. You're beautiful," while daring us with his eyes to make a comment.

Of course, we were too busy staying out of the way of the other creatures that erupted from the caves: hell hounds and demon dogs and wraiths and skeletons, not to mention the usual vermin that took shelter and grew to unusual size under the influence of the magic. The rats took a hard left, heading downhill, probably to some bog. Everyone else ran straight down the trail, treating the troll like a bump in the road. I almost felt bad for Gurlurk, except that he could have listened to me.

The last to emerge was Cerberus, who bounded onto Gurlurk's backside, paused to howl with all three heads, and then hurried off, presumably to return to guarding the gates to the underworld, which is what he should have been doing instead of playing poker in some fraternity labyrinth.

There was a moment of silence. Then, the mountainside collapsed with a huge boof! Dust, debris, leaves and pine needles, and one very angry squirrel fell from above, coating us in dirt, but fortunately, the slope was such that when the mountain crumpled, it didn't topple onto us.

We coughed and hacked. Thunderpaws started to shake until we all shouted, "No!" He stood, whining until Sam cast prestidigitation and the filth lifted from his fur. He scratched at one spot on his neck until a large bone from the poker game came loose. He plopped down to chew on it.

Gurlurk sat up, spat out dirt and scrub brush, and moaned. "Hate magic! Hate HMU! No want be mage! Want go home!"

He stood and stomped off. I heard him mutter, "Want be bard. Make pretty music. Get girls."

The female kobold finished her retching. She wiped her mouth on her sleeve, then looked up at the male who still held her hair. "You really think I'm beautiful? Even now?"

"Now and always."

She sighed and leaned against him. Together they made their way down the path after their kinsmen. Behind her back, the male waved a thank you signal to someone in the tree.

From where he hovered in the branches, Al'Beah waved back.

I was starting to smell a rat, and it didn't have anything to do with the pests that had infested the caves.

The genie floated down, applauding us as he did so. "That was amazing! Inspired. Sending the troll after me...well, not my favorite part of how all this worked out, but the rest! Wow! Wishes granted in style."

The dwarf stepped forward. "What are ye yammering about? I wished for a challenge that would make me famous."

"You what?" I asked, the rest of the party half a word behind me. Even Thunderpaws tilted his head inquisitively.

"The greatest challenge of your life. You just burrowed 18,150 tons and almost three miles, while facing supernatural dangers and bringing your companions to safety."

"And the evidence is gone! Buried under all the rubble." Colvert turned to the old man. "This is your fault!"

"Mine? I faithfully kept that spell going! I was supposed to be a hero and save my company from financial destruction."

"Stop!" I hollered. "Are you telling me both of you had wishes pending with this genie?"

Al'Beah pushed forward, so excited he was glowing an even brighter shade of orange tan. "It's really a very funny story. You see, a kobold, a dwarf, and an accountant walk into a bar—"

"Do you think this is a joke?" the old man—the accountant, no doubt—screeched. "I have been faithfully feeding that stupid spell every one hundred and eight seconds for years to keep that stupid maze put together and save Hermetic Industries the embarrassment and expense of failing to meet contract."

"And you succeeded. The warranty expired yesterday."

"What? It's been thirty years?" He sat down hard on some rubble.

"I thought you said you were saving the world," Ray said.

"You heard him. Thirty years! It got conflated in my head. Besides, work is my world! I had to save it. But thirty years?"

Al'Beah grinned like a madman. "You have such a retirement party waiting for you."

Colvert cleared his throat with a rumble that could have started an avalanche if the mountain hadn't already collapsed in on itself like a bad soufflé. "My wish was for fame for my amazing deeds. How is that going to happen if all the tunnels I've dug are now collapsed under a million tons of dirt?"

The genie smiled smugly. "This was a university project run by a fraternity. Surely you didn't think it went unmonitored?"

The accountant started to sputter. "But they'd have seen me. Thirty years, and no one came to relieve me?"

"What about the guy trapped on the rack as part of the holding spell?" Sam cut in. "He looked to have been there a hundred years."

"Oh, that was just because the spell was seeping his life energy. It'd only been a twenty...seven? Yes, seven. Twenty-seven years. Since the trolls destroyed the university."

Now, it was my turn to shout. "They did what? But I told them to go peacefully and retrieve Gurlurk!"

"Well, Vern, some of them wanted to, but the others were angry, and they got there first, and then the Piotas gave them attitude, and... By the time the leveler heads arrived, it was a mess, let me tell you, so when they discovered my lamp among the debris, the first wish they made was that people forget about it. The exact words were

'You make all landfolk forget HMU,' so of course, there was a little wiggle room."

"You made everyone on land forget, but the people in the dungeon remembered. That's why I had forgotten about the labyrinth and the Piotas until Rackman reminded me."

The Genie bowed to acknowledge my reasoning. "But back to Colvert's concern. Just because people had forgotten about the university does not mean the surveillance spells forgot. In the security department of Cavernous Insurers, there is a scrying ball that has been recording every event in the labyrinth since HMU took out the policy, which of course, goes well before your company was contracted to make improvements and reinforce the structure.

"It just so happens that a bored security officer was perusing the scrying balls and saw Colvert as he placed his hands on the first wall. And, wouldn't you know, he is a big fan of the slate league."

"So, someone saw me?"

"Someone? As soon as you announced your intent, he was hollering for a mage friend to put it on the scrywork. It was the night shift here. You had a dozen followers from the start, including the owner who happened to be there on one of his unofficial visits."

"He...was impressed?"

"He called in one of his bards to write the ballad just in case you didn't make it."

"Didn't make it?"

The genie shrugged. "He is in insurance. Be that as it may, you have survived and in fact, there's quite a reception awaiting all of you in a meadow about a hundred yards downhill. So, in one arranged adventure, I've..."

He pointed to the accountant, "...made you the hero of your company and secured you a hefty retirement salary with bonuses..."

He pointed to the dwarf, "...ensured your career as a professional, sponsored tunneler..."

He pointed to Thunderpaws, "...granted your wish. That is the Bone of Unending Delight. Chew it as much as you like, and the next day, it returns to its full size just as savory as the day Cerberus gnawed it off his victim. Is that a good bone? Is it? Is it?"

The dire corgi wagged his tail so hard his behind wiggled back and forth, knocking Ray off balance.

Then, the genie crossed his arms and smiled at me. "I helped Spitz the Kobold impress the female of his dreams, and I have convinced Gurlurk to go home (which was his parents' wish, by the way.) Ray got to experience an actual dungeon crawl; Linda's had her wish for all of you to go on one last big adventure, and..."

He jerked his head toward where Sam and Betts had sat down together under a tree holding hands and talking seriously. Sam leaned forward and kissed her.

"Wait," Ray protested. "You can make people fall in love? That's not really, I don't know..."

"That wasn't the wish," Linda said. "I wished someone would see Sam's true worth, and that I'd be there to witness it. Aw, I might cry."

"Owen might gag," Owen grunted. Linda punched his arm.

The genie, however, smirked and examined his nails in a feigning humility he knew was false. "Betts had wished for a loyal and brave husband.

Two more wishes, there. So go on, dragon; tell me I'm good."

Good? He was a conniving genie-us, and I told him so.

He preened. Like literally. His wispy backend morphed into peacock feathers and fanned out. He puffed out his chest. "And I'm not even done fulfilling all the wishes."

We heard a distant rumbling from the north, pounding in a complex rhythm that human ears could not distinguish, but which I recognized with an ache in my heart.

The accountant screamed and fled downhill. Apparently, he knew what it meant, too.

"What's wrong? Is a storm coming?" Linda asked.

"No," I said, my heart starting to beat in time to the wing flaps of my kin, "but it is a thunder."

I pointed to the sky.

Far above us, my fellow dragons dotted the sky, weaving in and out of complex patterns as they danced along their way. They were too far up for us to feel the pulsing of each downflap, and we saw only the shadowed silhouettes of each magnificent figure, but I felt my breath catch in my throat, anyway. Eight hundred and fifty-seven years. I'd not seen my kin in at least 857 years.

I saw a gap in the changing formations, subtle as the others altered their trajectories to make up for it, but one I noticed right away. My spot. I could feel the motions as my muscles remembered the moves. My incomplete memory didn't let me recall that last time I'd danced with my kin, but my body still knew how it had felt.

Dragons didn't cry, but they did rage. I spun and let out a stream of fire at Al'Beah. My friends yelped and scurried out of the way, backing up against the rubble. The genie jerked away just in time to avoid getting flamed.

"Well, that's some thanks," he said, putting out the fire I'd inadvertently started in the trees behind him.

"What game are you playing?" I demanded. "I didn't make a wish!"

"Didn't you?" he responded with infuriatingly good nature. "But you've been a great sport about getting everyone else their wish. I thought you deserved a treat, too. Really, it's not hard to guess what you want. Why should everyone else have all the fun?"

"Yeah, fun," Father gasped out. He was huddled up with his cloak around himself. Linda was opening another bottle of healing potion.

"What about Father?" I asked. He hadn't voiced a wish to suffer.

"Yeah," Ray said. "This wish-world runs on Care Bear rules, right? We can't die here, can we?"

"The risks are real here. But there are solutions."

Al'Beah raised a brow at me. I knew what he was implying. Dragon blood heals. But that handy magic was taken from me in my battle with St. George, and I'd have felt it if I'd gotten it back.

The thunder was passing overhead now.

Don't trust him, the sensible part of me said. Never trust a genie, especially the one granting wishes out of the goodness of his heart. Genius that he was, I did not know his vision for his "masterpiece." We should go home...

To what? Another part of me argued. A rundown human warehouse in a world where humans have a problem with me even sitting and smiling for a camera? What's awaiting me in the Mundane except disrespect and loneliness?

"God forgive me, I'm ready for this to stop," Father gasped. If he meant it—if he really meant it— he'd be fine. Wish granted. Suffering stage achieved.

"Yes," Owen said, his voice ringing with worry that cut through his orcish facade. Somehow, he'd figured out what was going on. "You stop suffering now. Good enough."

"I'm open to suggestions." Father groaned.

Al'Beah wouldn't end it. Someone else had to do it.

With a roar that shook the trees and upset the layer of dust, I stretched my neck toward the sky and sent out a long, brilliant pillar of white-hot flame into the sky. My friends yelped and shielded their eyes.

Despite my misgivings, I could not deny how good it felt.

Chapter Thirteen: If Wishes Were Dragons

Ray yelled and pointed, "Look!"

A single shadow disengaged from the formation and dove toward us.

A roar shook the mountains. My friends clamped their ears and cowered, oblivious to the music that was my name correctly pronounced for the first time in eight centuries.

The dragon circled us once. The light of the rising sun reflected off her pink and orange scales, and the translucent membranes of her wide, strong wings caught the light as if its only purpose was to illuminate her to the world below. She was a sunrise in and of herself. My breath caught in my throat so that I couldn't even call out a greeting. I know I'm always saying how glorious we are, but I'd forgotten what that really meant.

Around me, my friends gasped in wonder. "Oh, Vern!" Linda whispered. "Were you like that? I'm so sorry."

I didn't reply. What could I say?

As she came in for a landing, the forest gave way. I mean this literally. Where there were trees, suddenly, there was flat and gentle land. She backwinged once, creating a mighty breeze that knocked Ray off his feet and pushed Al'Beah back. Her feet touched the ground with the softness of a kitten's.

Her eyes, pale lilac under rosy brows, scanned the skies before looking at us. Her stance was wary and poised for launch. Her barbed tail swished with agitation. Worry showed in the tightness of her muscles and how her cheek crests pulled back. But in the shape of her face, I saw my own, and that brought back a flood of memories.

"Grislakeh! Twinkin!"

God created the entire drove of dragons all at once, with such rapidity that mortal creatures, for whom time was so important, could not tell the order of our Creation. But we knew with an instinct that told us who was elder as surely as we knew whose territory we were in. But there were two of us, created so closely together, that it was said God had a thought too grand to fit in one dragon, so he divided it up among twins. I was one of those.

And that majestic, awe-inspiring, terrifyingly beautiful creature whose worried expression turned to horror as she focused on my puny, diminished form? That was my twin "sister."

I grinned at her. I was sure I looked like an idiot. I was equally sure I didn't care.

She said, "Well, twinkin, I should have known when we saw the mountain collapse that we'd find you nearby." She looked me over, not quite circling. She didn't need to, she was so much larger than me. She sniffed me with distaste. "Vurnerrah! What happened to you?"

"Long story."

"I have time." It was an old joke among dragons, empyrie, and elves with a sense of humor.

Behind me, I heard Father's shallow breaths. I didn't have time for patience or humor. "Later. First, can you heal him?"

She gaped at me. "Is this what you've been doing? Playing with mortals? You almost missed conclave to play with your pets?"

"Vern," Linda said behind me.

I realized Griss and I were speaking in the native language of dragons, which involved a lot of growls, roars, tail swishes, ground pawing... It must look aggressive, especially as our moods shifted. How quickly I'd gone from awe and joy to annoyance. Was that what happened with familiarity? I felt like there should be a metaphor in there somewhere, but right now, I had more pressing concerns. "They're my friends. I'll explain later. My healing is gone. Help him."

"Friends?" She lowered her head, the better to examine them. Even with her chin nearly touching the ground, she was eye-to-eye with Linda, who was kneeling by Father and patting his head with a wet cloth. Linda gulped hard but maintained her composure as Griss sniffed at them and spoke in English.

"Oh, a priest...no, a paladin. Did you do this to my twinkin?" She indicated with a jerk of her head my diminished state.

Despite his pain, he managed a shrug and a weak smile.

"You think it's funny, Human?" she growled.

But Father had been around me too long. "A little. He gave as good as he got, but God was on my side."

She snorted, then turned to me. "Despite this, you want him restored?"

I shrugged. "It's complicated."

"Another long story?"

"I'm full of them. Is there somewhere else you need to be?"

"Yes, and you as well. Where have you been that you did not hear the call to conclave?"

"Collapsing a mountain?"

She gave me a queer look, then giggled. It was a lovely sound, and some of the woodland creatures who had originally fled made a cautious return to the area around us. "All right, then, Paladin. Show me your wound."

Father gritted his teeth as Linda pulled his pant leg away and removed the bandage. The bite area had blackened and the skin around it was sallow and oozing.

Griss made a disgusted sound. "I hate those spiders."

With a claw, she pricked her skin and let the blood flow into the furrow of the nail. When she had about a cupful, she poured it onto the open wound. Father hissed through clenched teeth as dragon blood battled with spider poison. Finally, his eyes rolled back, and he slumped against Linda.

My friends gasped. Owen stood. Even though he was shaking, he was ready to defend or avenge our friend priest.

Griss shook her head at him. "Relax. He'll be fine in a few hours."

Then, she turned to me and spoke in our language. "There. I fixed your plaything. Ready to tackle something more challenging?"

"I just collapsed a mountain!" I protested.

"Oh, were you victorious over dirt?" she teased.

"Envy is so ugly," I countered.

I thought she was going to match my sarcasm with more of her own, but instead, she looked at the deflated hill thoughtfully. "Was it fun?"

At the time, "fun" was not the word I'd have used, but looking back, I had to admit it was.

"Then tell the thunder. After the hunt. Can you keep up?"

Without waiting, she launched herself into the air with a great flap of her wings. The downdraft toppled Owen and Ray.

"That was awesome!" Ray said as he dusted himself off.

"Aye," the dwarf answered, "and worrisome. Dragons dinnae gather in such numbers unless something is terrible wrong."

Colvert was right, and my place should be with them. But this was the wish-world. I'd seen my twin. Wasn't that enough?

"Why are you hesitating?" Colvert demanded. My kind had formed a V formation so far ahead they could have been geese.

I looked at the sky. My heart was already soaring among them, but I had a responsibility to these Mundanes.

"Go on," Sam said. "I'll get everyone to the Summer Court. We'll wait for you there. Father could use some recovery time, anyway."

He was still out, but his breathing was steady and calm.

Al'Beah pointed a finger at me. "And as a bonus for being a good sport."

I felt warmth spread over my wings, and I unfurled them to find them healed.

I told my friends, "If you get a chance to leave, go. Don't wait for me." I took off before Colvert could protest that they were already going.

It took me less time to catch up with my kin than Griss suspected. Usually, when one of my kind is my current size, they're recovering from injuries. They're weak and need the help of others. But my size was the result of 850 years of recovering from my real fight with St. George. I took a spot at the back of the line behind her. She gave me a surprised glance but pretended not to be impressed. Brat.

No one else acknowledged my joining them, though I didn't feel snubbed. Rather, it seemed everyone was grimly focused on our destination or what we'd find there. Since I'd missed the briefing, I could not ask, but was expected to figure it out as we went along. That was fine by me. I'd had plenty of surprises today. What was one more?

We flew in formation for an hour or so, then by a signal we all understood on instinct, we changed position as those in the front moved back and those in the middle took their turn at the front. My elderkin, Agarrabarresheh, took the spot behind me. He made a snide remark about my deigning to join them.

"It's been a weird couple of days," I grumbled back, but really, I was just happy to be there, soaring so high the ground below was a patchwork of terrains and even the largest creatures were the size of ants. I reveled in the wind flowing over my wings. Magic flowed, too, and I closed my eyes, trusting proprioception to keep me in position as I concentrated on the sweet feeling of its energies against my scales. My friends were safe, and for a glorious while, I could enjoy being a dragon with my own kind. I think I sighed contentedly because behind me, I heard my older kin snort.

We didn't switch positions again before we got to our destination. My heart beat faster with excitement. This wasn't just a conclave for discussion and debate. We were on a hunt!

More than a hunt. Nineteen hydras—hydrae?— were terrorizing the elvish coastal city of Tannenreelahxbydahseey.

In my Territory. And I hadn't known. No wonder Griss had gotten mad. Nothing to do for it now except make a good fight. Besides, I'd also had to deal with a swarm of spiders. That had to count for something, right?

The elvish army had formed a picket line on the beach, spears pointed outward threateningly, while behind them, their archers led the offensive with volley after volley of arrows. In the ocean, the merfolk fought as well. Some shot arrows, but those that had run out were improvising by throwing whatever was handy, from rocks to their clamshell bikinis. Blood and corpses on the beach and floating in the water told of their valiant efforts and limited success.

The hydrae stood in the shallows, their many heads weaving, snapping at elves and merfolk, trying to push past to get to the tasty morsels in the nearest houses, and completely not cooperating with each other. Ironically, teamwork was never a hydra's strong point, something Griss and I had often used to our advantage.

We broke from formation, and Griss and I called dibs on the one nearest the merfolk. We both had a special affection for the ditzy species.

I swooped down, cutting in front of one head just as it was making a lunge toward a merman. I puffed enough fire to make myself the bigger target so it would follow me. Griss did the same with a second head. As predicted, each head focused on us to the exclusion of everything else. We crossed paths. Griss kept her hydra head occupied by staying teasingly just outside its reach.

Meanwhile, I feinted across her head's neck, and when my head pursued, I reached down under her neck with my tail, grabbed my head, and pulled it around. It almost caught my leg with its teeth when I let go, but I didn't worry. I liked having it focused on me.

Griss and I backtracked toward each other and repeated the maneuver. The heads stopped their pursuit of us with a jerk that gagged them both and turned toward each other in confusion at their knotted necks.

Right over left and left over right works just great when your hydra's not bright.

The entire creature turned in on itself, the free heads distracted by the other two as they alternately tried to pull away from each other (which only tightened the knot and choked them) and snapped at each other. The free heads snarled and chided the others with howls like a summer squawl. That only made the two tangled ones more agitated.

Griss and I backed away to admire our handi-work. We loved a good gag, and this one worked on a literal and figurative level. So did the merfolk. They paused to cheer then began their attacks with renewed vigor.

Even if the other two heads were gullible enough to let us repeat our trick, they were too far from each other. Griss flew around them to keep them occupied while I went for the tender area where the neck met the body. I bit down hard.

All four heads of the hydra screamed, and the creature writhed, but I sunk my claws into its back and held on as I pulled the neck from the body. The hydra was colossal, perhaps five times my size, but that just made it easier to ride as I worked to sever the spine. Now that I was thinking about it, I should have let Grislakeh do this part. Her jaws were ten times more powerful than mine at the moment. She could have done this in a single bite while my smaller size and increased maneu-verability would have kept them distracted.

Too late now. I bit harder and followed with a swipe of my claws.

Above me, I heard a meaty slap and Griss's cry of surprise. Apparently, the hydra had gotten a lucky shot. I didn't have time to call after her. I swiped again, and the neck came away and fell into the ocean. Cold water and hot blood splashed over me. I opened my mouth to breathe fire into the crevice to cauterize it before a new head could form.

"Vurnerrah! Look out!" Griss cried.

Blindly, I turned my fire upward toward the free head, but it wasn't enough.

Apparently, the other heads had learned from my example and gnawed off one of the tied-up necks. Two tiny, angry heads were already budding in its place, and the remaining mature ones were coming after me.

I caught the nearest one with a face full of flame, but the other chomped down on my back, its teeth piercing my wings. It was my turn to howl in pain and outrage. I'd just gotten them healed!

Fortunately, dragonhide is thicker than a hydra's jaw can press. It had a good grip on me but couldn't puncture me the way I had Old Seven Legs. As it tried to tear me off, I dug my claws in deeper and finished cauterizing the wound I'd created. Just in time; two tiny heads were starting to bud in the gaping hole.

The head holding me shook, like Thunderpaws playing with a chew toy. Caught between its jaws, my body twisted and my fire went wild. Griss had been diving for the other head, claws out to pierce its eyes, but swerved to avoid my flame. The mermen had advanced and were poking at its underside, while the mermaids continued their attack, but they were running out of useful weapons. Soggy seaweed slapped the head attacking me.

Meanwhile, the tiny heads had grown large enough to threaten the nearest merfolk. They hissed like cobras and struck out. Two larger heads from where the hydra had decapitated itself were surging at Gris, keeping her from coming to help me.

Suddenly the sky above us darkened. I looked up to see a dragon-shaped silhouette against the sun.

"You're in trouble now!" I told the heads. From somewhere above me, Griss crooned agreement.

Our eldestkin, Durrehkeh, swooped down, roaring joyfully. His black scales reflected the sunlight like mirrors. He stretched out his legs, each of which was easily as wide as a hydra's neck. His claws extended like a cat's. Long as scimitars and just as sharp, they gleamed with the same iridescence of his horns and back spikes. He smelled like gold and power and exuded a magical vibrancy beyond anything a dragon should possess.

Terrific is an odd Mundane word. The original meaning came from "terror": to shake with fear. Over a couple of centuries, it shifted to mean awe-inspiring, then huge or excessive, then amazing. My eldestkin embraced all of those at once.

Merfolk scattered as he let loose with a searing flame. The hydra arched and howled in pain, releasing me. I, in turn, leaped off its back, sending a targeted blaze at the tiny heads while Griss sent a funnel of fire into the larger head's screaming mouth. It reared, exposing its chest. Durrehkeh dove in for the kill.

Durr flew under the hydra, toppling it to the ground. Immediately, he and Griss were upon it. He bit down on its chest, coming away with a mouth of flesh.

But he hadn't gone deep enough, and our hydra still had a lot of fight in it. Plucky thing. It swung hard with its tale and slapped my eldestkin across the face, knocking him aside.

I saw my opening and dove in. Smaller and faster, I shot between the weaving heads, the tail, and Durrehkeh's bulk straight toward the wound. I breathed a pencil-thin blast of white flame straight into its heart.

The beast shuddered and fell dead.

One down. I scanned the shore. My kin had taken down two more.

Sixteen to go.

We needed tactics. We had plenty of big fighters. We needed someone wily with sneaky tricks they didn't know. Someone like Yours Truly.

I was tiny, but I was used to my shape and size. I had defeated false gods and true demons in my current state because I'd learned how to use everything to my advantage. Kind of the Krav Maga of dragons. Plus, I had centuries of fighting alongside mortals and hundreds of hours of watching movies.

I flew to the mermaids. "New game! Get strong rope. Then tricksy, brave merfolk tie up the hydra legs. Yes?"

They agreed it was a good game indeed. Others suggested slippery seaweed to trip them. Their eyes shone with anger and a desire to get back at these beasts that had taken so many of their own.

Next, I flew to the elves, but Grislakeh had already caught onto my plan. She was giving the elves instructions on targeting the hydras. They had stopped shooting when we arrived to keep from hitting us.

I saw a shield lying abandoned on the beach, its owner no longer in a position to need it. I snatched it up, dragging it across the beach until it was full of sand. Then I headed to the nearest hydra and flung sand into its eyes. I caught three of the heads in my sand cloud. They shrieked and shook as I easily swooped past, leaving the others to attack.

We spent the next hour in battle. Soon, my kin picked up on my capabilities as I distracted, tossed sand, dove in for a fast blast before skipping out of the way, and generally annoyed the hydras while my merfolk tangled them in ropes, nets, and seaweed, and the elves moved in to kill the ones that fell. They tossed me up a rope, and I grabbed it in my jaws and flew around one hydra who had managed to spring a dozen new heads in this fight. I circled them once, twice, and again as Grislakeh and Huerrah kept them distracted and snapping at them. After my fourth circumnavigation, I grabbed the other end from the mermen holding it taught and pulled.

All twelve heads jerked together with a chorus of "gerk" that was heard even above the other battles. At that moment, one of my youngerkin swooped in for the kill. Grislakeh laughed as it went down.

But I caught a glimpse of our eldestkin staring at us, and he didn't seem so amused.

Chapter Fourteen: Conflict at the Conclave

The lord of the merfolk and the City Elder of the Elvish town offered us treasure and gratitude, but oddly, Durrehkeh refused it on behalf of the thunder. He was rather rude about it, too: "What you offer, we do not need."

Maybe so, but when did tribute have to be something we needed? I held my tongue because I was, in essence, middle of the pack—lower, thanks to my diminished size and weight. I'd made an impression during the fight which had raised my status a lot, but not enough to contradict our alpha. Besides, dungeon-fun aside, I didn't think God would use the fact that I was in a wish-world to excuse my vow of poverty.

So we took the corpses of the hydras as the only prizes for our efforts. Durrehkeh did allow the elves to create for us a portal to his territory, so we had only a short flight to the hot desert sands of his home where we could dry off, soak in the heat, and enjoy our meal. The right of first bite was given according to a complex set of rules which included relative age, territory, and prowess in the fight. As usual, Durrehkeh ate first, but I was glad to have made the top ten.

As we ate, we shared stories. Huerrah, the youngest, recounted his latest battle with the Great Apes. He'd already been injured before joining the hunt and was in even worse shape than I, but he'd held his own. Now, he spun a good tale about how he'd toppled the statue of the ape king that they were all worshipping. It had landed on the high priest's toes.

"It's only fair," I quipped. "They'd been falling at its feet all day."

We spoke through the evening and into the next day. Storytelling had its own hierarchy, and thanks to my being late to join the conclave, I was last. I didn't mind.

Griss talked about how we'd spent a decade advising two opposing armies in Gaul in their war, keeping them evenly matched until in frustration, they sued for peace—and came to us to help negotiate the terms. She paused several times in the story to give me a chance to chime in, but I waved for her to continue as if allowing her to take the glory for us both. In truth, if this was a true story and not some wish-world construct, it had to have happened before my run-in with George. I didn't remember anything about it. I did enjoy hearing about my own conniving brilliance, however.

Earkurrer sounded annoyed as he relayed how Coyote decided to mimic his form and take women on flights before seducing them.

"Now, everywhere I go there are human women who..."

"...want to have your half-dragon babies?" I finished.

"How did you know?"

Agarrabarresheh defeated a Titan. No big deal, since he outweighed it; even he agreed it wasn't much of a fight. Which didn't stop him from bragging about every blow.

Loki swiped one of Rraurahashar's favorite trinkets and led him on a treasure hunt that lasted two years.

Big deal. Try that when the stakes are the destruction of all mortalkind. I held back a yawn, but not well enough.

"Are you bored, Vurnerrah?" Agarrabarresheh asked.

Around me, everyone tensed. Agarrabarresheh was secondkin, less than half a second younger than our eldestkin, Durrehkeh. If he decided I'd insulted the thunder...

My instincts told me to stand, unfurl my wings, and fight. Common sense said to lay on my side and stretch my neck, the dragon equivalent of showing my belly. However, I was too full of food to bother with either. Besides, I felt like he had something other than a challenge in mind.

"I meant no offense," I said instead.

Smiling as if that were the perfect answer, Agarrabarresheh concluded, "But we've heard all these stories before, haven't we? Have any of us done anything new?"

"I collapsed a mountain today," I offered. "It's kind of a funny story. See a kobold, a dwarf, and an accountant walk into a bar..."

Durrehkeh snapped his teeth at me to silence me. Just as well. I didn't know the punch line, anyway. Or maybe I was the punch line. That would make a kind of twisted sense.

When he was sure my submissiveness was genuine, Durrehkeh said, "Agarrabarresheh, what is your point?"

"What's left for us here? What challenges are worthy of us? Are there any adventures left that we don't connive for ourselves?"

"The hydras…" Huerrah started.

Agarrabarresheh silenced him with a look. "A hunt, nothing more."

Huerrah pulled in, cowed, but I sensed his doubt. He was the youngest of us by a full two seconds, the last, contented sigh of God after creating the universe. We all adored and protected him, but we didn't always listen to him.

As Agarrabarresheh pontificated about how this world lacked anything interesting, I edged toward Huerrah. Grislakeh followed.

"What about the hydras?" I asked.

"It's just… so many, and attacking the Elvish kingdom and the merfolk? When did we last see anything like that?"

He had a point. "The SOUSs overran Farrayway," I mused.

"SOU…?"

"Spiders Of Unusual Size. And number. They seemed to think they had permission to attack my territory. And Titania seemed to be of the opinion that we were shirking our duty."

Griss's eyes narrowed with annoyance at Titania's assertion, but as I expected, she thought past it. "What do you mean, 'permission?'" Griss asked.

Something was not adding up. Unfortunately, I could not interrogate any of the hydras. Wish I'd thought to ask one of the heads. I'd been having too much fun.

I shrugged. Permission or no, there was no reason monsters should be able to gather in such numbers. Why hadn't Levvy known and done something about it? Then again, why hadn't I known about the SOUSs?

Something niggled at the back of my mind, something about the real world's history. Post George, but not long after. My mind kept flashing back to the 30-or-so years I spent at the Vatican as the pope's pet. I was restricted to the pope's chambers, the chapel, and the library. My only duties were to learn the Catechism, eat, sleep, and hang out with Pope Pius. What could any of that have to do with our situation now?

I didn't know, but whatever it was soured my joy at being among my kin.

Around us, our kin were starting to voice their agreement with Agarrabarresheh.

"And respect!" one of my youngerkin, Djarrusheh, chimed in. "Has anyone else noticed how the mortals take us for granted? In this last fortnight, I drove back a legion of Anansi's feral children before they destroyed a human village. I spent myself to exhaustion, only to be told by the humans to leave their lands. Their lands! Their neighboring kingdom dared accuse me of driving the remaining spiders their way."

There, too? His land was south of mine, mostly along the African coast. It was a rich and beautiful land, but my swiss-cheese memory insisted on showing me an area of ruins and desolation. When was that?

"What kingdom was this?" I asked.

"Does it matter? I've seen it festering throughout my territory. These mortals have forgotten the dragon's place as the most exalted species."

Despite myself, I nodded. Farrayway had forgotten; else, they might have asked for my help, or if not mine, that of my kin. Prince Derek's disrespect had cost him his kingdom.

A memory tugged at me: I was in the Vatican, lizard-sized and useless, half-listening to Father Boniface drone on about the Trinity, something dragons understood instinctively. I turned my attention to the window, where George sat astride Bernice at the head of a group of armed cavalrymen. Their heads bowed as Pope Pius gave a blessing. Father Boniface followed my gaze, and his lecture faded to sorrowful silence.

My kin were now in a full froth of griping about the slights and insults foist upon them by the mortal races. Did I sound this whiny? Agarrabarresheh egged them on.

Grislakeh raised her voice to argue. "What of the Elvish king who offered us half his kingdom in reward, and the bards willing to immortalize us in song?"

I saw in her eyes how she wanted to add, "tribute you disdained," but she settled with a pointed look at Durrehkeh. He ignored it.

The others, at any rate, shouted her down. It was too little, too late, they said. It could not make up for the decades of increasing disrespect and apathy. They only recognized our greatness when it was useful to them.

As the arguments piled on, Griss turned to me for support. I could only shrug. I, of all of us, had experienced the worst of mortalkind, and I was tired of being used, too.

When the complaints started to circle back, Durrehkeh cut them off with a roar. "Agarrabarresheh, what do you suggest?" he demanded.

My hackles rose. Why did this suddenly feel scripted?

Agarrabarresheh replied, "The Age of Dragons has ended. This world no longer desires nor deserves us. I say it is time to leave it and return when time is ready to favor us again."

Hibernation. The words started as a whisper, then spread, growing in volume until it became a chant: Hibernation! Hibernation! The word pounded into my head, feeding worry itching at the back of my mind until my heart hammered in time to its beat. More memories came:

George returning bloodied and victorious, but alone.

Later, traveling with the pope through lands blackened by fire and towns with nary a building standing. Rich and poor alike in ragged clothes, working together, eyes vacant, and yet I felt their accusations. With my memory gone, I hadn't understood them. Now, I did: *Where were your kind, Vern? We needed you.*

"No!" I shouted.

"And why not?" Agarrabarresheh yelled back. In a single bound, he closed the distance between us to snarl into my face. His teeth were as long as my snout and still red from hydra blood.

Because I don't want to be alone! I could hardly admit that in the wish-world, could I? Would it make a difference in reality?

No. They'd insist I conform to the will of the thunder. For whatever reason, that did not happen. Besides, the visions which filled me with dread weren't about me.

"There's something not right here," I said.

"That is what we have been saying," Agarrabarresheh replied, but Griss moved in beside me, using her larger size to protect me from his wrath and to bolster my position.

"What are you thinking, Twinkin?" she asked

I was thinking how helpful it would be to know if I'd had this conversation before. But how could I, when I hadn't had the information I had now? Not that I had a lot as it was, just a vague feeling that when the world needed us, we were gone.

"Well, youngerkin?" Agarrabarresheh prodded. For some reason, that struck me wrong, too. This was Durrehkeh's territory. Why was he letting his second take charge?

"Give me a minute!" I snapped. "I've had a tough week fighting a paladin and my own spider invasion. My mind is not what it used to be, but things are not adding up. Rraurahashar, what did Loki steal from you?"

"A game, made for me by the elves of Ammuzmantferal. Two flat plates of silver separated by an onyx column in the center. Inside, a dragon stone runs the perimeter. It's very relaxing."

A cat toy. Loki had stolen Rraurahashar's favorite cat toy. "And when you returned, was anything else missing?"

My elderkin shrugged. "If so, it was nothing of consequence. Why?"

I tried to remember what Rraurahashar collected. Some instinct told me the cat toy was a diversion, and the real prize had been stolen and likely replaced with a copy that would pass a disinterested inspection. "I'll bet if you go back, you'll find something was taken in your absence. Kackerathah, did the dwarves say why they did not create a lair for you in their mine?"

It was one of the slights that had been raised in the griping.

Kackerathah tossed his head in annoyance. "What does it matter? The insult was made, and I ensured they paid for it."

The others mumbled agreement.

George waking up screaming something about a twisted underground maze full of spiders and their web-wrapped captives.

"Where was this mine?" I pressed. "What were they mining for?"

"What concern is that of ours?" Kackerathah countered.

"I don't think we're being disrespected. I think we're being undermined."

Durrehkeh laughed, and I don't think it was at my unintentional pun. After a moment, the others joined him.

"Little Vurnerrah! Always looking for a mystery. Have you any proof, or just a vague feeling?"

"No proof," I admitted, "but there are too many coincidences."

He ignored me, turning to the thunder. "And you! Has anything we've experienced been so unusual as to indicate conspiracy?"

They chorused denial. If anything, what they'd been through had become ordinary and expected. Some added that no one could outsmart us, anyway. We were the Eighth Day Creation.

Durrehkeh nodded at me indulgently. "Your objections have been noted and considered."

"Then what about the hydras?" I demanded. "Is Huerrah the only one to notice how unusual it was for them to attack in force? And the spiders? We've dealt with spider hordes in the past, but in this number, and across multiple territories? Even if you don't want to see some master plan behind this, it's obvious they aren't going to stop their attacks. Are we going to abandon our territories to them?"

Agarrabarresheh shrugged. "The Elves did not implore our help until they knew they could not defeat them on their own. The humans outright scorned both you and Djarrusheh. I say, let them deal with the problems."

Some of my kin nodded. Others shifted uneasily. We were indeed the prime species, and as such, we had always defended the lesser sapients against threats.

Several glanced Durrehkeh's way, seeking guidance. There was a gleam in his eyes as he watched Agarrabarresheh that I did not like. I didn't like the hesitation of my kin, either. I wanted to scream for them to think for themselves.

That would get me pounded into the sand fast. Instead, I argued, "They can't handle it themselves. We've already seen that. Djarrusheh admitted he spent himself, and there were still enough left alive to terrorize another township. And in my current condition, I couldn't save Farrayway. I had to flee. The hordes are growing and getting more aggressive. The mortals can't handle it alone. They don't have a chance."

Centuries later, I had learned the truth: My kind had abandoned the world, and the monsters knocked civilization back to the Dark Ages. And thanks to St. George, I'd spent that time on the sidelines, oblivious, until the Church brought me back again as a champion to a world who had forgotten who and what I was.

Agarrabarresheh snorted. "Then perhaps they'll appreciate us better when we return."

"Sure," I said, my voice dripping sarcasm like the poison of my memories. "Or maybe we'll awaken to be remembered as the species who abandoned the world in its time of need. If they remember us at all. Tell me: Is that what being an Eighth Day Creation means now, Agarrabarresheh?"

Faster than I or Griss could react, our second-kin shoved her aside and backhanded me. My kin ducked and scattered as I flew 50 feet and crashed into the sand. I leaped to my feet, teeth bared. "You want respect, any of you? Then let's earn it back. Together, we can—"

Agarrabarresheh tackled me and shoved my snout into the sand. "You've had your say, youngerkin. Now, you decide: Join us in the Great Sleep or spend your days alone?"

"Déjà-vu," I muttered.

If he understood, he ignored me. He pressed down harder, forcing my mouth to shut tight, waited a three-count, then turned his back on me. He flicked his tail: *Stay down unless you plan to challenge me.*

Past him, the rest of my kind, even my own twin, watched, unmoving and unwilling to come to my defense.

I stayed down.

Agarrabarresheh went to Durrehkeh and bowed low, asking the eldestkin's permission and blessing. Durrehkeh nodded regally.

Agarrabarresheh launched himself into the air. He hovered, a stark silhouette against the setting sun.

"Go! Prepare your nests. The Age of Dragons is at its end!"

He blew a narrow, yellow stream of flame into the air. Djarrusheh joined him, then Kackerathah. The air screamed as their fire passed through it.

Singly and in groups, my kin took to the sky, heading back to their own territories. The sky flashed with the opening and closing of portals. Grislakeh gave me one last, apologetic look as she followed the rest.

The final portal closed with a sucking of air that seemed to take my hopes with it.

Vultures flew in to rip at the carrion we'd left behind.

Chapter Fifteen: Be Careful What You Wish For

This is why I didn't trust wishes.

I don't know how long I stayed there, moping until at last, I gave in to sleep, then waking to the heat of desert midday. Whether it was the next morning or days later, I didn't know. The carcasses were picked clean, but I wasn't hungry, anyway. I wasn't even depressed anymore.

I was angry.

For centuries, I'd wondered what had become of my kin. Why they had abandoned Faeriekind. Why they left me behind. If the genie had decided my wish was to understand, he'd failed. My answer only generated more questions.

Was this an actual recreation of what happened before I fought with St. George? Even in my prime, I could not have beaten Agarrabarresheh. And if I had, I would have next had to challenge Durrehkeh.

...if Durrehkeh was on Agarrabarresheh's side. There was something about the way he stood back and let his second run the show that set off alarms in my mind. Durrehkeh didn't clamor for hibernation. He didn't add his flame to the others. But then again, he'd always held himself aloof, hadn't he? Even now, I could not remember how we had decided on the hibernations in the past, and there had been a few, so my feeling was just that—a feeling.

Or did I miss the conclave because I happened upon the righteous and overpowered Saint Pain-in-my-tail who challenged me to a fight I could not refuse? Whenever I asked about that fight, Church authorities gave me the same answer: God's Will.

A very unhelpful answer. Why would God want an undersized, underpowered, underwonderous dragon at the beck and call of His Church? Why not just order us all directly to do whatever He expected me to accomplish?

I filed that one away. No wish was powerful enough to discern God's will if He didn't want it known. I'd have to trust.

I'd told Agarrabarresheh that there was something happening, that someone was manipulating us. To drive us to hibernation? The others hadn't seen it, but why would they? We were the apex species. No one would dream of bending the thunder to their will.

How about a single dragon with his powers nerfed? I dismissed the idea. True, I'd spent over eight centuries being made to obey others, but I could not imagine a world-wide master plan to put me in the position I was in now. I may be arrogant, but I'm not that arrogant.

Suddenly, I was cast in a dragon-shaped shadow. Had Grislakeh returned for me? I looked up, but instead of her beautiful luminescent wings, I saw the heavy black form of my eldestkin. I realized with a jolt that I was still in his territory.

I held my ground as he landed in front of me. The thick sand cushioned his heavy thump. Funny. I remembered him being more graceful.

"Why do you smile, youngerkin?" he asked. "Shouldn't you be in your secret lair getting ready to nap away the boredom of this era while the world destroys itself?"

It was tempting now that he put it that way. I curled my lip in reply.

He settled himself in front of me, arms crossed, tail wrapped around himself. "You are angry, youngling, but I did not come for a fight. If I wanted to fight, I'd have driven you out of my lands by now. No, I am here to offer an alternative. You are not the only one to think hibernation will not solve our problems."

That wasn't what I said, but he was eldestkin and I was on his turf. Interrupting would have earned me a slap at best and a fight if he changed his mind about being magnanimous. Instead, I tilted my head in the dragon equivalent of a raised brow.

"The problem, which too many of our kind do not see, is not the disrespect or the routine. Those are symptoms of a greater issue."

My hopes rose. Maybe I had gotten through to him.

But no. "The fact is this world has become too small for us."

"I didn't know the world could shrink," I quipped.

He answered with harsh earnestness. "Because you have been shrinking with it, Vurnerrah. And I do not refer to your diminished size. You've adapted, youngerkin, contenting yourself with games and tricks like a common faerie. We were once the greatest of God's creations, the best of His Imaginings."

"We still are!" I retorted, but it felt hollow, like a platitude you give a dying man who wasn't ready for the truth.

Even my metaphors were mortal. The thought fueled my anger. I stood. "We are the Eighth Day Creations. I have not forgotten."

"No? You play with the mortals, travel with them. Treat them as equals, even when they fail to show you the respect due our kind. Humans are the worst. They cannot retain a sense of awe any more than they can retain the wisdom of our world. And how many times has a human or a dwarf or an elf, for that matter, come to you seeking advice? No, you are the laborer, a tool."

"The mortals have always come to us for help. All of us." Owen would have called my kind the nuclear option. It was true, though, that of all my kind, I and my twin had most often been sought out by the lesser species. Kings asked for our help and services. The fairy courts had considered us advisors. But then again, I helped create a dungeon just to get a frat pin.

And what had I done lately—was doing? Playing imaginary games with humans and getting fired from the jobs they gave me because one thought I wasn't subservient enough? Had my life become so small?

Even sitting, he still looked down at me. "Calm yourself, youngling. Again, I have not come to fight—and be glad of that. I am here with an alternative.

"I do not blame you for allowing yourself to decline. At least on some level, you had recognized the changing way of our world, and you tried to find some amusement in it. But truly, Vurnerrah, is that all you want? To play with the lesser sapients on their level, conforming to their rules? Becoming one of them? When was the last time you were a real dragon, magnificent and terrible?"

I didn't answer. I didn't remember.

His voice was cruel in its gentleness. "It's not just you, but all of us. Over the centuries, we have grown lazy. Weak. We have sullied ourselves with the lesser beings of this world and we are lesser for it.

"You are not alone, youngerkin. The world has forgotten what we are, what it means to be the last and greatest of God's creations. Over time, we have forgotten, too. We grew bored, we grew complacent, and we grew small. And now, it's too late. We are no longer a symbol of God's ineffable glory. When was the last time you inspired awe?"

I racked my brains, trying to think past the memory of a four-year-old whacking me with a sword while people chuckled at how cute he was. There was no reverence there. Since my true battle with George, I had been (in most cases) treated with kindness, but awe? What did it feel like to inspire amazement—real, slack-jawed, my-God-the-wonders-you-have-made awe? With my maimed and imperfect memory, I could not recall. Or was it that it had truly been so long ago?

"Would you like to return to those days?"

I perked up. Maybe this was the wish I had not voiced that the genie wanted to grant. "I'm listening."

"I've found us a new world, one where dragons are not known. We will go there, a new superior species, and retake our rightful place."

He'd done it. He'd broken the cardinal rule of dragons.

My heart hammered in my chest. "What new world?" I asked. I was afraid to know. I was afraid not to. There were no wishes come true, just more traps.

As he waxed poetic about this marvelous new world, I realized he was talking about the Mundane.

He'd sacrificed everything...for the Mundane world.

My eldestkin was going to be in for such a disappointment.

If dragons could cry, I'd have bawled like a child. Instead, a half-hysterical snicker escaped my tight-lipped grimace.

"How dare you mock me?" he suddenly roared. "You, who are called, 'Vern.'" He said the name in a completely human accent.

"Oh," I said, the sound smaller than I'd intended. "You heard about that, did you?"

"How could I not? Not only do you let a paladin take you down to...this." He put as much contempt as he could into the word as he poked my noggin with a claw almost as big as my head horns. "But how long ago did you let them debase your name?"

So wish-world Durr didn't know about my centuries with the Church or my time in the Mundane. I rolled my eyes to hide my relief. "They can never pronounce it right. They had to call me something."

"They used to call us 'Magnificent Ones!'" He roared, blasting fire that billowed across the sky. "They used to treat us with respect and obeisance. Have you forgotten, youngling? Do you not remember what it was like when our words were law, our whims, their commands? When the mortals fell before us in veneration, when we were the greatest of all God's creations?"

I remembered. The memory stuck with me like a permanent toothache. "We are still the greatest," I told him. "We are the Eighth Day Creation!"

"Yes! Yes, we are. Repeat it as often as you like, but do the other species see it? Where is our superiority? Look at yourself, Vurnerrah! Even before your fight with this human—which you dismally failed at, just look at you!—before then, what was your life like? Did you not dare just yesterday to lecture us on the grandeur of dragonkind?"

"No. On the responsibility of dragonkind," I countered. "I may be small. The lesser sapients may have chosen a name for me that suits their limited tongues, but I have not forgotten that we have an obligation to the mortal species."

Durrehkeh shook his head, baffled at my passion. I was more than a little baffled, myself. For all that my kind felt slighted, I'd experienced nearly a millennium of additional misery and in two different worlds.

"Durrehkeh, Eldestkin. Hibernation is not the answer. Nor is running away. We belong here, now, fighting alongside the mortals as we did yesterday. That is the only choice."

Either my posture or my seeming willingness to talk mollified him. He spoke more reasonably. "That is where you are wrong, youngling. While you have been adapting to our changing stature and others like Agarrabarresheh have railed against it, I have been pondering, and consulting."

"Consulting? With whom?"

"Is it truly that we are forbidden? Or simply that we are unable? Why would God deny us anything? Us—His greatest and most loved creation? Would He truly make us unending in days knowing that at some point, this world would become too ordinary to handle our grandeur and we, too great to find challenge and joy in it?"

I felt a shiver move across my scales. I did not like where this was going. "Who did you consult with?"

"No. It's not that we are prohibited. It has been that we are unable. No portal in the history of this world has been large enough, physically or in capability, to transfer the magical volume needed to carry us to another world. That has been our restriction."

"The world is yours, its creatures you reign," I recited. "But only this world is the dragon's domain. In this world shall dragons remain."

Now he smirked. "How sweet that you say it as the humans do. You really do not see how small you've become. No matter. It is simple reassurance and an assertion of the status quo. It does not prohibit us from seeking other worlds. But there are those who can make us such a portal. We are no longer limited."

"Who's making this portal for you?" I demanded. "Who could possibly convince you that this is a good thing?" Then, it hit me. "Oberon."

Durrehkeh shrugged. "We discussed the possibility. He makes excellent points. I shall go first, test the world…"

Yeah, I knew how that would turn out. Oberon would scatter my kind across time and the planet. Someone would decide burning down a village was a fun way to spend an afternoon, and it'd all end with me getting stabbed with a tainted lance thanks to an angry saint who decided to protect his world against evil dragons.

"Durrehkeh, you cannot fathom how bad this idea is. There is no wonderful new world that will hold us in awe. This is our world. This is our home.

"Besides, how can we leave this one undefended? The mortals can't handle the threats coming. The monsters will destroy entire kingdoms."

He shrugged. "What of it? We've slept through extinctions before."

"Not of sapients! Durrehkeh, Eldestkin. I don't know what 'advisors' have convinced you this is a good idea, but trust me: You will not find in another world what we no longer command here. We cannot abandon our responsibility, not by sleep and certainly not for worlds that are not ours. It's wrong!"

I steeled myself for another lashing. One did not tell the leader of the thunder that he was wrong.

Instead of hitting me, however, he stood and stretched languidly, dismissing my arguments as if my opinion meant nothing. It hurt almost as much as a lashing. Upon the sands, more dragon-shaped shadows told of my approaching kin.

"Who would have known that Vurnerrah, brave, curious, playful Vurnerrah, would turn down a chance at the ultimate playground? Stay then, youngerkin. Stay with your puny size and your puny name, and your puny playmates. We are done with you."

Durrehkeh launched himself with a powerful flap of his wings and a blast of magic that sprayed a storm of sand around us. For a moment, I was blinded, but even worse, I was obscured from sight of my kin. When the sand settled, they were gone, and I was forgotten.

From behind me, Al'Beah said, "Not how you'd hoped it would turn out, was it?"

I did not want his pity. "Where are the others?"

He knew I meant my friends. My human friends. "Safe, Vurnerrah. Safe. They are still with Titania. This was about your wish."

"I never made a wish."

"But you did. Do you not remember the Labyrinth of Locord?"

I groaned, and not just because Al'Beah was right. Locord was the mine where the dwarves had refused to build a dragon lair. Rather than gold and gems, the mine was specifically for weapons-grade metals for fighting the spiders. They'd been focused on preparing for the war they knew was coming, and Kackerathah had destroyed the interior settlement including the main defenses, all in response to a perceived slight.

The spiders had then moved in to take advantage of their weakened state. Unable to fight, the dwarves had dug deeper, no longer following the logic of the lode and instead concentrating only on what could help them flee the spider legions while trying to mine as much ore as they could to help the war effort. In the end, they'd failed.

Almost a century later, the sapient species of Faerie had at last defeated the spiders, but not before over half the population of the world had been killed and the survivors thrown into disarray. Mundanes had the Black Plague that led to the Dark Ages; for Facric, our global disaster crawled in on eight legs.

The dwarves wanted to reestablish the mine as a symbol of hope and renewal, but even their excellent sense of the ground was no match for the panicked burrowings of the previous generation.

They asked the Church for help.

I hadn't grown much past cat size. I could not fly. My inherent magical capabilities were laughable at best. But at least my senses, including an enhanced instinct for finding my way around caves, had returned.

The pope sent them me.

I still remember how the dwarfish minemaster snorted when he saw me. "No wonder your kind left you with the rest of us," he'd said and refused to explain his words.

We spend dismal weeks delving further and further into the mountain. At first, each tunnel was explored, promising areas marked, dead mourned. After a time, it became too much, and we fell into a routine of simply marking the tunnels to mine, collapse, or remove the dead.

Then, my instincts led us to a wide opening, filled with coins and jewels and trinkets. At some point, the previous inhabitants must have repented their lack of foresight and created a starter lair in hopes of appeasing my youngerkin and enticing him back to help them.

The minemaster had gaped at the treasure, threw down his ax, then turned on me. "Where were your kind? Why did you abandon us?"

And I hadn't known.

Now, in my eldestkin's territory, covered in sand and with the heat of the sun providing no comfort, I remembered.

I said to Al'Beah, "I'd missed the conclave thanks to George. I told Gark that, and that I wished I could go back and talk to them, knowing what I knew that day in the caves. Your lamp was in the pile?"

"Colvert had left it there."

Fewmets. I swore to myself. "That means Colvert...?"

He nodded. "He managed to keep his mining squad and their families alive for many years before he was killed in the tunnels. He is remembered as a hero more than a champion. In fact, all the mortals you met today in the dungeon died in the early years of the war. You could say these were their dying wishes that I granted. Poignant, no?"

Poignant? Wretched fit better. "Thanks for nothing, genie."

He spread his hands wide. "I can only grant the wishes. What happens after is up to you. The others are ready to return to your own time and place. Shall we?"

"No." Something had started to burn inside me. Not anger. Not remorse.

Purpose.

"But my tapestry is complete. A more somber tone than I expected, but a masterpiece, nonetheless."

"I don't care about your masterpiece. I got brought here for a reason, and I've not completed my mission."

He laughed. "Titania's subquest? The upcoming war? Surely, you know that you can do nothing about these. The past is written. The betrayed are betrayed. The dead are dead."

"But we never found out who was behind it all, and I'm wondering if that's because I—the right-now-me—had something to do with that. The thing about the spiders is that they continue to breed, but in my present, they are few and far between.

"Take me back to my friends. I want them to know what's happening, and I'm getting Titania to level me up. No self-respecting campaign ends without a big boss battle."

I grinned, feeling optimistic for the first time in ages. I might not have been able to protect Faerie.

But I sure was going to avenge it.

Chapter Sixteen: Squishies Go Home

Al'Beah returned us to Titania's palace. The Great Hall had returned to its normal summery décor, with clear walls that let in the light but not the heat, mossy floors dotted with tiny purple and blue flowers, and tall elms and maples in the place of columns, their leaves providing shady spots where the Summerfae lounged talking, laughing, and loving. In a corner of the grand hall, the saxophonist played his instrument, but this time without the magically forced urgency. Rather, he played sitting down, relaxed, and for a small audience of four besotted fairy women. He paused after one song, and I heard him asking his audience for feedback as he reworked a stanza. Titania herself was not on the throne.

My friends were seated at a bench not far from them. As Al'Beah promised, they looked safe and whole. Everyone's outfits were cleaned and, I noticed, upgraded. Father's had been restored to its original holy cleanliness, and while I could not see his legs from my angle, he didn't seem to move with any discomfort. Linda still had her bikini armor, but I caught the shimmer of magic energies coming from it. Some fairy had given her magical shielding. Ray had a new lute resting against his leg. Owen's furs looked well-fluffed, but that was about it. I'd guess Ti's servants didn't know what to do with an orc. They don't usually consort with humans—or anyone else—in our world. Betts was with them, and the fae had dressed her in a flowing robe with silver ribbons and flowers in her hair. I did not see Sam, however.

All of this I took in in the time it took them to realize we'd entered the room. With joyful cries, they rose and ran to us. Linda hugged my neck.

"How'd it go?" Ray asked as we headed outside where we could talk more openly.

"It was everything I expected," I replied.

Funny how my new friends understood me better than my own kin. Linda stroked my flank. "Well, you've got us, and we love you. Let's go home now. Stupid wish-world."

I grimaced. "Unfortunately, there's more I need to do here." Quickly, I told them about my suspicions that my kin had been driven away to give the spiders and other sentient monsters free reign in Faerie.

Father paled. "You, um, aren't expecting us to stay here and take on the spider legions, are you? Vern, this has been fun and all, but it's time we got back to the real world."

I sighed. "This isn't a wish-world. This is Faerie. My Faerie, in my past, maybe a couple of days after my encounter with Saint George."

Father said, "So if we went to the Vatican right now, we'd find you?"

"Yep, about six inches long, lapping up milk, sleeping on a velvet cushion, and resisting the urge to bite off George's toes out of spite."

"Awww!" Linda said as if I'd just described a kitten.

Father, however, was having a different reaction. "And when I got bit? The poison, the pain, almost dying...that wasn't just a wish to sacramentally suffer?"

Al'Beah blushed, though I wasn't sure if it was from embarrassment or pride that Father had thought there could be secret wishes. I still wasn't fully sure there couldn't be, myself.

Father seemed sure. He rounded on me, fury in his eyes. "When did you figure all this out?"

"A few hours ago? I don't know. I started suspecting something was going on when Al'Beah artiste started bragging about all the wishes he'd granted. They couldn't all be in a wish-world. And for the record, Griss did show up and heal you."

"Which I appreciate. I really do. And I'd have been willing to accept the alternative if that's how God wanted it. But now, we know that this is real and can really get us killed, yet you are suggesting we go after the evil mastermind behind the monsters that nearly killed me. Do you think inviting us to a Boss Battle is a good idea?"

He waved his arm to take them all in: a paladin, a warrior, a half-orc, a bard, a fairy warrior with a dire corgi...

Father had a stern look that nonetheless belied his fear. Linda couldn't manage that much. She hugged herself, unsure. She pulled her cape around her body and not because of the cold. Ray's new lute hung limply in his hand; in real life, he was tone-deaf. Owen's pot belly was fine on a half-orc but told of too many hours sitting at a counter or a gaming table. Not to mention, whatever the cancer was doing to his already weakened system. Samwise, the computer nerd who couldn't get a date, was still off wherever Titania had sent him, but his new love twisted her skirt in her hands.

Four wide-eyed nerds, a priest, and a dog.

What was I thinking?

"Find Sam and Thud, and take everyone home," I told Al'Beah. "You said it yourself. Their wishes are fulfilled."

"But Vern, what about you?" Linda asked in a small voice.

I gave her a reassuring smile. "There's no point in my being here, now, knowing what I know, if I don't do something. This is my world. More to the point, it's my responsibility. That's what being an Eighth Day Creation means. The rest of my kin may have abandoned the Faerie, but I've not forgotten what it means to be a dragon."

"But...alone?" she pressed.

"There was no mention of a future me in the records of this time. If I'd had allies and succeeded, some bard would have made a song or something."

"Did you succeed on your own?" Ray asked.

I smiled with bravado I didn't feel. "Ask me when I see you in Los Lagos. And have pizza ready. I'll have earned it."

"Where will you go?" Ray asked.

"I'll start at Farrayway, see if I can pick up some clues there. After I talk to Titania."

I accepted their hugs and started back to the palace. Father caught up with me. "Vern, I didn't mean..."

"No. You're right. This was never meant to be your battle. It was fun when it was a game, but now, this is my fight. Don't worry. I'm immortal, remember? I'll be fine."

Father knew me well enough to know that immortality didn't mean I'd be fine. But he accepted my statement and blessed me, then joined the others.

"Be careful!" Linda called, and I could hear the guilt in her voice.

I hollered back, "Would you stop worrying? I'm a red dragon. You're all squishies by comparison."

Another advantage of being the size of a pony was I could walk into just about any room created for sapients. I found Titania in her chambers, enjoying a bath while a Mundane read to her from Grimm's Fairy Tales in the original version. She enjoyed hearing what Mundanes thought of Faerie.

Her reader was a tubby, older human who would have filled my stomach for at least a week, although being a newly enlightened dragon thanks to my experiences in the Mundane, I would never dare comment on his weight. He sat with his back to her tub and read, completely absorbed in the book and seemingly uninterested in her bathing activities or my traipsing into the room. He did have an excellent, mellow voice, and I said so as I entered.

"You've returned," Titania said, equally uninterested in my entrance as her storyteller was. She stretched languidly and draped her arms over the edges of the tub. "My first toy was more of a tenor, but I couldn't get him back. Something about an acting job with a police box, whatever that is. But this one he does have the most beautiful voice. So relaxing. So, what news have you of my treacherous husband and selfish sister?"

"I didn't encounter either of them, but I daresay I came across their handiwork." I told her about the thunder and the decisions they'd made to leave this world to its own devices. "Most want to hibernate until the world changes its attitude, but Durrehkeh and apparently some others think the answer is to go play in someone else's world."

She glanced at me sharply. "So, my intelligence is true, then. I must admit, I'd hoped to be wrong."

"I wish you'd been, too, but apparently someone convinced Durrehkeh that our proscription was never really meant to be a permanent prohibition, but more of a limitation we had to overcome...with some help, of course. Sound familiar?"

"Oberon always did know how to play on Durrehkeh's ego, and Mab has always wanted to ride a dragon around the Mundanes." She slapped her fists on the water, splashing like a petulant child. "Why is he doing this now, instead of in her season?"

"Because it's a horrible Christmas present?"

"Leave me!" she screamed, indicating everyone but me. With a fluttering of wings and the shutting of the book, her servants scrambled from the room. She waited until they were gone and then burst into tears and rage.

I waited out her tantrum at a respectable distance because I didn't want to get wet. When at last, she'd spent herself, she looked at the sizable puddle around her tub, then glared at me. "You've ruined my bath."

I decided to be gracious about it. I had delivered some particularly hurtful news. Besides, I needed a favor. I bowed. "I apologize. You know you are my favorite, now more than ever. Oberon and Mab have not only hurt my kind but you. And, I fear, all of Faerie. I wonder if Oberon himself has been tricked."

She rose and with a snap of her fingers, was dry and dressed. She flew daintily over the spilled water and past me, motioning me to follow. We went to her meadow.

"Oberon, tricked? This could be delicious news. Tell me your thoughts."

"Tell me what Oberon would have to gain from helping the spiders."

"Those wretched beings? We've been fighting to keep them off our lands for months. There can be no alliance. They destroy the sapients! With whom would we play?"

"Perhaps you're right. He probably saw an opportunity and took it. He does like to make a big gamble." I let the subject drop; I'd planted the seed. It was up to her to nurture it to a logical conclusion and act on it as Queen of the Summer Court. I moved on.

"But I do owe it to all sapients—including your beautiful kingdom—to discover the spiders' plans. Or all monsterkind's, if they are just part of a grander organization. At very least, I have to do something about them."

She laughed. "You would fight all the spider hordes alone? In this condition?"

That hurt. She didn't have to rub it in. "I don't intend to take them all on. Just the spider queen."

She rolled her eyes and shook her head. "Is that so different? She's bound to be well protected."

"Then help me. I've got the paladin's blessings. Grant me luck and cast me in a glamour so I can get close to her, then portal me away when I've finished."

"What of your playthings? And my knight?"

"They have their own adventures to attend to."

Her expression softened with worry as she took in my implication. "Are none of your kind left? Grislakeh?"

I shrugged. "The thunder has split, but I am alone."

I swallowed down the lump in my throat. When you have a throat as long as mine, that's no mean feat.

At least she didn't make it worse by arguing or offering sympathy. Instead, she called for her greatest wizards to bespell me for battle. They cast spells to protect my hide. I made them double up on my wings. I was getting tired of having them shredded.

As the magic-wielding fairies layered protection spells on, other fairies entered wielding nail files and buffing cloths. Four servants, one at each paw, sharpened my claws to a razor's edge. Meanwhile, others rubbed enchanted wax over my scales.

"The spider silk will not attach to you," the head servant told me.

I felt like Jerry Costa's lowrider, but I wasn't complaining. I hardly ever got so pampered. Too bad I couldn't ask for a nice long soak in molten gold.

Titania returned when they had put the finishing touches on my horns—a spell that made them longer and sharper. She circled me, humming appreciatively.

"Were it not for your size, you would be as fearsome and awe-inspiring as I've ever seen you," she said.

I held up one paw to inspect their handiwork. I practically glowed. "As much as I appreciate making a grand appearance, I'll be more successful if I can be stealthy."

"I thought of that." She held up a large hoop earring. "I've treated it with a stealth spell. Tap it twice and it will last an hour or until you tap it again."

"Very nice, except I don't have ears."

"Do not be so ordinary, Vurnerrah. Here." She flicked her wrist. I felt a prick and the sudden urge to sneeze, and the ring was firmly attached to my nostril.

The fairies around me burst into giggles.

"Ti..."

"Nonsense, you look even more fearsome," she said. She managed to keep a straight face, but I saw the mischief in her eyes. It made her look younger and happier than I'd seen her since we got here, so I didn't protest. Let her have her fun. Besides, I was a dragon, and a buffed—and buffed up—one. I could make anything look good.

"Where do you wish to go?" the head mage asked.

"Put me in the skies above Castle Farrayway," I said. We knew the spiders had overrun the kingdom, and I remember it being a recurring battlefield during my time at the Vatican, so they must have made it a stronghold. I'd start there and see what clues I could pick up concerning the Spider Queen's abode.

I watched as the fairy mage opened a portal and spread it wide. He didn't bother with any fancy gestures. I wondered if Puck had been having some fun with his peers or if he was genuinely impressed by Sam's strange spellcasting style. Well, I wouldn't get a chance to find out. Either I'd accomplish my mission and get back home (hopefully to pizza) or I'd end up out of commission for a long time.

How would that even work? Dragons can't be killed, so would I ever meet my past self? Would I spend eternity trussed up in some spider silk prison, forgotten?

Would God make an exception to dragon immortality?

The sky beyond the portal shone a clear, late-afternoon blue, a mocking contrast to my dark thoughts or what I expected to find there.

"Something wrong, my dear dragon?" Titania asked.

There was plenty wrong, but I didn't know how I could explain it to her. Or if it would matter if I did. Instead of answering, I gathered my thoughts and my feet, ran to the portal, and leaped through.

Chapter Seventeen: Vern Says Yes to the Quest

As soon as I cleared the portal, I spread my wings. I dropped only a few feet before the winds and magic held me aloft. I scanned the area for airborne threats, and seeing none, turned my attention below me to get my bearings and to make sure no one had noticed me. I wanted to hold off using the stealth spell as long as possible.

The land below, once a peaceful patchwork of verdant treetops and fertile fields, was now a writhing mass of dark dots and shining spider silk. For miles, stampedes of spiders overwhelmed the land. I could breathe fire for hours and barely make a dent in their numbers.

I was gladder than ever that I'd discouraged the others from coming. No matter what buffing Al'Beah or Titania gave us, we would not have lasted more than five minutes. I had the urge to turn around and head home myself, but after all

my brave talk, I could hardly give up without trying.

All I needed to do was find and destroy the
queen. That would give the world a fighting
chance. And, since Faerie did manage to beat
down the spider hordes, that meant I must have
succeeded, and will thus succeed now. Right?

Happy thoughts, Vurnerrah.

For all that the landscape roiled with waves of
monstrous arachnids, there didn't seem to be
much going on. I saw no pockets of resistance, no
surges of activity. What were they doing just hanging around?

A storm was starting to blow in, and I flew to
meet it and use it for cover as I headed to the castle. Its courtyard was mostly empty, save the
detritus of battle: gouges in the stone walls, broken wagons, scorching along the wood beams and
in one of the stables. No bodies, spider or human.
Somehow, in the deepening overcast of the storm,
it seemed even more eerie for their absence.

A patrol of larger spiders bearing red stripes on
their legs walked the perimeter. Lieutenants? An
elite guard? That could work in my favor. I could
swoop in, grab one of the spiders, and be a

hundred feet up before its companions could react. Then, I could hold a little aerial interrogation.

I scanned the area for an isolated target, but something on the road caught my eye. A parade? A squadron of spiders marched toward the castle. At least, as close to marching as an arachnid could get: two columns four spiders deep, all moving in concert if not in actual step with each other. More curious, however, was the orc honor guard in shining plate armor and clean furs that followed. Behind them walked a half dozen trolls, then three draus on emaciated black steeds flanking a carriage drawn by skeletal horses. Sitting atop the carriage were two fairies snuggling close.

Oberon and Mab.

The throngs of spiders on the road parted as the odd group approached. Not prisoners, then. That would not have made sense, anyway, from the behavior of the non-spiders. Granted, escape was a futile hope, but orcs and trolls would have fought to the death rather than become prisoners to a spider, and Oberon could port away, anytime. No one so much as had their hands tied up in spider silk.

Allies. I remembered that some sapients had thrown themselves in with the spiders during the dark war. They preyed on those left in the chaos of the spiders' wake. But I didn't remember any being on their side from the start. Maybe I'd had incomplete information.

Or maybe I'd disrupted their alliance.

How hard could it be? a part of me, the part that sounded like my eldestkin, asked. Strafing run, roast them all dead, take one home as lunch. You're a dragon, after all, terrifying and bold. That would make them respect you for the dragon you are.

Except that I no longer was the dragon I'd been. I'd changed. Once upon a time, I would roast a knight in his armor and pry him open like a can of anchovies just for annoying me. But nearly 900 years of living under the Church had changed my ethics. I couldn't blatantly kill them no matter what it meant to my future self. Plus, there was a slim chance that they were hostages after all. In that case, rescuing them could be used in our favor.

If they were allied to the spider people, then I was going to have to give them a chance to repent and switch sides. Mercy aside, it would help the rest of the world to have them as on our side. If that didn't work, maybe I could spread confusion and make them think each species was scheming against the other.

Despite the severity of the situation, I grinned. Destroy alliances before they formed? That could be fun.

If all else failed, I could always fry them and deal with the personal consequences later.

For now, it was time to be clever and sneaky instead of terrifying and bold.

As the clouds at last opened and the lightning started to blaze across the skies, I watched the group disappear into the castle itself. There wasn't much more I could do from the air, and even though the rain slipped off finely waxed scales, I did not enjoy being wet. I tapped my nose ring twice to activate the charm and dove toward the castle. The rains decided to cooperate with a downpour that sent the spiders scurrying for cover.

There was a secret door Prince Geoffrey used for sneaking in to woo Princess Arlene back in the day. I rode the sheeting rain to the gardens, then ran to the door. I pressed the rock I remembered would unlock the latch and was rewarded by a click and the stone door sliding just slightly. I pushed it open and snuck into the dark hallway.

Dust stuck to my wet feet. Yuck. No one had used this passageway in years. I wonder if after my ill-fated scheme worked and King Daddy gave his daughter's hand to the valiant Prince Geoffrey, they had forgotten all about it, just like they forgot all about the "terrifying" dragon who was really a kindhearted and romantic matchmaker.

I shook myself, sending water to splatter the walls. It dripped to the floor, leaving muddy rivulets. I expended some careful fire to clean and dry my feet. Even the best stealth charm was no good to me if I left muddy footprints all over.

I blinked to adjust my eyes to the dark and made my careful way down the corridor, hoping that it wasn't just an escape route for the royal family and guests. I didn't want to exit into the royal bedrooms on the upper level. Fortunately, it forked at the stairwell, and I found an exit near the kitchens that serviced the main ballroom. Stroke of luck, that, since I wanted to meet with the Spider Queen's guests before she did.

The door opened partway, then stuck. I dug my claws in and pushed, wincing at the sounds of heavy boxes or casks scraping against the stone floor. I guess after a generation of peace, they'd forgotten about this exit or decided they no longer needed it.

I squeezed through the narrow opening, then pushed the door back and rearranged the boxes so I could get through the exit more quickly if needed. I had no problem learning from other people's mistakes, after all. Then, I took in my surroundings.

I stood in the staging pantry. The shelves were piled with baskets of fruit, breads, and desserts. The panel to the secret door held a wine rack, and the crates in front of the pantry held brightly colored bunting and new candles. Looked like they'd been planning a celebration. Too bad the spiders had to crash the party.

A preservation spell permeated the room. I smelled tart apples and yeasty bread. My mouth watered. When was the last time I'd eaten? Yeah, the hydra. You'd think it would have held me longer.

I heard the scratching of spider feet heading my way. Just one. Lucky me. I gathered myself and pounced as soon as the arachnid lieutenant entered the room.

"Please!" I mean no offense!" he shrieked.

"There's an odd choice of words," I retorted.

A second spider entered. He looked from his buddy to me and back to his buddy. I prepared to blast him with flame, stealth forgotten.

But instead, he rolled his eyes. It's quite a thing to see. With so many eyes, he managed to express multiple layers of exasperation and disgust.

"What have you done?" he asked—but to his buddy, not me.

With his head squashed between my paw and the floor, he couldn't really answer, but he raised two back legs in a shrug.

The second spider tried a different approach. "Honored guest, dragon, are you lost?"

Honored guest? They were expecting dragons. That was going to complicate things.

But in the meantime, I could milk it for what advantage I could. I stepped off my prey, playing innocent and a little offended.

"The carnage outside has whetted my appetite, so I came looking for a snack. This one approached me without announcing his presence." I cast a dark look at my former victim, who bowed in apology.

His buddy was not impressed. "You are the representative the dragons saw fit to send my queen?"

I reared up, eyes blazing in fury. "You dare question the will of the thunder?"

My accusation, posture, or both, broke his arrogance, and he bowed in obeisance. "Forgive me. I spoke out of turn. Let us escort you to the queen."

I shook out my scales and gave my wings a small snap as if releasing some aggravation. Really, I was amazed at my luck. The Spider Queen was here, after all. That could make life easier. If I could take her out, I could ruin the alliance before it was formed.

"Fine. Bring a large platter with an assortment of pastries and two bottles of wine—red. Something from the past century, if possible?" That would keep one minion distracted for a while, anyway. I spied a basket full of peaches and helped myself to a half dozen, holding the pits in a pouch in my cheek. I had a powerful spitting ability, and now I was armed.

Then I strolled out of the pantry like the queen's honored guest they thought I was.

I let the grumpy lieutenant lead the way. Meanwhile, my mind ran at full speed, pouncing at questions as if they were spiders. Who was supposed to be meeting with the Spider Queen? My guess was Durrehkeh or Agarrabarresheh. Durrehkeh made the most sense, since he was all about finding new worlds and had let himself be influenced by Oberon. Then again, Agarrabarresheh was so frustrated. He wanted to sleep through the next era in hopes a new flock of mortals would arise to treat us better. What if he wanted to expedite the process by culling the current batch of sapients?

I kept my head high, but I wanted to bow down and beg God for mercy for my entire species. That, or for me to be completely wrong. This is one time I'd love to have come to the wrong conclusions. Which probably meant I was right on track.

What was I going to do if my elderkins showed up? I could not defeat either in a fight, and they knew me well enough that neither was going to believe I had a sudden change of heart and just happened to hear about this meeting and invited myself... Well, they might believe I invited myself, but how do I explain knowing where to come?

I'd have to cross that bridge when I came to it. Maybe the best plan would be to find out as much as I could, then high-tail it to the nearest cathedral and share what I know with the bishop there. The Vatican has its own army. They could handle the problem while I made a clean getaway.

Speaking of clean, the hallways were remarkably clear of carnage. Nonetheless, the bloodstains, ripped tapestries, and new nicks in the stone walls and floor testified to the bravery of those who fought to defend the castle. I wondered if the queen had escaped and what the spiders had done with the corpses.

We entered the ballroom. There was a reception going on. At least, I guessed it was a reception. All the parties I'd seen earlier were gathered, eating and sipping drinks, but rather than mingling, they kept to their own groups and eyed each other suspiciously.

When I entered, they all turned to stare at me. I gave them a haughty look and waltzed in, my spider escort trailing behind.

Chapter Eighteen: Roll for Persuasion

Farrayway was a small kingdom, and its castle was built to suit. The grand ballroom wasn't much bigger than a large parish hall in the Mundane. It was partially decorated for whatever festival the spiders had so rudely interrupted with their invasion. Now, they'd added their own macabre touches to the décor. Spider webs wove among the colorful buntings, their clean whiteness a stark contrast to the bloodstained purples and golds. Hanging from the ceiling and between chandeliers were wide ribbons of spider silk, and caught in these were the corpses of humans frozen in fighting poses, wrapped in webbing and bearing weapons.

Creepy, yet creative.

The tapestries were bespelled to repel dirt and liquids of any kind and were as clean and bright as the day they were made. They showed the history of the unification of the kingdoms—or rather, the official history. There were intricate weavings of battles neither side clearly won, the suffering of the peasants as a result of those inconclusive war-wagings, the romance of the prince and princess of the opposing sides. Then...

I faltered in my steps at the tapestry of a giant dragon wreaking indiscriminate damage on the poor, already suffering population.

Rude!

"What is it, Your Magnificence?" my escort asked.

I jerked my head at the offending work. "They got my likeness all wrong." It wasn't a lie. It wasn't like me at all to burn down innocent villagers.

He looked at the tapestry, appraising it with his multitude of eyes. I can't imagine I looked good at any angle. Regardless, he tensed slightly, as he connected the massacring menace on the fabric to the mild-mannered drake standing beside him. His respect for me went up a notch. Guess I'd take that as a win.

Come to think of it, I'd been lucky he hadn't heard that an undersized dragon had run from his soldiers a few days earlier. Hopefully, that meant my hasty retreat had not reached the queen. When we passed another tapestry, this one of me scattering herds of sheep while the princess offered herself as a human sacrifice, I just gave it a dirty look.

But when I got to the one of the prince proudly posing over my unconscious body as if he were Michael the Archangel and I were some kind of hunting trophy, I lost it.

"Damsels and knights! That boastful, lying—"

"—human?" Oberon concluded from behind me. Amusement warred with suspicion in his voice. My spiders backed to a respectable distance.

I turned around. "Bet you find it funny, all things considered."

He looked me over. He had questions he wasn't sure he should ask. I had accusations I was sure he didn't want to hear. How much could we say in this company?

He took the lead. "It is a prank worthy of Puck himself. Are you here to exact some revenge before going to a long sleep? Or are you joining your kin in our fine offer?"

"Neither. Your wife asked a favor of me. You're shirking your duties again."

His eyes flashed. "It is my duties as a king and husband to both my wives that brings me here, and you know it. Or do you?"

So, he thought I was in on the scheme? I skirted the issue. "Midsummer Festival was only a few days ago. You belonged there. You couldn't arrange the timing better?"

"Who am I to question the timing of the Spider Queen?" he shrugged expansively, but his gesture drew my gaze toward the spiders lurking in the shadows. We were being listened to. No surprise, really.

I feigned boredom at his excuse. "And how do you explain excluding Queen Titania from your schemes? I see Queen Mab has escorted you."

"Mab understands me in ways Titania does not."

In other words, Titania would not have approved of whatever game he's playing, and since it involved the disappearance of my kind for perhaps the rest of her life, I couldn't blame her. "You have to go home sometime."

"You're not here to take me by force?"

"Do you need me to?" It was as much a threat as an offer, and he took it as such and changed the subject.

"And what of you, friend Vurnerrah? Will you accept my generous offer and make your way to new worlds?"

I snorted. "Maybe I'm looking forward to a long rest."

Oberon looked me over skeptically. "There is too much adventure in you. Too much fun. You are like the fairy that way. That's why you and your twin have always been our favorites. What has she chosen? It's hard to believe given the opportunity, you both choose sleep."

He didn't know? Interesting, if he had to arrange to transport my kind elsewhere. "Look," I said, "I had a long, painful fight with an overpowered paladin. Probably a saint in the making. I deserve a nap. And you deserve whatever heat the Summer Queen bestows upon you. I'd suggest you go back on your own, begging forgiveness and with a compelling reason for her to forgive you. You abandoned her for this business on the most important night for the Summer Court. Do not expect her to approve, and rightly so. You dismiss her feelings too easily, Oberon, and when has that ever worked in the favor of your people?"

I hoped that those around us would think I was calling him out for not attending the festival and that he would see I was referring to this whole scheme. I dearly wanted to address what he'd done to my eldestkin, but I didn't know how without implying my disapproval for the whole plan.

"As for my path," I finished, "I will choose it when I'm ready."

He bowed. "We shall be at your service, friend dragon."

I glared at his retreating back, then gave the last of my angry look to the tapestry. Finally, I snorted, shook my head, and went to where the trolls were dunking tankards into a large barrel of mead and guzzling down the contents. The barrel, nearly as tall as a human and even wider, was half-empty.

I stuck my nose in and slurped down a couple of gallons of the contents. Then I belched.

The trolls hollered approval.

"Good ale!" I said. "Enjoy now."

"Yes! Much enjoy! Spider Queen give much ale. Much enjoy."

"You join queen for ale?" I asked.

They laughed. "No. Humans bad. Humans need punish."

I looked over at the tapestry. "Some humans bad. That human tell lies. Lies about me. What human do bad to you?"

One troll, whose furs and armor were fancier than the others, spoke. "Humans trick prince. Make prince coward. Make him run away. King die. No new king."

Another troll took up the narrative. "Trolls make participatory democracy. Hate participatory democracy."

"Too much talk," one said.

"Too many countings," another added.

The first troll concluded. "Trolls can't decide new rule. Spider Queen say, 'I rule. You kill humans. Drink beer.' Life good."

Fewmets. Gurlurk! He ran off because he didn't want to be a prince. Could this work to my advantage? "Prince Gurlurk? I know Gurlurk. Not coward. Strong troll. And alive."

They gaped at me, processing the information. I didn't blame them; by all rights, he should be dead. Finally, the leader said, "Dragon lies.

Gurlurk coward. Gurlurk weak. Ran away. Joined tricky human. Human trick Gurlurk. Gurlurk dead much years."

I shook my head. "Gurlurk live. Stuck in time out. Gurlurk ate tricky human. Gurlurk broke school. Very strong to break school. Gurlurk strong, fight me. I lock Gurlurk up many years. Time out for being bad. Now Gurlurk fight me and get away."

"Gurlurk...free? Gurlurk...strong?"

The trolls looked at me, hope growing in their eyes. I nodded. "Gurlurk strong."

One shrugged. "Gurlurk old. Die soon."

The others looked at their beers despondently.

"No. Gurlurk in magic time out," I said. "Gurlurk young."

"Gurlurk go home?"

"Maybe? Gurlurk out of time out. Gurlurk go away."

"Gurlurk brave?"

"Gurlurk brave. Gurlurk maybe not like rule. You let Gurlurk sing. Say, 'sing song about rules, get pretty girls.' Then Gurlurk rule." No reason he couldn't do both, right? Why should Al'Beah be the only one to grant wishes. Besides, I kind of owed him.

The troll leader frowned in thought. I could almost see smoke coming from his ears. Finally, he shook his head and thumped his chest. "Trolls strong! Humans weak. Trolls and spiders defeat humans. Queen rule trolls."

I nodded my head. "Spider Queen better than Troll King?"

He paused, thinking. "Queen say trolls kill humans. Make deal. Trolls help spiders. Kill humans. Save some for spider food. Trolls in charge of humans."

I snorted. "Trolls in charge of spider food. Trolls spider slaves. Queen not Queen of Trolls. Queen master of trolls."

He paused, thinking. "Spiders boss trolls. Trolls fight back. Queen knows. Spiders good to trolls or trolls fight back. Trolls strong."

"Trolls very strong," I agreed with the enthusiasm of a parent encouraging a child. "How many trolls?"

"Many and many!"

I nodded. Trolls had a rudimentary counting system. Anything past hands and feet counted as many. Then you added manies or multiplied them or exponentialized them. Many and many meant up to tens of thousands.

I nodded. "How many spiders outside?"

"Many and many," he said.

I nodded. "Many and many here. Many and many in other places. Many and many other places. So many-many spiders." I paused to let them do the math, but essentially hundreds of thousands. "How many daughter spiders?"

"Fifteen," one replied. I gave him props for good intel.

"Fifteen. One queen makes many-many. Fifteen make…"

"Many by many," his companion, apparently the smartest of the group, said. They all went silent, the drinking stopped.

I asked, "Queen like be master of trolls. If spiders find Prince Gurlurk, think spiders let live?"

The leader said, but more quietly, "Spider Queen make deal. Queen rule trolls. Trolls no slaves. Else, trolls fight."

"Trolls fight alone? Trolls win?"

They didn't answer, but their eyes wandered to the horrifying decorations hanging from the ceiling.

I ignored them and took another long draught of the ale. I smacked my lips. "Humans make good ale. Enjoy now. Enjoy before humans no make ale, just be spider food."

One of the drau had been watching me spin up the trolls. Now, I glanced his way just enough to make eye contact, then moseyed back to the tapestry. I was tempted to set fire to it, but I wanted to make sure I did it at the best time for my advantage.

The drau came to stand beside me, also regarding the tapestry. He sipped wine that my nose suggested was laced by the bleedings of one of our decorations.

"It's all a lie, you know," I said, "just a lot of propaganda."

"It is the way of all sapients to lie for their own advantage—present company excepted," he replied mildly. He jerked his chin at the cloth. "What gain came from this?"

"A kingdom united. A war ended. An era of peace for their people. What would you expect?"

Fortunately, drau are more clever than trolls by a longshot. He picked up my drift. "Power, as always. A chance to move freely in the evening shadows."

"There's a reason your activities are restricted," I said, with just enough edge in my voice to remind him that I did not approve of drau evils.

He merely shrugged. "It will not matter soon enough. Besides, do you not know that this united kingdom fell in one evening to the Spider Queen's armies?"

"It was overwhelmed by superior numbers, and its ruler was more interested in harassing me than tending to his borders. There are millions of humans and hundreds of millions of sapients. They will not all be caught unawares. Like Farrayway, they will unite against a common foe."

"That is for the spider hordes to deal with."

"Perhaps," I mused. "Perhaps they will also look to their allies."

He sipped his drink. "We are not concerned. No human can match our kind."

I sighed. "Yeah, I thought that, too, until I tangled with a saint."

I gazed again at the tapestry. "I played their little game. I wanted to see the kingdoms unite and peace in their land. In return, I got an IOU I cannot reclaim and this slap in the face. All their lies, this fabrication...and their kingdom didn't manage to last two generations. Pity they didn't exercise more forethought before deciding who to make a friend and who to make their enemy."

I puffed a ball of flame straight at the king's face. Most tapestries are bespelled to be fire-resistant, but I had not spared the heat. It caught like dried tinder.

As the flames burned an expanding hole in the hanging, spiders chittered and ran to put out the fire before it spread to the nearby webbing. I strolled away. It didn't deserve any more of my attention.

That only left the orcs, who were in one corner of the room, leaping up and whacking one of the hanging corpses with their clubs like it was a piñata. That told me all I needed to know. Orcs have a kind of genetic caste system. You have the clever ones, and you have the stupid, violent ones. Spider Queen had either decided she needed stupid and violent or had been rejected by their smarter counterparts. At any rate, they were in it for the fight, and nothing I said would dissuade them.

Would anything I said dissuade the others? If history played out as I remembered, probably not, except for the fairy kingdoms, who did side with the sapients against the spiders. That was probably as much Titania's doing as mine. She could be a powerful leader when she wanted to, and even her husband would not deny her if she got into the right temper. I remember a few cases of human towns enslaved by orcs, and drau incursions. But by the time I was in any condition to pay attention to the world, the war was already in decline. I hadn't really bothered to read up on the history; I was too occupied with dealing with the present. I should probably have gone back and read up. Too late now.

The Spider Queen was nowhere to be seen. Was she coming to this shindig? Maybe I'd be better off making a quick exit and reporting what I'd learned. I knew the allies and their motivations. The Church could use that for negotiating them to our side. I knew there were 15 breeding females at least, in the local area; that gave us the main targets. If we could find Gurlurk, he might have some influence over his father; at least enough to get him to talk. There wasn't much we could offer the drau; D&D clichés aside, they were just a step above demons in Faerie. Narcissistic sociopath was the kindest classification you could give them.

I'd accomplished quite a lot in about 20 minutes. I should make my exit, hide out, and consider my next move. If I got lucky, I'd find the queen en route and kill two birds with one spider. If I got caught, I'd say I wasn't going to stand around being mocked by the decorations.

I started toward a side exit, when suddenly, all the doors opened, and spiders swarmed into the room. They took station on the walls, along the ceiling, and on the hanging corpses. The festive air of the room, strained as it was, died and was replaced by one of tension.

The spiders milled around a bit, but I got the impression they were finding their places, like an amateur dance troupe seeking their starting marks. I looked around, seemingly in interest, but counting spiders and trying to find the easiest exit.

Then, it turned out my analogy was on target. The spiders began to chitter and tap their feet in rhythm. I didn't think they meant to entertain us, however. They all faced the throne, and their beat rose in volume, speed, and intensity. And—because what was Faerie without cliché?—the storm outside grew fierce. Rain pelted heavily on the windows. Lightning crackled, followed almost immediately by thunder.

Just as the drau were starting to noticeably wince from the loudness, they stopped. All eyes were drawn to the thrones. Then lightning flashed, illuminating the area.

From above, the Spider Queen lowered herself, almost languidly, on a thick silk thread from the darkness of the tall ceiling.

Chapter Nineteen: Schtick Gets Real

The queen was huge. Her thorax was black with a greenish tint, almost leathery in looks. Her face was pale and veined as if she were a cadaver rather than a living spider. Each eye was as large as a dinner plate and gleamed darkly. Her front legs stretched and swayed as her back ones wove the threads coming from her spinnerets.

She should have been a horrifying sight, yet I couldn't help thinking I'd seen this scene in *Star Trek: First Contact*. I bit my cheeks to hold back a snicker. If she had a voice like Alice Krige...

I may have spent too much time watching Mundane movies.

The Spider Queen perched on the throne—or, more accurately, she used the king's and queen's thrones as a framework for her own seat, a cloud of spider silk threads suspended hammock-like from the chairs.

Behind her was a tapestry of the prince and princess on their wedding day. Unlike the others, this one had been ripped so that prince and princess hung separately, their bodies twisted grotesquely, yet somehow reaching for each other. I had the feeling that if I looked at the back of the fabric, I'd see spider silk holding each fold in place. Some artistic arachnid had a sick talent.

The queen settled herself on the throne, legs splayed, making me think that Owen would have thought she'd be perfect on the cover of a comic book or in a monster manual. Yeah, too much time in the Mundane was making me see things in weird ways. At least when she spoke, her voice did not sound warm and mellow like the Borg Queen's but clackety and harsh.

"The Age of Man ends!"

Trolls, spiders, drau... all burst into cheers. Oberon, I noticed in my peripheral vision, stayed quiet but attentive...and he was grinning at me.

The shouting died down.

The queen didn't rise from her seat, but she did lean in my direction, and I knew all her eyes had focused on me. "Dragon. Why are you here?"

"You weren't expecting me?" I countered with a haughty edge to my voice. Not too much, because I didn't want to overplay my hand. In my peripheral vision, I scanned for the exit that would be easiest to fight my way to.

She regarded me with some confusion. I realized four of her eyes were focused on my snout. I pointed at my nose ring.

"Like it? I wore it just for the occasion."

"Approach!"

I stood my ground. First off, I was not her lackey, and I didn't think any of my kin, even if they did deal with her, would do so from a position of subservience. Secondly, I wasn't sure what her game was. I wanted to see if she'd send her soldiers to drag me forward or if they'd attack me on the spot. Neither were good choices, but I could probably break free and bust through a window more easily from my current position than on the dais.

But then, she dipped in a small bow and waved one long graceful leg in invitation. "Please, honored dragon."

Well, she did ask nicely...

I climbed the short steps. In the meantime, she indicated with a wave of a second front leg that the others should continue their celebrations. This was good. Dragon business first. Or, more to my point, the others could get good and distracted so I could lunge at her, get in a quick bite to the brain, and run before they could react.

Two of her lieutenants flanked me. Figured. Guess I was going to have to deal with doing this the hard way. This was going to hurt.

"You're early," she scolded. "Agarrabarresheh said I'd have more time with my new plaything. He said he'd fetch her after I'd thoroughly punished her."

I cocked my head, the dragon equivalent of a cocked brow, but my mind was racing. Punished? Who had Agarrabarresheh brought her? If I killed the queen now, they'd probably kill whomever they had captive. My mission just changed, but maybe I could still accomplish both.

I shrugged. "Not my problem. Shall we?"

She glared with six of her eyes as the other two kept tabs on what was going on with her guests. "There is only so much arrogance I will tolerate, dragon. You came to me in the middle of my finalizing my alliances. I was assured the thunder would not interfere."

I gave a small nod. "As you wish. I only thought you might enjoy a final act of...punishment...before I take her."

The mandibles on the sides of her mouth closed slightly in thought. More eyes focused on the group. They were waiting patiently enough, though the trolls had finished their keg and were breaking it down to play with the rings.

"Prepare the table and the knives," she told her lieutenants. "I shall return shortly."

Knives? That meant contracts signed in blood and probably magic. Yeah, I needed to remove the queen. It'd been a long time since I purposefully set out to kill a sapient. The rules were different for dragons, but after so long in the Church, I found myself hesitating.

Fortunately, she helped me work past that. As we walked to the room where she kept the prisoner, some of her soldiers following along, skittering on the ceiling and walls in an almost puppylike fashion, she spoke in sinisterly happy tones about how her children were ready to overrun the world and how she relished laying eggs for more generations to ensure the victory. The "bipeds" as she called the groups most likely to stand against her, would become little more than farm stock.

"That won't last long," I said. "They'll fight."

She tittered, a fleshy clicking of mandibles and lips. "At first. But the drau have made me a spell to alter the venom of my children. Just as I make some spiders to fight and others to spin webs, I can now birth children with a special venom. Rather than kill, it makes one complacent, unaggressive, and dumb. Stock animals."

"That's a neat trick," I said. "Have you started laying the first batch?" If so, there was an egg sack around I was going to have to torch.

"The drau will perform the ceremony after we've committed to our alliance. I must say, it's refreshing to have an equal interested," she said. "The other dragons do not ask questions like you do. They mostly complain."

"I'm naturally more curious. It comes from being the cleverest," I said. I politely ignored the insult she set upon me by reducing me to her "equal."

We came to a door guarded by two of the largest lieutenant spiders I'd seen. Fortunately, they parted before her without giving me so much as a suspicious glance. They really were expecting a dragon. What prisoner could be so important that she would require a dragon to retrieve her?

The queen gave a genteel twist of her mandibles to express approval at her guards as they moved to open the doors. "Is that why they sent you? Be careful. This one, too, thought she was clever. We certainly enjoyed teaching her the errors of her ways."

Something about how she said "this one" made my hackles want to rise. Up until that moment, I'd been open to the idea—hoping, even—that this prisoner was just someone from Agarrabarresheh's territory, and this was a last gesture of protection. Now, I braced myself against the shock of what I was afraid to see.

The door opened to what had been the chapel, only now the pews were toppled, the statues swathed in webbing, and the area crawling with spiders. Rain pounded against the stained glass, so one could imagine the saints weeping and swaying in grief. Lightning flashed, illuminating the room in a myriad of colors.

On the altar, like a horrific sacrifice, lay an all-too-familiar shape cocooned in spider silk, wrapped so tightly, she could not move. Not that she was moving. I could see the rapid rise and fall of breath, and my keen eyesight saw the swathing sag in places. Only one creature could turn mass into healing energy. Then, I saw a tip of a wing peeking out through a gap in the cocoon. It was the delicate pink of a sunset at sea. Grislakeh!

Agarrabarresheh had sanctioned this? I shook against the urge to flame everyone in the room.

At least until the door had finished shutting.

Then I backed against the door and let loose with a wide, hot stream of fire. Everything started to burn around me: wood, webbing, spiders. The flames licked at the cocoon holding my twinkin captive. It wouldn't hurt her; if she was conscious, she'd know it was me and that I had come to help. If she wasn't, it might wake her enough to defend herself or run.

A din rose as spiders started to shriek and flames roared. Behind me, I felt the door bump against my back as guards tried to make their way in. I dug my claws into the polished wood floors and held my ground.

The queen, taken by surprise, had nonetheless managed to skitter up the wall behind me, which saved her from the brunt of my attack. Now, she moved in with a bite. I caught sight of her in my peripheral vision and jerked away just in time. Her teeth scraped against my buffed scales.

Still, my move had cost me. The guards were able to shove one door open enough to see the conflagration. One dashed in to engage, while the other wisely ran for backup. If I'd still had the peach pits in my mouth, I could have knocked him out cold with one well-aimed superspit. but they'd burned up when I spewed my fire. Fewmets! I had to move fast.

Ignoring the rest as targets, I concentrated on reaching the queen. I swung my head around to snap at her, but she'd launched herself out of my reach. I inhaled to let loose another stream of fire when something body-checked me. I went tumbling down the floor, flames spraying wildly. On the bright side, most of the minion spiders were engulfed in flames or running for safety.

Except for three that went straight for my kin. I heard a familiar groan, then a scream as they bit into Grislakeh' s wings.

Knowing they were trying to exploit my weakness and that I was letting them succeed, I bounded toward the altar. My twinkin was thrashing, but whatever they'd done to her had weakened her horribly.

I slashed out with my razor-sharp claws and sliced two before they even registered I was there. The third chose the better part of valor and fled. The queen was heading back to the door.

Griss blinked at me. "Vurnerrah? How?"

"Never mind," I said, laying down cover fire—literal fire. I blocked the queen's path out. "Can you fly?"

She raised one shredded wing.

"Then you need to hide. But wait a moment."

I leaned against her and concentrated hard, willing the fairy magic to leave me and coat her instead. I didn't know if it would work, but I had to do something.

Please, I prayed. For my twin.

I felt a kind of crawly tingle, and she gasped as the magic oozed its way over her. "Vurnerrah! What...?"

"Best I can do. Find cover and defend yourself. Run if you get the chance. I'll find you if I can. I'm sorry. I have to get the queen."

"The queen is a pawn, twinkin. There's more to this. We're not the only ones who play this game."

I half-heard her. It didn't really matter, anyway. The queen couldn't be allowed to lay mind-enslaving spiders. I left Griss and started after the queen.

Lieutenant Rugby bounded toward me, but I was ready. I leaped just as he dove for me. I sprung off his back and soared toward the queen, who had made her way to the highest point of the cathedral ceiling.

She twisted her back toward me and blasted out a net of spider silk.

I barely had time to register her skill as I made a desperate flap. The netting tangled in my legs. I flailed my legs to untangle them. Rather than strike at her like I'd planned, I resorted to fire again, scorching the beautifully painted putti smiling from the clouds. Unfortunately, my distraction gave her the time she needed to get out of the way of my flame. She dashed across the ceiling, then jumped and landed on my back.

"My children!" she screamed. "You'll pay for this."

I flipped over and dropped, hoping to dislodge her or crush her against a pew. She bit hard into my wing muscle, then jumped away.

The pain distracted me, and I barely had time to twist before crashing into the pews. I felt ribs crack. Great. Could this get any worse?

I felt a meaty hand grab me by the tail and yank me up, so apparently, yes.

The troll leader held me at arm's length. I fought the sense of déjà vu. The Spider Queen rode on his shoulders, whispering something in his ear I could not make out against the tumult going on outside and in the chapel.

"Go find Gurlurk!" I yelled. "Prince live. No need spiders."

"Bad dragon," the troll leader countered. "Queen say you lie."

Then he whacked my broken ribs with his club.

I saw red, then everything grayed. I fought my way back to consciousness, but the poison was starting to get to me, too. A large, dark disk was moving across my vision.

Wait. That wasn't a blind spot. It was a deep-dish pepperoni with extra cheese—and it hit the troll in the eye.

Behind me, the familiar voices of my friends chorused, "That's amore!"

The troll dropped me, screaming as he clawed at his face. Cheese stuck to his eyeballs. I caught sight of red pepper flakes, too. Nice touch. Too bad it hurt to laugh.

From the corner of my eye, I saw a portal open, and a band of fairy warriors, led by my friends, poured out. They all seemed hazy and were moving in slow motion.

"Healer!" I gasped out, "and stop the Spider Queen."

Before I totally blacked out, I slashed with a front and back leg, shredding the troll's ankles. He screamed and collapsed. A gust of wind blew past me, shoving the big lug to the side before he crushed me. Unfortunately, he landed just far enough that I couldn't reach him. At least he was too concerned about his own pain to bring more on me.

Thunderpaws bounded beside me. Thud growled and snapped at anything coming at us and Sam swung his sword and shouted out spells. Ray jumped off Thud's back and poured a healing potion into my wound while singing a healing song. My wound burned, then cooled, and my head cleared. I leaped to my feet just in time to slash out at a spider that had gotten past Thud and Sam.

"You're a squishy, Bard," I scolded. "Get some-place safe."

"Got a suggestion?" he shouted as much from fear as to be heard. "Half this place is on fire and the rest is full of things that want to kill us."

"Target-rich environment!" Linda shouted. She and Owen were back to back, making quick work of the soldier spiders. Linda swung her broadsword with the strength and grace of her D&D character. Her barbarian bikini top and her skin glowed with magic. Her tight leather pants looked as buffed as my scales. She had a grin on her face more appropriate for a roller coaster than a boss battle.

Owen swung his broadsword with one hand while the other worked spells to hold the creatures at bay with elemental magics. Where he could, he directed a wind attack to blast a spider away from Linda.

A spider slashed at her leg. She swung low, cut off its claw at the joint, then kicked it between the eyes with a high-heeled boot. She let out a triumphant laugh.

I wondered for a second if someone had given her a berserker spell, but no. Once Linda made up her mind about something, she resolved to enjoy it as much as possible. I was going to miss her.

Think about that later. We had to survive first. I glanced around. It was pandemonium as Summer Court soldiers on dire hounds chased after drau and spiders. There were two other trolls in the room; winged fairies dashed in and out of their reach, stinging with swords. I caught a glimpse of Father on Bernice. He practically glowed as they dashed along the side aisle, him slashing at spiders and shouting about the glory of God. It had gotten crazy-crowded fast, and it looked like our side might win. But I didn't see the queen, and if I didn't exterminate her, we'd win the battle at the price of the war.

Wait! There she was, ducking into the sacristy behind the altar area.

From under the altar, I caught sight of weak bursts of flame. "Sam, my twinkin, Grislakeh is at the altar. She needs help. Take Ray!"

I waited only long enough for his acknowledgment before I sprang onto the troll king's lap, raking in my claws as I scrambled across him.

"Father!" I called, as I leaped off the troll, tearing his stomach with my claws, a trick I'd learned from Mundane cats. He swung, but too late. My wing screamed protests against their use, but it kept me above most of the fighting.

Father Rich heard me, and with a move worthy of a rodeo cowboy, spun Bernice on her heels, leaped her over a pew, and charged toward the front of the chapel. By the time we'd entered the sacristy, however, the queen had already passed through it to the hallway beyond. I caught a glimpse of one thin, black spider leg as she rounded a corner.

Together, we ran after her.

"What are you doing here?" I asked.

"We couldn't leave you to have all the fun and glory," he snapped, but I knew what he meant. *We couldn't leave you.*

"And the army you brought?"

"Titania wants her husband back. They're supposed to clear her a way."

The hall split, but I let my instincts choose the right path and turned without slowing. Bernice's hooves scraped the floor as she made the turn.

"He was in the ballroom," I said. "He's not going to get anywhere near this fight."

Father tapped his ear with his sword hand and relayed the information. Somebody must have convinced Al'Beah to give them some tech.

My senses were telling me we were heading back toward the outer part of the castle, so when we came to another set of double doors and burst through, I had just enough forewarning to skid to a stop and fling my tail out to block Bernice from charging off the short balcony. She reared up, her hooves slipping and straining for purchase. Father shouted words more suiting a cowboy than a paladin, but somehow kept his seat.

Then from the wall behind us, the Spider Queen dropped down on him.

Chapter Twenty: Brothers, Bros, and Boss Battles

Queen Nasty-on-Eight-Legs knocked Father off Bernice and pinned him to the ground. Before she should bite him, I grabbed her leg between my teeth and pulled her off. I bit down, cutting it off at the joint, and swiped at her with my paws as I spat it out. She shrieked, unable to react fast enough to stop me from gouging her abdomen. I bit again. At the same time, Father took off a leg on his side. She spun toward him.

This time, I chomped on her abdomen, but instead of biting down, I flung her hard against the stone wall, then followed with a full force of fire.

She struggled but could not get away. I blew flame until her struggling stopped, and her corpse started to smoke and steam in the rain. Then I blew more until I dropped to the wet floor gasping and coughing.

Father dropped his sword and braced his hands on his knees while he caught his breath. "You okay?" he asked.

"Yep. You?"

"Yeah."

Then we looked at each other suspiciously.

"Maybe we don't need a big boss battle?" Father asked.

Bernice let out a horsey scream and ran back indoors. We spun around.

A dragon-shaped shadow, darker than the night storm clouds, sped toward us.

"Friend of yours?" Father asked hopefully; then seeing me tense, he groaned and snatched up his sword.

Another shadow emerged from within the clouds.

"How about we go home?" I suggested instead, and the two of us ran back into the castle.

We'd made it down the long hall when I felt a change in air pressure that told me one of my kin had stuck his head in the porch entrance. I shoved Father in front of me and spread my wings. Just in time, too; a rolling cloud of flame splashed over my back. Remember how I'd said fire was language? This one told a story of arrogance, anger, and hate.

I shoved Father. "We can't defeat the eldestkin. Get to the others. I'll catch up."

"You have five minutes. Then I'll send Al'Beah."

When he rounded the corner, I turned to face my eldestkin. "Durrehkeh, what are you doing?"

"I? I am securing the future of our kind. What are you doing, Little One?"

The insult, in our language, referred not just to size but also to stature, ambition, attitude... It stung that it was true.

And yet, I hardly recognized the dragon staring at me, his face filling the entry. It was my eldestkin; the one we all looked up to. The one who since time began led us, inspired us, took us down a notch when necessary. The one whose eyes burned the passion that fueled dragons.

Now, behind that fire, I saw only cold blackness and death.

"What's happened to you?" I could not get past that emptiness in his eyes. I stepped toward him.

"What happened?" he sneered. "I have been betrayed on all sides, it seems. The decline of the mortals' respect we've seen for millennia. But that you and your twin would choose your pets over your own kind..."

"My twin? You knew that Agarrabarresheh gave Grislakeh to the spiders?"

"She defied our authority. She was told to leave things alone, and she came here anyway. She got caught. We simply allowed her to be punished before we came to get her, hopefully wiser and more willing to submit to the wisdom of the thunder. Apparently, that is not to be so. The two of you always were so bothersome with your questions and thinking you are so clever. How clever are you now, Vurnerrah, now that the ones you feel so responsible to defend could bring the two of you so low?"

"I don't understand," I whispered. But I did. I just didn't want to admit it to myself. Griss was right; the queen was just a tool. Someone had manipulated her.

He smirked at me. In the past, I'd have seen some affection—grudging, if he were annoyed, but it'd be there. Now, there was only disdain. My value was in following him. "You do. Publicly, we play the equal, but oh, Vurnerrah, if you could have seen how the queen groveled. I am their new master. It was the way it used to be, the way it should be."

"We have a very different memory of the past." My mouth worked on automatic while my brain struggled to think my way—our way—out of this. I could not see past my eldestkin's big head to the sky beyond, but my instinctive ability to sense my kin (something I'd forgotten I had) told me only Agarrabarresheh had joined him. Still, two dragons were more than a match, even for all the Summer Court's soldiers and my friends.

He laughed. "You used to love the groveling. Have you forgotten? Has your pet paladin taken so much of your memory?"

He had me there. I did enjoy seeing some wayward mortal cower and beg for forgiveness—and, usually, his life. It was a perk of being a dragon.

I refused to answer. "So, what? Now, because the sapients are becoming too strong-willed to treat us like we think we deserve—that's an excuse to destroy them all?"

"Extinction is inevitable. You know this. Why are you so concerned when your favorites will die eventually, anyway? That, or they will grow tired of you and move on. Pah!"

That struck a little close to home, too.

I said, "We're supposed to protect the sapients. God didn't sanction this."

Durrehkeh growled deep in his throat. I took heart in the sound because it meant I'd scored a point. "No. Nor have I said I was going to allow a complete extinction. Just a significant diminishing of their numbers. Then we would return, refreshed and strong, and rid the world of the vermin. The sapient races would recognize our grandeur once again. They'd be beholden to us. Do you remember those days, Little One? When we commanded authority that surpassed any political position? We were revered because of what we were!"

"You can't really think this will work? They'll find out. At very least, they'll know we abandoned them when we could have prevented this."

"That's why some of us are awake. To make sure that does not happen."

To kill anyone who suspects, he meant. I felt sick in a way no poison could make me.

"Durrehkeh, eldestkin, grandest of our kind. What happened to you? We're not supposed to be the masters. You know this!"

"We are the greatest creation!"

"Yes, I know! Top of the food chain and master of no one. We advise, we inspire, we punish when necessary. We do not command."

"Maybe we should have. Maybe the beings of this world would not be in the mess they are if we had ruled, if we had been—"

"What? Like gods? Want to ask Zeus how well that worked out? Or maybe Baal? He had to come to us to get rid of those ravens, remember?"

"Do not accuse me of forgetting. I remember only too well the glory we commanded."

"Reflected. That was our job—to reflect glory."

"And we will when we set up our new kingdom!"

"God's is the kingdom, the power, and the glory!" From behind me, Father yelled it like a battle cry. I heard hoofbeats galloping toward us, and then Bernice jumped over me, Father hugging her neck, the two threading the opening between me and the ceiling.

He charged Durrehkeh. He had a new lance; it gleamed in the light.

My eldestkin had shoved his head into the doorway and down the hall as we'd spoken. Father had a clean shot up his snout, into his mouth, or through his eye. But Durr was no dragon of Mundane legend. It would hurt, but it wouldn't be enough.

"No!" I yelled, and I didn't know if it was for Durrehkeh's sake or Father's.

Durrehkeh let out a stream of fire. It splashed harmlessly against shields I hadn't sensed. Definitely Armor of God stuff. Father and Bernice rode through it.

Durrehkeh saw what was happening and backed up fast, but not fast enough.

Just before he'd fully cleared the doorway, Father's lance speared him in the cheek just below the eye.

Durrehkeh howled in pain and reared back, crashing through the doorway, shredding the threshold and destroying the stone wall above. It was so sudden, Bernice's hooves left the ground before Father's boots escaped the stirrups. Father had had the lance tucked under his arm and gripped tightly; he was twenty feet in the air and flinging around before he knew what had happened. I was sure his guardian angel was helping him keep hold of the lance, and good thing, too. We were several stories above the ground.

I ran to the entrance and launched myself off the balcony.

Durrehkeh had dug his claws into the side of the castle, the only way to keep himself steady as we'd argued. Disoriented by pain and fury, he didn't think about taking flight but held on with three paws while he freed the fourth to pull the lance out of his face. Father, however, kept kicking his claws away. He'd wrapped his arms tightly around the lance and was holding on for dear life.

As my feet left the balcony, my eldestkin lost his patience, and ignoring the pain, flung his head violently back and forth. Father flopped like a rag doll, and finally, the rain and the sudden motions made him lose his grip.

I caught him on the way down.

"I thought you were sending Al'Beah!" I yelled at him.

"He's kind of busy. There's another one in the chapel," Father yelled back.

Durr flicked out his tail and knocked us hard into a wall. Fortunately, we were almost to the first story. Father's sword clattered to the ground. I bounced and landed on my feet. Father slid the rest of the way, then flopped prone, dazed. He rose to his elbows, shook his head, and made a halfhearted lunge toward his sword as Durr set a paw on it. He'd pulled the lance from his cheek and had it stuck in his mouth like a toothpick. He was already healing. Show off.

Durrehkeh laughed. "Did you think it would be so easy against a real dragon at the height of his power?"

I cut in, "Real dragon?" A roar of fury and defiance tore from my mouth and I splayed my wings.

He laughed and swiped at my head with his tail.

I flipped back and sank all my claws and my teeth into it.

He shrieked as much in surprise as pain, but before he could flick me off like an annoying tick, I let go. I'd planned to dive back in by another angle, but he reached out and snagged a claw on my nose ring.

"And this, 'real dragon!'" he said as he flung me around by the snout. "Are you an ox now? A common beast of burden to plow the humans' fields?"

Considering I'd done just that for a hundred years with the Silent Brothers, insult added to injury. I told Ti the nose ring was a bad idea.

Well, it had done its job, anyway. I dug a claw beside his and pulled sideways. The latch popped open, and his next shake yanked it out of my nostril. The edge raked the interior of my nose. I sneezed and breathed fire, and we both swore with pain.

But I was free to attack. I pounced on his back. My fairy-sharpened nails speared through his scales and left narrow but deep gouges. I didn't have the advantage of size or weight, but I had skill and acrobatic grace.

As I danced the Merengue of a Thousand Paper Cuts on my kin, I watched Father pull himself up and stand. He swayed, but I knew if I told him to run, he'd ignore me. He'd come back twice already. I wouldn't insult him by asking a third time.

"Stay away from the tail," I called out in elvish. Tolkien's Elvish, that is, which is unknown by

Faerie creatures but well-known by nerds like my friend. "Don't bother with the big muscles. Stab him in the armpits or the joints of the hips. Our scales are less thick there. That's your best chance to lame him."

I paused to duck Durr's back kick and got smacked by his wing. "Wings—slash the membranes. Stab the joints."

"Got it!"

"What are you saying?" Durr shouted. I couldn't tell if he was frantic or annoyed. He whipped his tail and circled my waist. I dug all my claws in as he tried to pull me off. He howled, then blasted fire at Father, who managed to score on his ankle before skittering out of the way.

Father got lucky that time. I didn't want to count on his luck holding out.

"Do the thing with the rain!" I shouted. It was still coming down in hurricane-level torrents, probably the only thing keeping the entire area from going up in flames. The spiders, too, had abandoned the courtyard, though I didn't know if it was from distaste for the rain or fear of us.

"What thing?" Father shouted. He yelped and ran as Durrehkeh sent a shot of flame his way. He made a wild swing with his sword and managed to slice the large membrane of Durrehkeh's wing. I bit him in the other wing. Durrehkeh's fire paused as he gasped in pain.

"Like Saint George did to cancel my fire!" I shouted.

"How?"

Damsels and knights! He didn't know. He wasn't really himself when we were having our fight. He screamed as my injured but plenty dangerous kin let loose a truly marvelous stream of renewed fire. He managed to jump behind a pile of water-laden bricks. They blocked the flames, but from how they steamed and popped, the bricks would not last long.

I scrambled up Durrehkeh's neck.

I dug my claws into his cheeks and wrapped my tail around his throat. There was one gland in our necks that acted like an igniter. Put pressure on it, and we couldn't breathe fire. It was ridiculously hard to find, much less squeeze. My kin had made a game of neck-and-tail out of it. I'd been reigning champion three centuries running. Durrehkeh, naturally, never played. He was always above that kind of silliness. Today, that was his loss. I was just glad my tail had grown long enough to reach.

His flame ended with a choke, but I underestimated his strength. He flung his head backward. He almost dislodged me, but I tightened my grip. As I was whipped to and fro, I saw the castle, parts of it burning. I saw a silhouette of my secondkin, Agarrabarresheh, rearing back as a flurry of arrows struck his chest. He was inside—that meant he'd already sacrificed more than half his size to healing his wounds.

Something from above fell on his head, and I sensed it was magically done.

Just like I would not have won against the overwhelming numbers of the spiders; at this size, Agarrabarresheh would not win alone against the forces of Titania's army and my friends. But how many would die before he gave up?

Durrehkeh danced about, stomping hard and lashing his tail. Father had left his hiding place and was again harrying my eldestkin. I didn't know how my priest friend was managing to keep going; I could hear his breathing even through the raucous spattering of rain.

I pulled myself closer to Durrehkeh's ear. "Please, eldestkin. Listen to me. We can stop this now."

"Traitor!" he choked out. "I will hurt you so you need a thousand generations to recover!"

Every muscle in me tensed in anger. My claws dug deeper. "Traitor? You betrayed us. You broke our prime law, betrayed our responsibility to the sapients. You let them hurt Grislakeh!"

For a wild moment, all I wanted to do was rip his eye out and breathe fire straight into his brain. Maybe when he recovered a thousand generations later, he'd understand what I was capable of. "Real dragon." I'd show him a real dragon.

He howled as Father scored again. In the ball-room, I heard my twinkin cry out as well. Was she sacrificing herself to defend the others against our secondkin?

We'd trusted them. They'd led us with strength and mercy and love. What had happened? I jabbed a claw into the hole Father had made with the javelin and dug in. "No one's putting anyone out that long. Now calm down so we can figure out how to get everyone out of this."

"Is that your answer for everything, Little One? Talk? Where has talk gotten you? You fight your own to defend the one who has hurt you more than any creature in millennia. We shall command all the species of this world and others!"

"You've lost your mind. That's not our job!"

"And our 'job' is to coddle the mortal races as they persist in sin? When I am done, I will reign supreme and we will force them to new ways of our choosing. I—aargh!"

Father must have scored on a sensitive spot. Durr launched himself in the air. I heard a heavy thump and a cry. I turned my head enough to see Father lying on the ground, breathing but not moving. Then Durr flew over the castle, climbing high, and dove fast until all I saw were rushing rock and rapidly approaching cobblestones.

He twisted and jinked, and my claws spasmed in a desperate desire to not get thrown off. He howled and threw his head back, slamming me against the wall of the castle. My spikes jammed into my back with the agony of a hundred stubbed toes, but Titania's magic kept them from breaking. Stones and mortar fell as we crumbled the masonry. Blurry, black spots dotted my view of the already dismal sky. I thought the cliché was to see stars.

Durrehkeh grabbed hold of the walls, twisted, and smashed me against the stonework. He rubbed his head, back and forth, scraping me against the walls. Soon, the slickness of the rain and the buffing of my scales was not enough to combat the friction as he ground me against the stones. Scales ripped off my hide, and my left wing was shredding.

Even as I fought to free myself from him, I remembered a movie line about a "rudimentary lathe." I laughed. He slammed me hard for my impertinence.

My tail's grip slipped, and he breathed a blast of fire in front of us. Reflexively, I tightened my hold, this time to the point of choking. The flame ended abruptly, revealing a small, winged blur, pink against the storm.

I blinked water from my eyes and forced myself to focus.

Grislakeh!

"No!" I gasped. "Run!"

My words were lost in the howling wind.

Durrehkeh dug his shoulder deeper into my side and flung his head against the wall thrice more, willing to increase his pain to inflict more on me. I felt the crunch as my shoulder shattered. I bit his snout, but he stuck a claw between my teeth and his skin and stabbed me through the palate, one of the few (and most painful) ways to get a dragon to release you from its jaws.

Only, I wasn't letting go. I had to keep him distracted from my approaching twinkin.

While he grabbed at my lower jaw with one claw and tried to force my mouth open, Grislakeh shot toward him like a bullet. She was small, not much larger than I was after my fight with George, and my rage burned away the dizziness. Unfortunately, it took all my concentration just to keep from getting strung up like a fish on a hook.

Griss landed on Durrehkeh's snout. She lashed out with both front paws and stabbed his eye.

He shrieked and jerked his head back, scraping my already flayed skin against the stone, making me scream as well. He retracted his claw, releasing me, but I wasn't fast enough to react before he swiped at Grislakeh, slicing four deep gouges in her stomach and flinging her away.

At least he tried to fling her. She held onto his eye with everything she had.

Half-mad with desperation, he shoved at her harder, not thinking of the inevitable outcome. When he succeeded, she went careening away. She hit the ground with a hard splash and lay still. But she held his eyeball in her grip.

I didn't think. I faced my eldestkin and breathed fire straight into his empty socket.

He jerked and spasmed like one being electrocuted. He plummeted.

I shoved away from him, but my broken and shredded wings could barely unfold. Fortunately, I'd spent a lot of time around cats lately. I landed on my feet. My right leg gave way. I ignored it. Grislakeh still hadn't moved. I staggered to her, putting myself between her and our eldestkin. My wings screamed as I unfurled them, and my cheek crests sent shooting pains as I flared them, but I hissed defiance, nonetheless.

Lightning crackled across the sky, followed almost immediately by thunder. I hoped I looked worthy of a comic book cover.

Durrehkeh gazed at me with fear and surprise.

And then, he turned his back on me, flicked his tail, and flew away. His movements were jerky and hesitant, like a stroke victim's, but he managed to stay aloft. A moment later, there was a crash of glass and stone and Agarrabarresheh followed.

I collapsed. With the last of my strength, I managed to twist my neck so I could bump Grislakeh with my nose. "Griss?"

She still didn't move, but I felt her breathing, light and too fast, against my snout. My eyes felt heavy. I let them sag.

The rain started to let up. Figured—perfect timing as usual. I heard footsteps splashing into the courtyard: human, fairy, canine. People shouted my and Father's names. Then someone yelled, "There they are!"

I opened my eyes long enough to see vague shapes heading my way. They seemed friendly. Then, it was too much effort to stay awake.

Chapter Twenty-One: All is Mended, Mostly

I came to in the stables, with no recollection of getting there or how long I'd been out. I did feel marginally better, which considering my last memory of how I felt, was actually a big improvement. At least the hay was comfortable and dry.

"Gris..." I started, then stopped because it hurt and my voice sounded wheezy. I remembered I had a hole in my snout.

I heard familiar human snoring beside me and gingerly moved my leg far enough to tap Father with my pinkie.

"Wha...? I'm awake."

It comforted me that he didn't bounce up, ready for a fight, but rather sat up slowly and with a grunt of effort and discomfort.

"I'm cured of LARPing for the rest of my life," he told me. "Besides, fighting three dragons is enough for one man's lifetime."

"You only fought two, and one was me," I protested weakly. "And I did the heavy work against Durrehkeh."

"Let's not quibble over details."

"Is that story going to grow each time you tell it?" I asked.

"Probably. And when you tell it?"

"Probably."

It hurt to laugh.

The next time I remembered waking, I was in a fairy garden, but not one I recognized. It was simple, a grassy meadow by a small lake with only a single weeping willow, its branches drooping lazily into the still water. The night sky had a silver tinge, and I could not make out constellations.

I was under a shield of obscurity. Probably not a bad idea, considering.

At least I felt stronger. I rose, stretched—gingerly because everything still hurt to some degree—and shambled to the water. Fortunately, my nose had fully healed, so I wouldn't have to deal with the potential pain and certain indignity of water pouring out the top of my snout. I drank, savoring the clean taste and how it cooled my throat.

"I asked Titania, She Who Burns with the Heat of a Thousand Summers, to keep just a wee hole in your momentous snout. Alas, she refused. Pity. You could have used it as a blowhole," said a familiar voice. I looked up and saw Al'Beah lounging among the branches of the willow.

The simple act of drinking had worn me out. I didn't have the energy to make a retort or even sneer. I tilted my head in his direction—the dragon equivalent of raising an eyebrow.

He floated down beside me. "How are you feeling?"

"Depends," I said. "Did I succeed?"

"In fact, you did. The queen spider is dead before she could create a breed with mind-controlling venom. Titania's army, combined with your friends, routed her alliance for now, and you caused such a conflagration that it caught the attention of some crusaders that were coming to check on Farrayway. They are seeking out the female spiders. You've prevented the destruction of the sapient species of Faerie. But you must know that, since you never saw such an extinction."

I didn't feel like arguing temporal physics. "Grislakeh?"

There was a shimmer behind him, and Titania floated over to us. She answered the question as if it had been directed to her. "Hidden and healing. She won't wake for a long time." The way she said it made me think in terms of centuries rather than weeks.

My first instinct was to offer to take her to her lair, staying with her as she hibernated back to health. I caught myself. We'd challenged Durrehkeh like none of our kind had ever challenged an elderkin. Together, we'd defeated him.

I shivered, remembering what we'd done. We didn't just defeat him. We'd insulted him, using our diminished sizes to our advantage. We were always declaring ourselves the cleverest, and we'd pitted our wits against his superior everything else, and we proved our point. He wasn't going to let that slide. He'd come back after us.

I glanced at the sky. Ti had realized it, too, and had us hidden.

"Where is she?"

Titania waved her arm, and the branches of the willow parted, revealing a gnome-sized dragon curled up tight, waves of healing magic flowing over her too-pale hide. However long I'd been healing had been barely enough to touch the damage done to her. I saw angry red welts of spider bites violating the mellow pinks and tangerines of her scales. I caught just a hint of a huge but healing gash on her abdomen; one of the four Durrehkeh must have given her.

I did not remember ever seeing one of our kind so gravely wounded. If I ever had, I didn't want to know. I shook with anger and grief, but she wasn't the end of my concerns.

"My friends?" I choked out.

Titania set a hand on my flank. Her touch was warm and soothing, but I didn't want to be soothed. "They are alive and healing. The genie has explained the strange adventure you have been on. Worry not for them. We will make them whole before we send them home."

"Good. They need to get back to their lives."

"As do you," Al'Beah said. "I cannot leave you here."

I didn't bother to answer. I pulled myself up and went to my twinkin. I circled myself around her, careful not to disturb the halo of healing. One of her front claws peeked out from the spell. I set one of mine against it. Only the rise and fall of her flank, slower and gentler than when we were in the ruined courtyard, told me she was recovering.

I closed my eyes.

I was back in the rain-slicked courtyard, standing protectively over my twinkin as I curled my teeth in challenge to Durrehkeh. The rain had slowed to a drizzle, but clouds still obscured the moon from view. It made everything worse: I could see the red flaring of the ballroom windows every time Agarrabarresheh breathed fire, and I heard my friends screaming my name. There was nothing I could do. I could not leave Grislakeh.

"Al'Beah!" I yelled. "I wish you to take my friends home. Al'Beah!"

Durrehkeh chuckled, a low gravelly rumble that sent shivers down my spine. He turned toward me, and for a moment, all I saw was the charred eye socket. Then, he tilted his nose toward his paw, and I realized he held the genie's lamp.

"So, this is how small you've become, Vern," he sneered. "Shivering in the rain, wishing for someone else to help you. There is no help for you or your twin this time. I will take you down to nothing, and I will let you recover just enough to take you down again and again and again."

He slammed the lamp on the ground. It shattered like glass, not brass.

Then he lunged at me.

I snarled.

"Vern!" a human voice squeaked. "Vern, it's okay. It's me! It's Linda."

My eyes snapped open, and I took in the peaceful surroundings of the hidden fairy cove. Linda was on her butt, her hands behind her. I must have startled her as she was coming near, and she'd fallen back and crab-walked to get away.

"Linda! I'm sorry. I was having a nightmare. I..."

She cut me off with a nervous giggle. "I can't blame you. That was a little more adventure than any of us hoped for, hey?"

"Are you...?" I couldn't ask if she was okay. The answer was obvious. The right side of her face and neck was thick with pink scar tissue. From her loose clothing, I was sure that was not the only part of her that was burned by my secondkin's fire.

She reached for her cheek but stopped short of touching it. One of her fingers was missing a nail. "Oh, this? Don't worry. It's not fully healed yet. They said I should be good as new by the time we're ready to leave."

I released a breath I hadn't realized I was holding. "Thank God," I said and meant it. "The others?"

"Oh, we're all a mess," she said with forced cheerfulness. "Ray made it to the altar and hid there, but he got bit by spiders. He's only just stopped throwing up. The orcs took offense to Owen and broke through his defenses and just...just mauled him. Sam got his wings cut off, which I know considering he's really human doesn't sound like much but he screamed like it hurt for real. Thunderpaws was beside himself; he went berserk attacking anything that got close to Sam. He was such a brave doggy. He got stabbed and bit and singed and he never left Sam's side.

"But don't worry about us!" she said just a little too quickly and forcefully. In fact, her phrases were getting more staccato and manic as she spoke. "We're going to be okay. The fairies are healing us and Titania said we can stay as long as we need to and Al'Beah will get us home and... And I just wanted to see how you were doing and say... I'm sorry..."

Her eyes filled with tears, and her lips trembled. "I'm so sorry, Vern. This is all my fault."

"Linda, no."

"But it was my wish that brought us here! If I hadn't wished for one stupid adventure... I should have been in my new apartment and Owen setting up the new month's comics and... And instead, Owen got beaten half to death and Father and Ray got poisoned, and...and Thuddy's scared of everything and...your sister..."

She buried her face in her hands and cried.

Dragon instincts told me not to leave Grislakeh, but she was safe and lost in healing sleep. Meanwhile, my human friend was in pain. Of course, comforting damsels was not really my talent. So, I did what I had done with my twin. I circled around her protectively.

Is this how small you are, Vern? Durrehkeh's voice jeered in my mind. Would you leave your own kind to comfort your toy?

I told his phantom to blow fire out his butt.

She stayed pulled in on herself, cross-legged on the grass, her hands covering her face, sobbing loudly.

"Linda, can you listen?" I asked. When I thought the sobs had quieted marginally, I continued. "This is not your fault. You made the wish, but it was the trigger—that's all. The gun was already loaded. I had to get to this time and this situation somehow. I know, because my past would have been far worse if I hadn't taken out the Spider Queen. But because of your wish, I wasn't alone."

She didn't reply, but at least she'd calmed to weeping.

I tried again. "Your wish brought Sam and Betts together. I think he'd have given anything for that, don't you?"

"I suppose..." she murmured.

That was progress. "Because you were here, you brought an army to keep Agarrabarresheh busy while I confronted my eldestkin. My twinkin and I could not have managed against both of them."

I remembered what Durrehkeh had said in my dream, and I shivered.

"We barely managed against one," Linda said. "Vern, he was terrifying!"

And she leaned against my flank, sobbing all over again. I wondered if Thunderpaws was the only one who would be jumping at shadows from now on.

Then with a small pop!, Puck appeared beside her. Gently, he stroked her hair.

If we Faerie have offended
Think but this, and all is mended
That you have but playtimed here
While these adventures did appear.
And this weak and idle theme
No more yielding than a dream

She sighed and leaned more heavily against me, dozing.

I tilted my head at Puck. "Nicely done. Sounded familiar."

Puck shrugged. "I picked it up from a Mundane bard. Dragon, do not reprehend."

I grinned, "If I pardon, will you mend?"

He smiled and spread his hands. "Else the Puck a liar call. Don't worry, Vurnerrah, Brave and

Daring. The genie has revealed all to us. We understand these adventurers are but simple Mundanes. They handled themselves exceptionally. We will soothe their minds as well as their bodies. Even the dog."

I braced myself. Nothing came without a price, and this was deep magic. "What shall the Queen of Summer Sun 'N Fun want in return?"

Puck squatted down in front of me. "'Tis a funny thing, that. She sought to extract the price from your priestly paladin."

I groaned.

"Oh, aye! And such a vision to behold when my queen strives to seduce a stalwart human male. But your paladin would have none of it. I would have thought he was of 'the other persuasion,' if not for the fact that such preferences mean nothing when compared to the persuasions of My Lady of Heat and Passion."

Impatience bit at me. "Well? Obviously, she didn't kill him, or Puck a liar be. So, what happened?"

Puck laughed. "He told her eros was not the love she needed, and that she knew it. Then, he offered her what he said was the best love he could give—the love of Christ."

"He heard her confession," I guessed. Did he have any idea how incredibly brave that was? He just challenged the soul of one of the most powerful beings in my universe.

Puck shrugged. "She said she didn't think he could handle it. He told her Christ could handle anything, and with Christ, so could he. They were gone for seven hours."

I winced, and not because of the amount of time or what I could imagine Titania's sins included. No, this was more about how insufferable he was going to be now. Fought two dragons, sacramentally suffered to the point of near-death, and heard the confession of the Fairy Queen? And he didn't even wish for any of it!

At least we didn't have to throw a ring into a volcano.

Puck clapped his hands and rubbed them together. "And now, I must bring the fair Linda back to the healers. She has been aching to see you and apologize. I will ensure your assurances remain written in her heart."

Despite being half her size, Puck lifted Linda with strength and grace, shifting so that her head lolled against his shoulder. Then, with a wink, he disappeared.

In his place, a stack of meats and sweets appeared. I finished them off almost too quickly to taste them, then wandered to the lake to drink and decided I had enough energy for a quick bath. Then I returned to my place forming a circle of protection around my twin.

The next time I awoke, someone was caressing behind my cheek crests in the exact spot I liked. With each gentle stroke, warmth flowed through me. I lazily opened my eyes and purred. "I'll give you a year to stop," I quipped.

Titania snorted daintily. "You have already overstayed your welcome, Vurnerrah Great and Brave. You have caused much trouble for the Summer Court."

"I think your husband did that."

She thwocked me with her fingernail. "Do not contradict one who has been so hospitable to you. In fact, my wise and cunning husband was working to protect all the fairy. He agreed to play his little trick upon your kin in exchange for keeping the Summer and Winter Courts out of this vendetta against the sapients."

I growled, offended. "If he'd come to the dragons in the first place, we might have taken care of the problem before any species was in danger."

"Are you so sure of that, Vurnerrah, Born Twin and Middle Child?"

I thought back to the conclave and my attempts to sway Durrehkeh and the others. Ti—well, Oberon, much as it hurt my teeth to admit it—was right: They were tired of the way we were being treated.

Even if I'd been there when Oberon was confronting my eldestkin, I didn't have the power or the rank to force a decision. Grislakeh and I were 34th and 35th—or 35th and 34th—in the line of dragons. In all our immortal lives, we have always followed the birth order of the thunder in terms of leadership. Challenging a dragonkin was only for small matters or in the spirit of fun. There were rules of conduct more binding than the Geneva Convention.

Grislakeh and I had violated them all.

Titania sensed my change in mood. "Now, you understand the situation we are in."

I remembered Vatican envoys being sent to the Summer and Winter Courts, coming back defeated and frustrated. The fairy folk had stayed out of the war. "Oberon's renegotiated?"

She spoke airily yet with authority that would brook no argument. "We shall keep our original agreements. My army's valiant deeds in battle have been explained away as a lover's quarrel, and Oberon has assured the new spider leader that I have been 'put in my place.' We will supply portals to other worlds for those of your kind who wish other climes."

"Isn't it 'fairer climes'?"

She shrugged. "That was not specified."

I didn't know whether to laugh or be angry. Oberon really had played off my eldestkin's ire. "And Grislakeh and me?"

My twinkin was still curled up in my protective circle, asleep and unmoving. Healing energies continued to play over her, like rainbows reflecting in sunset-tinted waters. She seemed a little bigger, a little more comfortable, but I knew that this would not be a fast recovery, even by dragon reckoning.

"You delivered an insult none of your kind have ever seen. I'm at once impressed and disappointed in you, Vurnerrah. You moved with the bluntness and impatience of a mortal."

"Ouch!"

"They will not forget your insult easily, nor do they seem willing to forgive. However, Agarrabarresheh remembers the value of patience. He has gone to his Long Sleep. Durrehkeh, in the meantime, has begun his search for you in the Mundane."

"What?" I half stood, furious and terrified. They had no idea what awaited him in the Mundane. If he went blasting through the Gap, demanding my hide and destroying anything or anyone that got in his way, the Mundanes would not surrender like frightened villagers. They had tranquilized me and locked me in a zoo for getting uppity. If he reigned destruction on them, they wouldn't stick to simple guns very long. They had machines and weaponry that would match my kin in might. And then, they'd come after me.

"Titania!"

"Sit. Calm yourself. Do not undo the work my healers have done. He demanded we send him to where you are. He and some of your kin are in the Mundane, but now, they are learning their own lessons in patience."

I settled back down, grinning. Human history was rife with legends of dragons. Then something clicked, and my smile faded. Durrehkeh had, at one point, returned to my old stomping grounds. There, he'd attacked a village who called upon a saintly man for help...

Said saintly knight, St. George, just happened to see a demon talking to a dragon through a portal...

Without thinking, St. George rushed in...

Spearing the demon and starting a fight with an already angry dragon. Me.

It was like the dragon version of being my own grandfather.

I heaved a sigh. "What happens now?"

"Now you take your Mundane playthings and return to your time. They have their own lives to lead, and in appreciation for their valiant deeds, I will return them—even Samwise and

Thunderpaws, though I chafe at losing such a stouthearted pair of warriors."

"Yes, send them home. I have to stay with Grislakeh."

"Impossible. There is already one of you here in this world at this time. That is sufficient."

"So hide us away. Or I'll take her to a hibernation spot, stay with her until she heals."

"And how will you hunt without making your presence known? You cannot stay with her and you cannot bring her to the Mundane in this state. There is not enough magic for her healing."

"Give me some time. I'll figure something out."

"You no longer have the luxury of time. It is not only Durrehkeh who searches for you, you know. You have made enemies, enemies who will destroy anything to get to you."

I closed my eyes as understanding and defeat washed over me. That's why I had been stuck in the Vatican for so long. It wasn't just to let me recover or to imprison me while I got my indoctrination in the mortal religion. It was to keep me off the spider kingdom's radar until they were defeated.

And by hiding us, Titania was risking the neutrality of the Fairy Courts.

She continued, "We are expending great resources keeping the both of you hidden here, and thanks to the timing of Oberon's mission, we are already diminished. Fear not, my dear, dear dragon. You and Grislakeh have always been good to my sister and me—the twin dragons as companions to the twin queens. We will do what is necessary to keep Grislakeh safe and hidden until she is whole, and then we will send her to you."

I glanced back at her, so small and vulnerable. My heart ached not just for her but for myself. How many more lonely years would I have? What trouble would our reunion bring to the Faerie and Mundane dimensions?

Chapter Twenty-Two: Ya Get What Ya Get

Grislakeh never regained consciousness before I had to go. Every cell in my body protested my leaving her side. Literally. I'd forgotten how strong dragon instincts would be. I was achy and cranky when Puck brought me out of the hidden meadow and to the fairy hound stables where my Mundane friends and Al'Beah waited.

But when they all cheered my name and rushed to envelop me in hugs, it eased the pain. I also caught their excitement as they all started to chatter animatedly about getting home. Thunderpaws circled us, yapping and wiggling his entire body.

"No offense, Puck," Ray said, "This has been the most amazing adventure ever, and your people have been crazy generous. I mean, the Winter Court brought us X-Boxes! But I'm jonesing for a burger and fries."

"And they're still playing World of Warcraft," Owen muttered to me. "All this time, we thought it was the Chinese who were farming."

I snickered. "You're all okay, then? All healed up?" Myself, I was back to about to where I was before we started this cockamamie quest, which, to my ire, meant my fire breathing was gone again.

I blame you, George.

Everyone nodded, and from the grins and bright eyes, I knew Puck had been true to his word and had healed them emotionally as well.

"They couldn't quite fix everything," Linda said. She pulled up her tunic to reveal a 2-inch scar on her abdomen. "Drau longsword. Went straight through me."

"Bye, bye, bikini armor?" I quipped.

"Yeah, I'll bet she'll look terrible in them now," Ray finished the quote from *Avengers: Winter Soldier*, making Linda chuckle and blush. She smacked his arm.

Ray yelped and rubbed his bicep.

She did a woman bodybuilder's pose, giggling as Owen pretended to swoon, then she turned to the genie.

"Hey, Al'Beah," she wheedled, "If I have to keep the scar, can I keep the body? Please? I'll take care of it, promise."

"You've all earned the musculature, so yes," he said. He grinned indulgently, but his eyes twinkled as she squealed and gave a little jump for joy. Sam cheered, too. He'd gotten rather trim himself during our adventures.

I didn't think it would last long, however, not if things worked out with Betts. Faerie women, even the human ones, liked their men well-fed. She snuck under his reach and wrapped her arms around him. He kissed the top of her head and pulled her closer. Yeah, he wouldn't mind losing the abs, not if she was at his side.

Ugh. I had become a romantic.

"Shall we get out of here?" I asked. "I'd like a pizza that hasn't been splattered against a troll's eye."

"That's amore!" my friends sang.

Puck lifted his hands at me to show his confusion, but I didn't bother to illuminate. He came up with enough jokes and pranks on his own.

"One question," Father asked. He'd been quiet up until now, and he kept turning back to the stables. "What about Bernice? She wasn't really George's actual horse, was she? What happens to her now?"

"Do you want her?" Al'Beah asked.

Father bit his lip. Of course, he wanted her.

"Go on," I said. "Don't your parents have a ranch?"

"The Sabletons do, too; I bet they'd board her for you," Linda said.

But he shook his head. "No. She's a warhorse. She's made for the excitement, and she's still in her prime. Much as I'd want to keep her safe in our world, she'd be restless and undervalued. Can you find her a good warrior, one who will treat her as a companion as well as a ride?"

The genie bowed, acknowledging Father's wisdom. "I know several worthy crusaders who would wish for such a partner as Bernice. I will see she is well cared for."

Father let out a breath. "Okay, then. I'm ready."

Puck bowed low, arms spread theatrically. "Then I shall inform my queen. Prepare yourselves to receive her blessings."

He disappeared. The others looked at each other, then shuffled to arrange themselves in a lineup, with Father to the left, then Sam with Thud sitting at his side. The corgi was still dire hound size. His head stood equal to his master's. Then came Linda, Ray, Owen, and Betts. With a shrug, I took the spot to Father's left. I knew a pecking order when I saw it, and I was top rank.

A fanfare sounded around the meadow, and a dozen dainty fairies fluttered toward us, tossing flower petals. Behind them came a silver carriage pulled by what looked like horses, except they were made of flower blossoms. The carriage pulled to a stop in front of us and the door opened of its own accord. When Titania stepped out, carriage and horses dissolved into petals and mist and blew away. She herself wore a gown of bluebells sewn with silvery thread.

Linda and Betts cooed with admiration.

Titania clasped her hands in front of her and smiled at each of us in turn. It was a regal smile, with some affection, but also a hint of relief.

"My dear, dear guests. Your adventures here have come to their conclusion! I understand that it is customary for adventurers to come away with treasures and magic items after such valiant deeds..."

My friend's faces lit up, although they were wise enough not to say anything. Good thing, too. I knew where this was going.

"But as Ray, once a bard, had only moments ago said, we have been most generous already. I would neither tempt you with excesses nor insult you with such base rewards."

And...the smiles faded. I could almost hear Father Rich's sister chanting, "You get what you get, and you don't get upset."

Titania pouted her lips at them like they were precious children. "Now, do not be disappointed. I still have something special for each of you."

She sauntered up to Father. "You, Father Richard of Little Flowers Parish of the Mundane Catholic Church: You have the honor of being Confessor to the Queen of the Summer Court of the Fairy."

She twisted her hand in the air. With a flash, she held a stole woven of sunlit magic and the delicate fibers of a purple flower—hyacinth, the flower meaning forgiveness, nice touch. Father bowed down enough for her to drape it over his neck. He grinned and touched the delicate cloth. Then, however, he gave Titania a stern look.

"I am pleased to accept this honor, Your Majesty. However, do not wait until we meet again to seek Reconciliation. There are many worthy priests who can hear your confession as well as I."

Her pout turned sulky. I fought back a smile; Father had seen right through her intended loophole. *Bless me, Father, for I have sinned. It's been 850 years since my last confession, but since you weren't around, it's really your fault...*

It was a pretty little pout, but Father was not swayed. He kept that priestly, paternal gaze on her until she sighed and promised to seek out other confessors.

Next, she went to Samwise. "Your wish brought you into my employ without my knowledge or consent. Fortunately for you, I can appreciate a well-executed trick, and you did indeed show yourself to be true and equal to any of my warriors. Waif!"

Apparently, that was how she normally called Betts because the young woman dashed out of line and fell into a deep curtsey before her. "Yes, O Queen of the Summer Skies?"

She took Betts's hand and set it on Sam's, holding them both between her own. When she pulled them away, each wore a mithril ring. "I trust this is sufficient reward?"

She moved away before either could reply, but the answer was obvious in how he pulled her close to him.

Titania paused long enough to declare Thunderpaws a "good, good doggy," then moved to Linda. She reached out and traced the line of Linda's bicep. "I'm told this body pleases you?"

"Yes, Majesty."

"Good. It pleases me, as well. You may keep it."

"Um..." Linda bit her lip and glanced toward the genie.

I cut in. "I think She Who Brings Warmth and Light to Growing Things means that it will be easy to keep your figure."

Titania glanced sharply at me. "I do not need you to translate my intentions! However, my dear, the dragon is correct." She touched Linda on the neck, near her thyroid. Linda blinked, surprised by the sensation of magic enhancing her metabolism.

"Thank you!" She curtsied low, but Ti had moved on to Ray.

"You have amused us these many weeks with your unique music."

He made a fancy bow. "It has been my honor, Queen Most Beautiful and Tremendous."

"Give me your hands." She held them between hers a moment, then released them. "Now, any song you learn to your satisfaction shall be forever retained within your talented fingertips. But mind you; you must practice."

"Thank you, Your Majesty!" Ray stared at his hands with rapt fascination. Apparently, no one had told Titania that before Linda's wish had given him bard powers, he'd only been plucking out bad renditions of Hot Cross Buns and Yankee Doodle.

Finally, she came to Owen. "So, half-orc who is not. You were stronger than all your companions and yet more frail. It was quite a challenge restoring your health."

He bowed, embarrassed. "I am grateful beyond words, Queen of Summer Light."

She frowned and shook her head. "Yet here you are, fretting over your return. Should I let you remain here, a half-orc warrior in my armies?"

He gulped. "No, please."

She gazed at the top of his head, and her voice grew just a bit teasing. "Oh. Perhaps you wish to remain a half-orc upon your return?"

"Uh, no, thank you. Really. I'm just grateful to be healed. If you would, I am content with that."

"Oh, well, if you are content with that, so be it." She cupped his chin and tilted his head so he had to look into her eyes. "Then this health shall of course follow you into the Mundane."

His eyes widened, then swam with tears. "All of it?" he whispered.

Beside me, Father crossed himself and whispered a prayer of thanks.

She left him shivering as he tried to control his emotions. The others gathered around him, confused, but he held up a hand to forestall any questions, so they rubbed his back and arms, or in Ray's case, stood awkwardly to one side, trying to make a lame joke to break the mood.

In the meantime, Titania came to me. She changed her form to that of a dragon so she could say my name correctly. "Vurnerrah."

I let out a deep sigh, committing to memory the sound of her gift and the bittersweet emotions it stirred in me.

"Vurnerrah, created twin with Grislakeh. The two of you have always been favored among the Fairy Courts. That has not changed, nor shall it."

She turned back to her queenly form and wrapped her arms around me in a hug. "Until we meet again."

Then she backed up and snapped her fingers. The petals which had been strewn along the path gathered in a whirlwind around her. She rose in the air.

"Return now to your Mundane world, richer for your experiences here. Let nothing cause you to forget that you are heroes. Allow no mortal being to doubt your worth. For you are all comrades to the cleverest of dragons and friends of the Fairy Courts, and this is no small honor," she declared. "Live your lives with courage and joy, and perhaps we shall meet again."

Then the flowery whirlwind surrounded her, and she was gone. The petals fell to the ground in the pattern of a rosebud.

"She certainly has style," Ray said.

"Ready?" Al'Beah asked.

We gathered around him. Ray started to ask if we should click our heels three times, when suddenly we were engulfed in a cloud of blue smoke. With a poof, we were gone, without disturbing a single petal of Titania's design.

Chapter Twenty-Three: All a Dragon Can Wish For

After a moment no longer than the flip of a page, we were back at the Los Lagos RenFest, near our table, the food still there and not yet attacked by flies. Around us, people screamed in surprise, then fell into confused silence.

Then, they started to cheer.

"We're home!" Linda squealed, and they all gathered in for a group hug, pulling me into the circle as well. Thunderpaws, now back to his normal size, danced around us yapping until Sam reached down and scooped him up so he could lick faces.

The applause continued a bit longer; then, show over, people went back to their meals and other diversions. Mundanes have such short attention spans.

My friends broke apart and began to examine each other. They wore their upgraded armor and weapons. Even Thud had his Faerie armor, plus the Bone of Unending Delight strapped to the side of his saddle, all shrunk to accommodate his regular size.

Owen's outfit also fit. Linda's probably could have benefitted from being a bit larger. A couple of teenage boys watched her with such focus one walked straight into a bench and toppled over it.

"Don't look now," Ray said to her, "but someone just fell head over heels for you."

Instead of squeaking and looking for cover, however, Linda punched Ray in the arm.

"Ow!" he complained. "What?"

"Why'd you have to open your mouth? We could have had treasure. I could have paid off my student loans. Sam, too!"

"I'm happy with what I got," Owen said. "It's enough."

"What was that about?" Ray asked.

Owen shook his head. "I'll explain when I know for sure what she said is true."

Sam spun around wildly. "Betts! Where's Betts?"

"Sam!" Betts called from the vendor booths. She was dressed like a noblewoman in a gown that looked like silk but was finer than even that. Like Father's new stole, this one was woven from flower petals; this time of cerastium tomentosum—Snow-in-Summer. I wondered if Titania had suggested it to the genie.

Betts had her skirts gathered into her fists as she ran full-out to Sam. He ran to her. She all but leaped into his arms, and of course, he was ready to catch her. He spun her around. When he set her down, we could see her start in with questions, but he took her face in his hands and kissed her soundly. This time, my compatriots started cheering. They ran to join them.

I started to mosey behind, but Al'Beah appeared before me. "So, friend Vurnerrah. Are you content?"

"No."

I spoke truly. I was happy enough for my friends. They'd had a wild adventure and, Linda's comment notwithstanding, had come out of it richer than before. Me? I understood better what had happened to my kind, but I paid the price in knowing my twin was injured and in hiding, and that we both were exiled from the thunder. And I needed to keep half an eye open for a vengeful eldestkin. I would not have changed my actions, but the result was the same. I was stuck in the Mundane, undersized and underpowered, among humans who would die too soon if they didn't leave me for their own lives.

I was alone.

I didn't get any treasure, either.

"I can only grant the wishes made," Al'Beah replied, seeming to answer my complaints, "but let me leave you with a prophecy: Soon, you will know Grace, and then you will not be alone."

"That's not a prophecy. That's a Christian fortune cookie," I complained.

Al'Beah chuckled. "I must return to my lamp. Thank you, Vurnerrah, for helping me complete the greatest wish tapestry of my life. Pass on my gratitude to the others? Oh, and let them know their original clothing is in a bag under the table."

"The one that guy is making off with?" I snarled and dashed off after the thief, who yelped and ran full tilt, screaming that the dragon had gone crazy while I yelled for him to drop the bag. My friends heard us and started after me, also screaming "Stop, thief!" even though they had no idea what was going on.

I was going to get kicked out of RenFest for this, I thought as I tackled the thief and tore the bag from his grip. But before people could come to his defense by throwing things at me, my friends rushed around me in a protective circle, standing up to the crowd. They were going to get banned as well, but I knew to the one, they'd say it was worth it. They had my back.

I guess that's all a dragon could wish for.

Ready for the next book?

Don't hesitate! Click now to get
Nun of My Business on Amazon!

Acknowledgements

This book has been a looooooong time coming. It started with Regina Doman suggesting her publishing house could take the Vern series, but that I needed to start again with an origin story that explained a little better how Vern wound up alone in our world. That deal fell through for reasons that still leave Vern muttering under his breath about GK Chesterton, but it did get the idea firmly rooted in my head.

The story went through multiple iterations over about five years. I spent a lot of time mulling over dragon theology, the life of the Faerie, and how the Faerie Catholic Church worked.

I ended up with a hot mess of a novel, a lot of which didn't work, but some of which I adored. Think of it like an antiques store—where there are treasures among the dreck.

So I took it to a workshop with a mentor who was a best-selling author. (I also did this with parts of <u>Murder Most Picante</u>.) Let's just say Vern did not work for her, and she did not work with Vern. After telling me the twinkin interaction smacked of incest and that the best way to save the series was to gender-bend Vern, I left that group and joined the CWG SFF crit group. They gave me useful advice and rebuilt my flagging confidence, for which, I'm forever grateful.

However, I still didn't like the story when we were done.

So, I gave up starting his story in Faerie. Really, the fun begins when he's thrust into the Mundane, anyway. I wrote *Murder Most Picante* (which you really should get if you haven't), started the Space Traipse series, and launched into self-publishing, which has been more fun than I expected.

However, those gems in the original story didn't want to be left alone, so I pulled them out and put them into the story you see here. Moral of the story, fellow writers: No writing goes to complete waste, and sometimes a great scene just needs a different plot.

Many thanks to...

Vern fans who kept asking about Vern. He remained alive and kicking (if not breathing fire) thanks to you.

Regina Doman, for encouraging me to start at the beginning.

Matthew Souders, for being a friend in the awful crit group and encouraging me to move on when it didn't work out.

The CWG spec-fic crit group: Cesar Chacon, Sarah Crickhard, Colleen Drippé, Ann Lewis, Patrick McCarthy, Matthew Schmidt, Allen Shoff, Matthew Souders, Karen Ullo, Alyssa Watson, and Mary Woods. You guys are more than critique partners. You're great friends.

Beta readers: You guys are the best! Thank you, John Earle, K. Ann Seton, Monique Ocampo, and Carol Wilson. You caught my typos, noted problems, and (most important to Vern) told me you loved the story. (Vern appreciates ego-strokes.)

The Go, Go Nano Writers Facebook group: Especially Kim Mutch Emerson, Diane Gardner, and Jan Verhoeff. When I was tempted to not write, I would hop onto the site for a sprint or five. You got me to the finish line in record time!

Rob Fabian, the best husband a writer could have. You are my inspiration, my support, and my joy. Plus, you always have a great idea when I need one! Thirty years together, and you are still my inspiration and my own wish-come-true.

Keep in Touch

If you want to learn about future books, please
- Sign up for my newsletter. https://fabianspace.substack.com/subscribe for extra Vern stories, updates and a free book!
- Visit my website (https://karinafabian.com)
- Follow me on Facebook: https://www.facebook.com/Karina-Fabian-Speculative-Fiction-with-a-Grin-2233839790277963
- Follow *Vern* on Facebook: https://www.facebook.com/DragonEyePI

There's More Fun in FabianSpace!

Thank you for buying this book. If you enjoyed it, click to see the others in this series or discover one of the other worlds of FabianSpace.

Science Fiction

Space Traipse: Hold My Beer: Redneck ingenuity and common sense in a Star Trek-ish universe. Enjoy the adventures of the *HMB Impulsive*.

The Rescue Sisters: Intrepid women doing dangerous missions in space for the love of God and humankind.

The Old Man and the Void: Dex is a relic hunter on the edge of the black hole, desperate for the catch of a lifetime.

Jovian Heat: As the next Great Storm of Jupiter rises, Cass must find the father of a baby in peril—but the father died before the child was conceived.

Fantasy

DragonEye Story: Vern's a snarky dragon on the wrong side of the Interdimensional Gap, solving crimes, battling evil, and saving the universes on an all-too-regular basis.

Madness of Kanaan: Deryl isn't crazy; he's psychic, and aliens of two worlds thinks he can save them. Maybe he can—but can he regain his sanity in the process?

Horror

Neeta Lyffe, Zombie Exterminator: Neeta's an average exterminator, taking out bugs, rodents, and the undead. Can she keep her friends alive, pay her bills, and find romance?

Frightliner and Other Tales of the Supernatural (with Colleen Drippé): Truck-driving vampires terrorizing the road, Southern women doing what needs doing, a zombie wedding—a great story collection for horror lovers.

www.ingramcontent.com/pod-product-compliance
Lightning Source LLC
Chambersburg PA
CBHW070619260626
47161CB00007B/2493